# Road
# of
# Vanishing

# ROAD
## of
# VANISHING

*Book Four of the Latter Annals of Lystra*

## Robin Hardy

Westford  Press

*Road of Vanishing:*
*Book Four of the Latter Annals of Lystra*

Westford Press
6757 Arapaho Rd., Suite 711, PMB 236
Dallas, TX 75248-4073

ISBN: 0-9761964-4-1
Bookland EAN: 978-0-9761964-4-0
LCCN: 2005938712

Cover image © 2001-2006 www.arttoday.com

The daryoles mentioned in Chapter 3 were taken from Cindy Renfrow, *Take a Thousand Eggs or More: A Collection of 15th Century Recipes* 2nd edition, Vol. 1 (Unionville, NY: Royal Fireworks Press, 2003) p. 51. For the recipe, see the Appendix.

The Scripture in Chapter 19 is Gal. 3:13 from the King James Version.

The hymn fragment on the back cover is from the cover of a 1564 book by Girolamo di Manfredi, courtesy of http://www.fromoldbooks.org.

*To Sancia*
*whose questions changed*
*the history of Lystra*

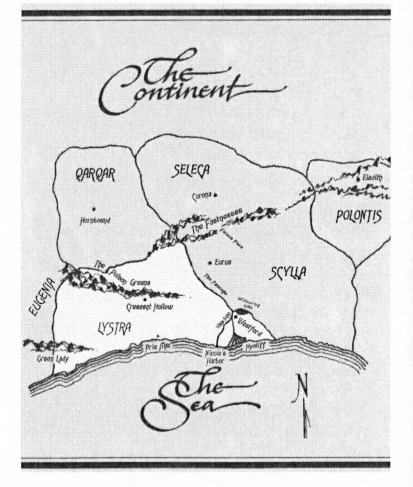

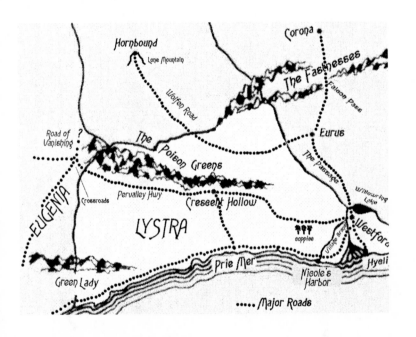

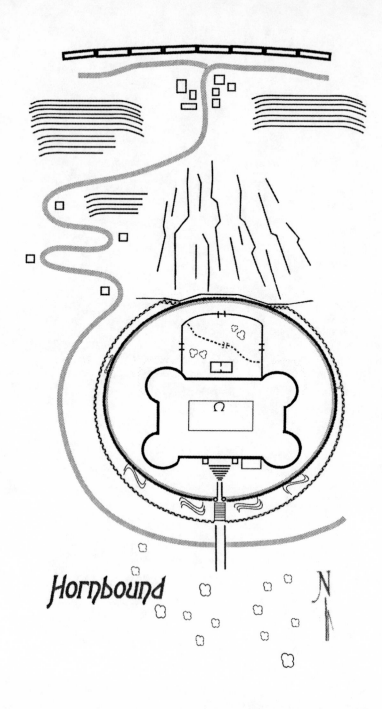

Hornbound

N

*T*ime, like an ever-rolling stream,
Bears all its sons away;
They fly, forgotten, as a dream
Dies at the opening day.

**O** God, our help in ages past,
Our hope for years to come,
Be thou our guard while life shall last,
And our eternal home.

Isaac Watts, 1719

# 1

"Where is he?"

"In Gretchen's room, in the lower corridor."

"Oh, well, then—" the Steward Giles began to advance in the direction of said corridor when the other shot out a hand to grip his upper arm firmly, despite the plush layers of velvet and satin that swaddled it. Startled, Giles protested, "Commander, really! The coat is Lord Preus' handiwork, and if you rip it, you shall certainly recompense me for it!"

The muscular hand did not release Giles' arm or coat. "He gave orders not to be disturbed. When he comes out, you shall have his ear after I do."

"Hmmpf!" Shrugging out of the grip (which would have been impossible had the Commander not relaxed it) Giles indignantly rearranged the sumptuous folds to regain his unruffled state. Unfortunately, the wild fringe of kinky brown hair that ringed his bald head seriously detracted from the polished appearance he endeavored to project. Glancing in lingering offense at the Commander, his gaze swept the other's hard blue eyes and short, bristly beard. Lips pursed in disapproval, Giles noted, "You looked much more courtly without that bush on your face, Thom."

The Commander might have smiled—it was hard to tell with that bush on his face—and replied, "I don't aim to look courtly,

Steward. And if you dislike it, then I have met my aim."

They remained in a silent standoff within view of the entrance to the lower corridor from the palace foyer while the hurly-burly of a normal business day in Westford coursed around them. It was early summer, a bright morning, and the great palace doors stood open, making the pitiful, half-starved fire in the massive foyer fireplace appear unnecessary and unwelcome. But it was always kept burning, year-round, night and day.

After a quarter-hour of waiting, during which time the Commander received two messengers who whispered in his ear and the Steward none, Giles finally threw up his hands—accentuating the gold dagging on his sleeves—and stepped toward the corridor. Thom stopped him with a battering-ram of a hand to the chest. Giles coughed and sputtered, "This is ridiculous! It was only a servant, and I have important matters to attend!"

"*No one* disturbs him. That was his word to me, which I will certainly carry out," Thom uttered.

While Giles was groaning and fretting, a little girl in a plain brown dress pushed her way through the stream of bodies in the foyer to stand beside Thom. He looked down at her, but Giles did not notice her. She was five, with thick chestnut hair gathered back in an untidy ponytail. Her green eyes large and serious, she addressed the Commander: "Where is Papa?"

"In Gretchen's room, Chataine," Thom nodded toward the corridor.

Seeing her, Giles offered a cloying smile. "Hello, Chataine Sophie. Are you looking for your father? We are waiting for him, too, dearest, and you need to wait your turn." With a glance at him, Sophie tossed her ponytail and turned to run down the corridor. Neither man attempted to stop her.

Coming to a closed door, she reached up to pull hard on the handle, straining with all her might to open the heavy wooden door, and succeeding. A masculine figure in black sat in an old rocker facing the opposite wall. The head was bowed, but at the sound of the door, it raised slightly, turning barely. Those who knew him well froze at such slight, deliberate movements, for they signaled serious displeasure.

Heedless, the child went directly to him and clambered up on his lap. He folded muscular arms around her, shifting her so that she sat more comfortably, and laid his cheek on the top of her head. She nestled deep in his black brocade jacket, closing her eyes.

After a few minutes, she murmured, "I'm sorry Gretchen died."

"Me, too," he whispered, kissing the top of her head.

She raised up to look in his face. "Will you miss her because she was good at cleaning our clothes?"

His answering smile was rather wan. The lines in his face, particularly the lines of sadness around his eyes, seemed to lessen the severity of the deep, jagged scar that ran from his eyebrow to his jaw. Sophie had only lately learned that the scar was not the distinguishing mark of a Surchatain—it was the result of an assassin's attempt on his life when he was a child himself.

He replied to her question, "I will miss her because she was loyal and faithful in everything she did. Had she not tended you and your sister so well after you were born, when your mother was so weak, you might not have survived—"

"I'm the firstborn," Sophie informed him gravely.

"And even that information we owe to her. I owed her much . . . but never thanked her. Your mother was the only one who thanked her." He glanced at the dinner gown hung reverently on the wall above the sleeping pallet. Sophie's mother Nicole had innocently caused a palace uproar when she gifted several favored servants—Gretchen among them—with formal gowns.

Sophie snuggled back down in his lap. "Mama was looking for you."

He blinked, a shadow crossing his face. "I know."

Several quiet minutes drifted by as he rocked her, eyes partly closed. Sophie, growing troubled, twisted to look in his face again. His eyes were uncharacteristically moist. She did not know that he was waiting for them to clear completely before showing his face to the palace again. "You were sad like this when old Dr. Wigzell died," she observed.

"Yes," he sighed, feeling another quarter-hour added to

his waiting. "I am very selfish. I cannot bear it when the Lord reclaims good people He has loaned to me."

She laced her little arms around his neck. "Will you cry when I die?" she asked leadingly.

"No," he said stonily. "I will be the first to greet you to our Father's house. But you may be a trifle put out when *I* die." She giggled at the unreality of the proposition. Other men died—not her father. Not the Surchatain of Lystra. In his role as Surchatain, he asked, "And why are you here, and not at your lessons?"

"Aunt Renée took Bonnie out for a fitting, so I left, too," she said defiantly, lifting her chin.

Eyes suddenly clear, Surchatain Ares stood with his daughter. "We shall return you and your sister to your lessons, and remind Aunt Renée that she does not interrupt to have Bonnie try on dresses." He opened the door and carried the child up the corridor toward the foyer.

Sophie's lips curled in disdain. "Why do Aunt Renée and Bonnie make such a fuss over dresses? It's silly. It doesn't make her prettier than me. We look just the same."

"That is a very good question which I cannot answer, dear one," Ares said tightly. Vindicated once again by her adored father, the man everyone else bowed to, Sophie kissed his torn cheek and cuddled his neck.

As they emerged into the foyer, Giles bowed flamboyantly and Thom straightened, opening his mouth. Before he could utter a sound, the Steward said breathlessly, "Surchatain, I implore a brief word with you." Thom shut his mouth, eyes glazing over.

"One moment, Steward," Ares said, lowering Sophie to the floor. He made eye contact with a nearby sentry, who hastened over. Ares instructed him, "The Chataine Sophie wishes to return to her lessons in the library. You will locate the Chataine Bonnie and likewise return her to the library. You will then request that the Chataine Renée favor me with an audience," he finished dryly.

"Yes, Surchatain." The sentry knew to salute him, not bow. He then inclined his head to the royal daughter. "Chataine, if you will," he said, extending his hand toward the broad staircase across the foyer. She indifferently headed for the staircase while he glanced back at her father, who watched with grave approval.

Ares turned to Giles. "What concerns you, Steward?"

Caught off guard, Giles paused. "May I speak with you in private, Surchatain?" The tumult of the foyer was not the best place to confer.

Ares jerked his head toward the lower corridor. In the instant before he turned down it, he flicked his eyes in Thom's direction without actually looking at him. Thom then knew to unobtrusively follow them far enough down the corridor to remain within earshot.

In the middle of the quiet corridor, Ares turned to Giles (who had his back to Thom) and repeated, "Yes, Steward?" Apart from his rank, Ares' physical presence was daunting enough, reminding Giles to collect himself before speaking. At the ancient age of forty, the Surchatain had apparently lost none of the iron from his frame. He was as taut and strong as ever, only more deliberate about proving it and deadly when he did.

"Surchatain, I trust that I performed adequately as overseer in Crescent Hollow?" Giles began his practiced speech.

Ares visibly hesitated before replying, "Yes, overall."

Dismayed by his hesitation, Giles nevertheless plunged ahead: "Then frankly I must protest your naming this upstart Vogelsong a Counselor before myself, when he was a mere copyist and I have had so many years of service and Carmine is—" Ares' eyes went hard—"somewhat—incapacitated," Giles stumbled to a finish.

Ares' face smoothed. "I am sorry that it appears to be a slight to yourself, Steward," he said thoughtfully. "When the fact of the matter is, I cannot afford to name you Counselor because I cannot replace you as Steward. A Counselor traffics in mere words, as you noted, but who else is honest and competent enough to handle the number of accounts and sums of money that pass through your hands?"

"Well—that is true—" Giles stuttered.

"I desire your indulgence to let me use you where I need you most. Have you not been well compensated?" Ares asked, glancing at the outfit that rivaled any of Renée's for sheer cost.

"Well—somewhat—" Giles admitted, passing a jeweled hand

over the gold brocade coat. It was certainly splendid in comparison to the dull black brocade that the Surchatain wore adnauseam. As a matter of fact, the mere action of comparing his clothing to that of the Surchatain's, and the illusion it produced of who cut the finer figure, was enough to soothe his ruffled vanity. While Ares watched, Giles arrived at a conclusion. "Since you put it that way, Surchatain, that's actually satisfactory. If you will excuse me, I have a number of accounts to audit."

"Thank you, Steward," Ares nodded. With a bow, Giles departed, turning up his nose at Thom's dull military attire on his way to the foyer.

Ares watched Giles depart with a half-smile, then turned his attention to his Commander. Thom quietly relayed, "We're ready to launch the strike against the slavers' camp, Surchatain."

Ares' eyes lit up. "Ah. Good. Let me—"

"No, Surchatain," Thom said tightly, and Ares looked at him in surprise. "You shall not lead this strike. If I have to draw blood to prevent your going, I will."

Eye to eye with him, Ares coolly regarded his implacable face. There was a moment of palpable tension, then Thom sagged, whispering, "After what happened a month ago, how am I to face the Surchataine if we bring you back on a pallet? I might as well hang myself in the courtyard."

Ares glanced down guiltily. A month ago he had been leading a similar raid on a small slavers' camp on the Scyllan border—it should have been so simple! But his horse had stumbled going down a ravine. The animal flipped hooves skyward and Ares had been pitched onto the rocks, striking his head. The minutes that he was unconscious created consternation among his men—the raid was called off in confusion and a rider sent off in utmost haste to summon young doctor Savary from Westford, hours away.

Then the slavers, having been alerted to their presence, attacked, so the raiding party was forced to fight a desperate defensive battle while their Surchatain lay at the narrow bottom of the twisted ravine, half submerged in a shallow stream. That whole time his page, Ben, had bent over him, holding Ares' head on his lap while sitting in the cold stream, making sure his lord's face stayed clear of the water. But as long as the fighting raged above them on the edge of the ravine, Ben kept him as much concealed as possible in the stream, even pulling sedge over them both. Ares had awakened, groaning, while the fighting was at its peak. But at Ben's insistence he lay still, his dark brown hair swirling in the water, watching what he could see of the battle above.

It went on like that for several hours. By the time Thom and his men had killed the last of the slavers, Ares' head had cleared enough so that he could sit up. He stripped off most of his cold, wet clothes to watch the slaves released and salvage gathered. By the time those tasks had been completed, Ares felt well enough to ride—slowly. They had met up with the doctor on their way back, and upon their arrival at Westford that evening, found the Surchataine Nicole waiting with smoldering fire in her green eyes.

Despite Ares' studied disavowals, she knew he had been hurt. (As Ares remembered nothing of his fall, his men recounted it to him in detail.) The doctor had ordered bed rest, which Ares ignored. But Nicole had gone privately to Thom to inform him that the Surchatain would not ride out to fight again unless it was a matter of life or death. Thom had agreed. Ares had not tested these restraints . . . until today. Sullenly, he told Thom, "Report to me immediately upon your return." The Commander saluted and went away satisfied.

Entering the foyer, Ares encountered the sentry he had sent off with Sophie. The young sentry saluted and said, "Surchatain, the Chataine Renée has granted you audience in her chambers." Ares nodded, turning toward the broad stone staircase. Another sentry approached—one Ares didn't recognize. Thom rotated them so much, Ares didn't have a chance to get to know all the new ones.

The youngster started to bow but then remembered to salute, which resulted in his saluting the floor. Ares, careful not to smile, watched him. "Surchatain, I have come from the Surchataine in the orchard, who requests that you remember your promise to her." The Surchatain acknowledged this without replying, then trotted up the stairs.

On the second floor, he turned down the Surchatain's wing

and stopped at the entrance to the Surchataine's apartments, then shook his head at his error. Renée had been occupying these quarters until very recently, when it was determined that Surchataine Nicole needed them to entertain visitors and store dresses. But she did not sleep here—she slept with Ares, still, every night.

After constructing the rooftop reservoir and diverting part of the underground stream that ran through Ares' first-floor quarters, his engineers were able to provide running water to the garderobes in the Surchatain's wing and the kitchen beneath it. Only then had Ares been persuaded to move to the Surchatain's spacious apartments, leaving Thom to snap up his previous quarters, and displacing Renée to the Surchataine's suite. Twins Bonnie and Sophie occupied the remaining set of rooms in the wing, while Renée suddenly decided that she preferred her old quarters in the opposite wing. Accordingly, she set to having a nice large window carved out of the stone of her sleeping chambers and set with exquisite colored glass—not the cheap greenish glass that was in the windows of the Surchataine's rooms. So Ares turned on his heel to cross the second-story landing toward her present chambers.

Arriving at her door, Ares nodded at the sentry to announce his presence to the Chataine Renée. Being the granddaughter of the usurper who had taken the throne of Lystra by murder, Renée's title was, at this point, a generous fiction. She retained it, as her half-brother Henry retained his title of Chatain, due to kindness and affection on Ares' part.

He was granted entrance into her opulent receiving room. While waiting for her to appear from the bedchamber, Ares glanced around the room in grim satisfaction, cluttered as it was with fantastically expensive knickknacks and furnishings. Upon annexing the province of Calle Valley, Ares had given the palace at Crescent Hollow to his friend and counselor Carmine, Renée's husband, and had given Renée the task of renovating it. After she had spent thousands of royals bringing the palace up to her exacting standards, she lived there for exactly three weeks before deciding to come home to Westford. Here, she had persevered in her practice of dropping outrageous sums on whatever caught her fancy, laughing at anyone's attempts to restrain her. Giles suffered acutely over the losses to the treasury, but Ares was reluctant to deal harshly with the Chataine.

Then Nicole—beautiful, resourceful Nicole—had hit upon a plan. Whenever Renée bought a new gown, Nicole would sneak into her wardrobe and remove an old one that Renée obviously no longer cared for, and take it to the treasury. If Renée bought new jewelry, Nicole removed some old pieces; if knickknacks or art, Nicole carefully dug out dusty objects from Renée's apartments that had long been obscured by newer pieces—all of which were taken to the treasury. Any fears that Renée would discover the subterfuge were quelled long ago, as this had been going on for over two years now.

Ares turned when Renée entered from her bedchamber and extended her hand. He bent to kiss it; as he straightened, she leaned forward to kiss his cheek, holding his hand against her chest. "What is it, Ares?" she whispered, confident in her beauty.

He gently withdrew his hand. Yes, with her golden hair and perfect features, Renée was a beauty, but . . . less so now that the years of self-indulgence had begun to take their toll. At twenty-five, she was only two years older than his dove, Nicole, but—her face was getting rather puffy, and the makeup she once used sparingly was now applied so thickly as to resemble a mask. Ares found it frankly revolting.

He got right to the point: "Chataine, I have asked you before not to disturb Bonnie at her lessons. You have many hours during the week to play with her and dress her up, but you must respect the time that she is with her tutors."

Renée gave a clear, ringing laugh, at which he straightened slightly. "Oh, Ares, you will go on so! She's a child! Why should she be burdened with lessons?"

"Because I am her father, and I wish it," he said in a low voice.

"But I am her aunt," Renée countered (a relationship in spirit only). Brighter: "Besides, I am a tutor, too! I am teaching her the finer art of charm. Dearest Sophie would do well to attend, occasionally," she said, turning to a golden pitcher of spring wine. She filled two golden cups, one of which she offered to him.

He took it, then set it untasted on a table with inlaid mother-of-pearl. "Your lessons must not take precedence over reading and writing."

Renée waved him off. "How tiresome you are! You cannot expect a girl that age to pay any mind to books!" Sipping her wine, she watched his discomfort with amusement. She thought she had struck a salient point, while in reality, he was recalling his own service under her father and grandfather. The office of Surchatain, however attained, demanded respect. Then she added, "Besides, Bonnie is mine."

His brows elevated slightly, and she persisted, "It's true, you know. She loves me more than her own mother." Ares' face smoothed as it did whenever he wished to make himself inscrutable. "Oh, Ares!" She put her goblet on the table to draw close to him. "You and I were meant to be together from the beginning. You know it."

Years ago, when he was madly in love with her, he would have died of happiness to hear these words from her lips. She had teased him and kissed him and laughed in his face at his earnest declaration of love. It was all a game to her. Studying her now, he accurately perceived that it was all still a game. "Chataine, the old toy is rusted and broken. Leave it and go on to a new one." Then he left her chambers while she grinned wickedly after him.

He went on down the corridor, where Carmine, Henry, Vogelsong, and Giles had their quarters. On the way, yet another sentry apprehended him: "Surchatain, the Trade Council is ready to meet."

Absently, Ares said, "Have Lord Faguy preside today. He knows what I want done." As that sentry saluted and moved off, Ares approached the closed door of the library, where Sophie and Bonnie took lessons with their reading tutor. Addressing the sentry across the hall, Ares asked, "Are the Chataines within?"

"Yes, Surchatain," he affirmed.

"Good. From now on, when they are here, the Chataine Renée is not permitted to take either child out. If you have any—

difficulties in carrying out my command, you may summon me or the Surchataine, and we will deal with whichever Chataine does not wish to cooperate."

The sentry kept a straight face as he acknowledged, "Understood, Surchatain."

From there, Ares went to stand before Carmine's door. There was more than reluctance, there was pain on Ares' face as he laid his hand on the door latch and drew it open.

The room was bathed in a soft glow of red, yellow, and blue as the morning light shone through the colored glass in Carmine's window. In recent years, panes of glass (mostly uncolored but for a faint greenish cast) had been installed in many of the palace windows, but Carmine was the first to use it. The furnishings of his room were luxurious, if dusty, for Carmine could no longer abide servants coming in to clean, and there was a mildly repugnant odor laying about the stuffy room—the odor of a neglected body.

Ares approached the figure slouched in the richly upholstered chair. The once-coifed hair was matted and stringy; the elegant fingers trembly. Kneeling before the chair, Ares righted several empty bottles and cups littering the carpeted floor. The figure grunted and shifted, rousing slightly out of a perpetual haze. Ares regarded his friend's bloated face that sprouted occasional, irrational hairs. Looking back at him with bloodshot eyes, Carmine exerted his old gift of acuity and chuckled, "I haven't shaved for weeks. Can't tell, can you?" Ares opened his mouth, but Carmine added, "We're both eunuchs, now, eh?"

Ares shut his mouth again. While serving under Renée's father, Carmine had been found out as her lover. As punishment, he had been castrated. It was only after Ares had ascended the throne that Renée and Carmine were permitted to marry. But by then . . . much water had passed under the bridge.

"Strange that the lovely Nicole has had no more babies, eh? But then, it was a hard birth. A hard, hard birth. . . ." Carmine lay his head back where there was already a dark grease stain on the upholstery, and closed his eyes.

"Carmine," Ares whispered. "I need you. You are too valuable to kill yourself."

Carmine's eyes barely opened. "What have I to live for?" he mumbled. "Day after day, day after day. . . ."

"I will allow you to divorce Renée," Ares said suddenly. Once Carmine absorbed that, he pushed himself up in the chair a bit. "If, I say IF, you drink no more wine but at dinner. Show me my old Counselor, sober and useful, and by the end of this month I will grant you a divorce from her."

As Carmine stared at him, some of the cloudiness dissipated from his eyes. He gathered his wrinkled, soiled robe about him and unsteadily stood. Making his way to the door, he opened it to gesture to the sentry. "You! Come. This room stinks. Get someone in here to clean it up. And have sent up a wash tub with water, and a servant to assist. I have duties that wait. Go on!" He shut the door emphatically and turned back to Ares, who was now standing.

"It will not be easy, Carmine," Ares said. "And for the damage it will do to Renée, I will permit no backsliding. Your life hangs on your obedience."

"For the first time in my life, I understand that, Ares," he said, and from the clarity of his voice, Ares believed him.

Ares exited his quarters, thinking about when, and how, he should broach the topic with Renée. But then he looked up and his heart stopped—there, in the corridor, eyeing him, was Nicole. Fresh from the orchard, she was dressed in the simple cotton frock she wore when working in the gardens, which she loved to do. While he stood there dumb, she came up to him, her glossy chestnut hair tousled, her cheeks flushed, her lips parted.

"You promised, my lord," she murmured with the vaguest smile.

"Nicole," he breathed out. "I . . . cannot. It was—too hard, to go through that. I cannot go through that again."

"Oh. Was their birth harder on you than me, my lord? But I have healed. I think you should have healed, too," she observed, drawing close to him. "And you promised." She leisurely unbuttoned his black jacket, parting the white frilled shirt to press her lips to his chest while he stood there stricken.

Then, eyeing him, she loosened the lacing of her bodice until it suddenly fell open. Ares came to himself with a start, grasping the gaping bodice and glancing around wildly. "Lady! Have you lost your mind? Don't—"

"You promised," she said in a harder voice. "And you will keep your promise—right here, if need be." She shrugged so that the drooping bodice fell off one white shoulder. A sentry advancing from the staircase took one look at the scene unfolding in the corridor and made a sharp about-face.

Almost panicky, Ares hustled her down the corridor to a storeroom and tossed her inside. But he followed her in, and when he had turned around from securing the door, saw her sitting on a pile of blankets, legs spread, dress half off. The room was dim and slightly musty, ventilated only by the crack at the bottom of the door. He found himself standing over her while she raised her eyes to him, running a hand up his leg. He dropped on top of her, yanking fabric out of the way, and she threw her head back in victory.

He pressed his lips to her chest, her neck, her face, and she gasped when he made himself her husband again. He stifled her laughing moan with his mouth, grunting, "Shh! Do you—wish to make known—that—unh—that the Surchatain—lays his wife—in a—in a—storage closet—? Oh . . . Nicole. . . ." She merely smiled into his shoulder.

In the corridor outside, the sentry and two maids were crouched with their ears to the door, grinning and hushing each other with wordless gestures.

All the rest of that day, Ares was more relaxed and cheerful than he had been in a long time, and everyone in the palace knew the reason for it.

When the bell tolled eight that evening, dinner at Westford commenced. Long tables were pulled together in the great hall to seat upwards of sixty people nightly, illumined by beeswax tapers on the tables and hanging chandeliers fitted with hundreds of candles. The food was always delectable, the wine clear and sweet, but most important, Ares was a gracious, tolerant host. He did not impose his own will on trivial matters, nor did he take offense at inadvertent slights. True, he was often quiet and preoccupied, but if he gave someone leave to address him, he paid attention.

Tonight, before Ares and Nicole were seated, the guests took their places as usual from the foot of the table up; high-ranking administrators who sat at the head were announced by Georges, the dinner master. They stood behind their chairs to wait—no one was seated until the Surchatain and Surchataine arrived. Doctor Savary, Counselor Vogelsong, Steward Giles and his wife Genevieve entered, then Thom's wife Deirdre and Rhode's wife Soucie were escorted in by servants, as their husbands' places would remain vacant until they returned from their mission. (Since the death of Oswald following the Battle of the Crossroads with the Qarqarians, Rhode had been promoted to Thom's Second.) Lord Faguy graciously escorted in Lady Vivian (Renée's mother); after which Georges announced, "The Chataine Renée."

Stunning as always, she swept in on Georges' arm, and the table bowed to her, as always. Taking her place to the left of the head of the table, she blinked at the place across from her. That chair—the only seat higher than herself, other than the Surchatain and his wife—had been empty for a long time due to Carmine's incapacitation. But tonight the place was set with pewter dishes, awaiting an occupant. (While goldware was available, Ares seldom gave permission for its use, considering it ostentatious.)

"Who is sitting there?" Renée demanded. Giles, who was to sit next to the mystery guest, was intensely interested to know, too. He had been denied that seat when Carmine stopped showing up for dinner.

Then Georges announced, "Counselor Carmine," and Renée's whole side of the table turned to look.

# 2

Though pasty and unsteady, Carmine was clean, combed, and outfitted in his usual luxury (which always made Giles burn with envy). He entered with dignity, standing behind his appointed chair, discreetly holding on to it. While the rest of the table bowed to him, Renée surveyed him in frank disgust: "What are you doing here?"

"Awaiting dinner, dear Chataine," he said, inclining his head to her.

"I, for one, am thrilled that you are feeling well enough to join us, Counselor," Giles said fawningly.

"Yes, aren't you?—since Ares hasn't seen fit to promote you in his stead," Renée muttered to Giles, whose courteous smile stiffened.

Renée turned her relentless attention to her husband. "What made you decide to eat dinner instead of drink it tonight?"

"The Surchatain," Carmine replied simply, at which point Georges announced, "Surchatain Ares and Surchataine Nicole." She entered on the arm of her husband, who escorted her to her chair with a certain self-possessed gravity.

When the ruling couple was seated, the others at table sat. Ares' nod to Carmine was so pointed as to arouse Renée's keen curiosity. He gestured to the wine steward: "You may begin pouring, Steward." To Georges, Ares said, "You may summon the Chataines." After filling the goblets of the Surchatain and his wife, the wine steward so adroitly changed pitchers that almost no one realized that Carmine received a different beverage: water. Given the chance to think about Ares' ultimatum, Carmine had realized that there was no way to exorcise this demon but cut it off altogether. He had no illusions as to how difficult that would be. But if he needed inspiration, all he needed do was look across the table at the unnaturally white face of his wife.

Bonnie and Sophie were brought into the great hall, as usual, to be presented to the table before being excused to the side room off the kitchen to eat their dinner with the other palace children. The girls entered hand in hand to bow to the table. Ares nodded gravely and Nicole beamed. The twins wore equally fine, though different dresses; Bonnie's hair was arranged a bit more elaborately than Sophie's, and she carried herself differently: chin lifted, back straight, with the cool, distant look Aunt Renée had taught her. Sophie, on the other hand, tended to straightforward intensity, never walking when running was possible. On the few occasions they dressed alike (or once, for a lark, exchanged clothes) hardly anyone had trouble telling them apart. But they loved each other very much, and were very close.

They curtsied to the table, and Ares asked his standard question: "What did you learn today? Bonnie?"

She clasped her hands in front of her proudly. "I learned the sparrow dance, Papa! Watch!" Lifting her arms, she performed a series of steps with glides and turns.

Sincere murmurs of admiration at her grace rippled around the table, and Renée led the guests in a round of applause. Ares did not clap, but he said, "Very good, Bonnie. Very nicely done. Sophie? What did you learn today?" Propping his elbow on the arm of the great wooden chair, he leaned his chin on his knuckles to await her reply.

The child glanced at her mother before fixing her eyes on her father. "I learned the Ten P'ecepts of the Law of Roman, Papa." She began laboriously ticking them off on her fingers. "Wisdom, hum'lity, pudence, jus'ice, mercy, reason, goodwill, cleanness, mod'ration . . . and . . . and . . . faith!"

The guests murmured their approval while the royal parents reacted with restrained delight: Nicole's lips were parted and flushed in pride; Ares' hand dropped to his lap. Learning the Law of Roman (of which the Precepts were but a bare outline) was the first and most crucial responsibility for anyone who would rule Lystra, or even participate in its government. The Surchataine Nicole was the first woman in the province to be certified in the Law since Roman's wife Deirdre. Sophie continued, "Surch'tain Roman wrote the Law, and he was my great-great-great grandfather!"

Ares pressed his lips together briefly. "That's true, Sophie. That's very good. You both are dismissed to dinner." Satisfied with themselves, the girls curtsied again and took each other's hand to skip out.

After pausing to clear his throat, Ares waved for the serving of dinner. Following braised fennel and rye bread, servants brought around terrapin with mushrooms and scallions arranged in the shells. For some minutes after the dishes were brought, everyone was usually so focused on eating that the table was generally quiet until someone said something to stimulate conversation. Tonight, the Chataine Renée was the first to find such a topic. "That is so sweet," Renée murmured into her cup, "Sophie memorizing all those big words that she doesn't understand."

Nicole answered quickly, "Oh, but she is learning them everyday just by watching her father." Ares turned to look at his wife, and Nicole smiled at him, regarding his scar. Sophie had come to her recently in great distress that she herself did not have the mark of the Surchatain, and would it hurt very much to get it?

"Still, it is so wonderful that the girls have each other for company. How I miss dear Henry," Renée mourned, looking at Giles' place, where Henry used to sit. Now, everyone who heard the comment knew that she had never paid any attention to her much younger half-brother, but Ares lowered his head in dismay at the mention of his name.

Ares had been Henry's guardian from his birth, but when Henry's father was assassinated and Ares gained the throne instead of Henry, their roles had significantly changed. Not quite eight at the time, Henry had not understood what *abdication* meant, other than the fact that he would not grow up to sit on the big, fancy wooden chair in the great hall. But the older he grew, the more he began to understand and resent his change of fortune. Add to that the uncertainty of his present status despite Ares' oath of protection, and normal teenage angst—about six weeks ago the thirteen-year-old had taken a horse and disappeared. Ares had not been able to locate him. Thom, convinced that Henry was capable of gathering an army of malcontents in Lystra, or journeying to Eurus, Corona, or even Hornbound to solicit aid in overthrowing Ares, wanted to place a bounty on Henry's head. This Ares could not bring himself to do. Meanwhile, Henry's room was kept just as it was in faint hopes of his return.

Carmine suddenly spoke: "After the Chatain Henry has experienced his fill of how hard life can be outside the palace, I believe he'll come home. The Chatain, of course, learned the Precepts when he was almost as young as Chataine Sophie. Perhaps, dear Renée, you could elaborate on her recital and give us the rationale behind each precept?" He lifted his elegant eyebrows encouragingly at her.

"Oh, yes, Chataine, that would be splendid to hear," Giles said quickly.

"Don't be absurd," Renée sputtered. "Everyone here knows them."

Lady Vivian, seated five places down and across the table from Renée, said, "I do not know them, and I would be most interested to hear you expound on them, dear daughter." She had been waiting a long time for an opportunity such as this. Ironically, having been Surchataine once herself, Vivian *should* have known them.

Renée tossed her head in disdain, trapped on the verge of having to admit that she knew less than a five-year-old. "Lady Vivian, the precepts of wisdom, humility, and prudence are based upon inward thinking—that one must discipline his thoughts to attain those attributes, rejecting evil and concentrating on good. The precepts of justice, mercy, and reason reflect the outward behavior that must result from the constructive discipline of inward thinking. The precepts of goodwill, cleanness, moderation, and faith describe the lasting effects of such thinking and acting. Building a life—or a province—pleasing to God requires these foundation stones. That is the short answer, though books have been written on the Precepts," Ares answered.

"Thank you, Surchatain," Vivian inclined her head, hiding her disappointment.

"Do you suppose Henry went off to try to find Melva?" Doctor Savary asked.

His question plunged the table into another awkward silence. Six years ago, the Chataine Melva of Qarqar had been brought to Westford immediately before a usurper, Ulm, killed her father and took the throne. Ares had kept her at Westford to safeguard her until just a year ago, when an assassin sent by Ulm attacked her outside of Lord Preus' shop in the city. She escaped harm, but her Lystran bodyguard died defending her, and the assassin was also killed. Ares, knowing that Ulm would not rest until the legitimate heir to the Qarqarian throne was dead, decided that she was no longer safe in Westford. The seventeen-year-old Chataine was escorted out of the city with a favorite maid in the dead of night, and no one but Ares and Nicole knew where she had been taken to live. Henry, of course, had been severely smitten with her, so that her removal sent him into a pit of depression that he had not found his way out of before disappearing himself.

"I almost hope that is the reason he left," Ares finally allowed.

Renée, having wrung all useful drama from the topic of her missing brother, refocused her attention on her husband. She studied him as one would a new and possibly dangerous species. "So," she murmured, delicately stirring the fennel around her plate with the fork, "what could the Surchatain have said to convince you to sober up for tonight?" Her instincts were uncanny, and if she believed a matter had something to do with herself, then it probably did.

"Weren't you going to handle the problem with squatters at the Harbor for us, Carmine?" Nicole asked. The proper name of the new port town was Nicole's Harbor, but she never could get the exact words out.

"Certainly, Surchataine," he said. "I have arranged for a

carriage to go inspect the situation tomorrow." Which was, remarkably, true.

Renée eyed him humorously. "Why, Carmine! How good of you. I think I shall go with you—it's been far too long since I've seen the Harbor." Renée had trouble with the proper name of the town, too.

Carmine dared not react. But Ares leaned back, inhaling, and looked at Renée. She glanced at him, then away, pretending that his hard gaze did not affect her, and no one else spoke while Ares so obviously deliberated his choice of words, fingering the base of his pewter goblet. Nicole, sensing something unprecedented, waited with eyes lingering on his hand. She had learned that his hands gave away secrets when his face was stone and his lips unmoving.

Ares, making up his mind, withdrew his hand as if he were withdrawing a favor. He leaned forward, resting his elbows on the elaborately carved arms of the great chair. "Chataine," he said, "I think it time to inform you that I have been receiving offers of interest for your hand from around the Continent. I am seriously thinking that, for the good of Lystra, I may make you available to entertain such offers."

Due to his veiled language, it took a moment for his meaning to sink in. Renée looked flabbergasted. "But—I am already married!"

"A divorce is possible, if both parties desire it," Ares said. "Your behavior toward the Counselor clearly indicates that you desire it."

"But—" Renée stammered, then looked across the table at Carmine in the sudden horror of realizing that *he* wanted it. Her lips parted in shock; her eyes glazed over. Nicole pitied her greatly, but said nothing to rescue her from this very public humiliation.

"Who have you received offers from, Surchatain?" Giles asked in mild offense and strong curiosity. He was usually privy to matters of this magnitude.

"That will be discussed later," Ares said, leaning back for the servant to take his empty plate, placing before him the dessert of baked pear stuffed with raisins.

With Renée abjectly quiet for a change, other more benign

conversations were free to flourish. Since almost everyone had finished eating, Ares motioned to Georges, who bowed and withdrew to summon the children from their dining room. In moments, a horde of laughing children, ranging in age from toddlers to teenagers, invaded the hall to assault their parents or other favorite targets. Those adults who were not overjoyed with this nightly invasion were free to retire to the gardens for quiet conversation, or to the other end of the great hall where musicians stood ready to play dance melodies. But anyone who wanted the Surchatain's ear immediately after dinner had to compete with Sophie for it, and she usually prevailed.

In the children's mad rush to the table, Sophie made haste for Ares' lap, though it was always open to her. Bonnie, as usual, headed straight for Renée, to Nicole's continual disappointment. Tonight, when Bonnie threw herself on Renée, the child gushed, "Aunt Renée, you promised to make up my face tonight!"

Nicole corrected her, "Bonnie, my dearest, you may not wear makeup."

In distinct imitation of Renée, Bonnie turned to her mother and sniffed, "Pooh!"

Eyes widening, Nicole glanced at Ares, but he was preoccupied with Sophie's demands. So Nicole gestured to one of the sentries lining the wall, who sprang forward. Ares looked up as Nicole instructed the sentry, "Take the Chataine Bonnie up to her room. Candace is to dress her for bed." Looking at her daughter, Nicole added, "I will be up presently."

Sullenly, Bonnie kissed Renée's cheek but avoided her mother as the sentry stood by to take her upstairs. Ares watched this, then looked at Renée, who begged leave from the table to go dance. He turned to Nicole, and she leaned over to whisper to him.

A while later, Nicole brought Sophie up to the Chataines' apartments (which used to be Henry's suite before he was moved across the landing to the room next to Carmine's). Nicole handed her daughter over to her maid, Kara, to get her ready for bed. Bonnie, already bathed and dressed in her nightgown, sat pouting in the big feather bed that she shared with her sister. While Kara undressed Sophie to bathe her in the tub near the fireplace, Nicole came over to sit on the downy mattress. Bonnie folded her arms and looked away. The Surchataine still wore her full-skirted, off-the-shoulder dinner gown in peach silk. It was one of Tailor Gathing's creations: simply cut but becoming and much less revealing that most formal gowns. Following her example, many of the palace courtiers were requiring higher necklines from the favored dressmaker, Lord Preus. Renée led the remnant of diehards who clung to plunging necklines.

Sitting beside her daughter, Nicole told Bonnie, "I am sorry I had to send you away from the table, dear. But if your father heard you being so disrespectful to your mother, he would not stand for it. He would also be very angry if I let Aunt Renée make up your face. I am afraid he would say, 'Since Renée is not teaching Bonnie the kind of things I want her to learn, I am going to stop letting them spend so much time together'"—something he had already said, in fact.

Bonnie glanced at her mother in apprehension. From the tub, Sophie chimed in, "He thinks the makeup makes her look ugly!" Bonnie shot a dark glance at her sister.

Scooting closer to take Bonnie's hand, Nicole went on, "I told him that as long as you mind me, I don't see the harm in your playing with Aunt Renée. Do you understand, dearest?"

"Yes, Mama," Bonnie murmured, eyes downcast.

"Now. Do you want me to tell you a story?" Nicole asked, smiling.

Bonnie looked up, eyes brightening. Sophie cried, "Yes, yes!" Then to her maid, "Hurry, Kara! Don't do my hair; I didn't get it dirty today."

Nicole sat against the great scrolled headboard to snuggle Bonnie under one arm. "What story would you like to hear?" Mother asked.

"Tell me about the poor little peasant girl who goes to the palace to visit the beautiful Chataine!" Bonnie said.

"Wait for me!" Sophie cried in the agony of being left out. She scrambled into the nightdress being held by the maid, then clambered up onto the bed so eagerly that it rocked on its rope supports.

"Uh-uh," Nicole said, lifting her chin slightly at Sophie in correction.

Whereupon the child just as adroitly climbed back down and went over to put her arms around the maid's neck and kiss her cheek. "Thank you, Kara. Night-night."

"Good night, Chataine," the maid said fondly, proceeding with her duties.

As Sophie bounded back into bed, Nicole gathered her underarm as well, and said, "Now. You want to hear the story of the peasant girl who goes to the palace for the first time in her life?"

"Yes!" the girls cried.

"And she meets the tall, strong Commander with the terrible scar on his face," Sophie said breathlessly.

"And he falls in love with her the first time he sees her," Bonnie sighed.

"She is afraid to marry him, but then she finds out how good and kind he is!" Sophie exclaimed.

"You seem to know this story quite well. Why hear it again?" Nicole hedged.

"Because it's true!" Sophie cried.

"And there may be something you left out," Bonnie added.

"Well. Listen then, dear hearts: Years ago there was a poor little girl who lived by the Sea. She loved the Sea—she still does—but she and her father lived all by themselves in a little house with two rooms."

"Just two rooms?" Sophie asked, squinting to try to visualize it.

"Yes. Just two rooms, a garden in back, and a chicken coop. She was a wild little girl—her father worked sewing clothes all day long, so she went roaming all over the coast and the marshes all day."

"She had to gather food," Sophie said solemnly. This also was a foreign concept, and what she visualized was a little girl much like herself picking up prepared sweetbreads or lamb croquettes right off the ground.

"Yes. She set crab traps, and caught frogs, and gathered bird's eggs. Once she found some snake eggs, and didn't know what they were, so she brought them to her father. He spanked her and burned the eggs," Nicole related.

"Why did he punish her? She didn't know," Bonnie said plaintively.

"I think . . . because he was afraid she would get bit by the mama snake," Nicole said slowly, a troubled look crossing her face. Why had he punished her so harshly? All she remembered was his shouting, *"They're no good to eat!"*

"She had Uncle Purdy to watch out for her," Sophie countered.

"True," Nicole smiled. And under Purdy's wise husbandry, the Surchatain's livestock had increased tenfold in the last five years. "Anyway," Nicole resumed, "one spring when the peasant girl went with her father to the Fair to show all the clothes he had made, she met a beautiful Chataine—"

"Was the Chataine more beautiful than the peasant girl?" Bonnie asked.

Nicole said slowly, "The peasant girl thought she was, yes."

"Then why didn't the Commander marry the Chataine?" Bonnie asked, cupping her chin in her little palm.

"Because . . . he was beneath her in rank, dearest. She was supposed to marry a Chatain," Nicole said uncomfortably.

"That's stupid. I would rather marry a brave Commander than some weaselly Chatain like Henry," Sophie said spitefully.

Nicole opened her mouth to rebuke Sophie but Bonnie observed, "Aunt Renée says that she wanted to marry Papa, and he wanted to marry her, only her father wouldn't let them."

Nicole turned to Bonnie in shock at the lie—Renée never would have considered marriage to Ares until he became Surchatain, by which time he was already married to Nicole. Sophie screeched in reply, "No, he didn't! Papa doesn't even like her! She's mean and a tart!"

"No, she's not!" Bonnie screamed, leaning over her mother to hit her sister, who retaliated with force.

"Girls! Stop this instant, or there will be no more of the story!" Nicole threatened. The two settled down warily on either side of her. Nicole resumed the story, hampered by troubling suspicions about Renée that surfaced yet again.

When the twins had heard enough to satisfy them—barely—Nicole kissed them goodnight and left their quarters with the sentry standing guard at the door. Still troubled, she walked the shadowy stone corridor to the Surchatain's chambers and entered the relatively austere receiving room. A large table surrounded by straight-backed, unpadded chairs stood in the room; within easy reach was the ceiling-high wooden honeycomb structure that held all the many maps that Ares or his administrators required on a daily basis. Against the opposite wall underneath the banner of Roman was the stand holding the Westfordian Book of Families, the oldest known copy of the Law of Roman, and the book of Holy Scriptures. A separate stand held parchment, ink, and quills that were continually replenished.

The fire in this room had burned down to ashes, so Nicole took one of the few remaining candles on the large round table with her into the bedchamber. With the shadows cast by the low-burning fire in this chamber, all she saw was that her maid was not here. Nicole uttered a frustrated exclamation—"Ursula!"—and began to turn out of the room to summon her. Finding someone to replace the irreplaceable Gretchen was vexing.

"You don't need a maid tonight." The low voice startled her badly, and she swung the flickering candle around the room. Then she saw Ares, in his breeches, sitting up in bed.

"Oh," she breathed out, trying to calm her pounding heart.

When he slid off the bed, she could see that he had been waiting for her. "Your bath waits, lady," he whispered, coming up close to barely brush his lips against her bare shoulder. She looked over to the corner of the room where the tub had been set in the floor, permanently enclosed in the surrounding stone. Heated water from the hidden conduit (that could be stoppered up) ran down to the tub over artfully arranged stones in a waterfall. Encompassing the tub were potted ferns, water lilies, and other water-loving plants.

Standing very close but barely touching her, Ares reached around her to begin unfastening the long row of pearl buttons down the back of her dress. "I do not have to beg tonight?" she murmured with a half-smile.

His chest expanded. "I have been a fool to listen to my fears. You were right," he admitted a little reproachfully. The dress fell from her shoulders, and he lifted her out of it. Shucking his breeches, he lowered himself into the recessed tub and held out his arms. She stepped into the water to stretch atop him.

They were very quiet, but for the gentle lapping of the water over the edge of the tub. (Soon after the conduit was built, Ares had discovered how reliably sound carried through it to the kitchen below.) Nicole allowed herself only deep-throated murmurings into his ear, which caused him to press her harder. As she clutched his shoulders, they heard a loud pounding on the outer door and shouts from the corridor: "Surchatain! Your attention, sir! Surchatain!"

Ares sprang up, lifting her out of the tub with him while water coursed over the stone floor. He seized his breeches to jerk them on as she clung to him, trembling. He kissed her before turning to fling open the bedroom door, since the pounding and shouting had not abated.

Nicole found her velvet robe in time to don it and slip into the receiving chamber seconds after Thom and Rhode had entered. They were sweaty and grimy, having come straight off the field. Ares had just closed the door behind them and asked, "What happened?"

"Surchatain, the raid was a success. We killed twenty-eight slavers and brought one back for questioning. He goes by the name Lazear, and you will want to question him yourself," Thom replied, still winded from hastening an indeterminate distance.

"Why is that?" Ares asked.

Thom replied, "Because, in bargaining for his life, he claimed to have had a boy Henry's age pass through his hands some weeks ago. This slaver was impressed by the boy's repeated assertions that he was a Chatain, and the description Lazear gave of him answers to Henry."

"What happened to the boy?" Ares asked in a whisper.

"The slaver said . . . he was taken to the slave markets in Corona," Thom replied.

Nicole gasped at the news, but Ares did not notice, being intent on the crisis at hand. The slave markets, of which Corona formed the hub, were an old institution going back hundreds of years. Despite the pledged efforts of the provinces to subdue them, they thrived due to the continual demand for cheap, expendable labor. No one who lived very far from armed protection and high walls was safe from the slavers, who kidnapped the vulnerable with impunity. And the suffering they perpetuated was horrific.

After quashing the Qarqarians under Ulm who had invaded Lystra's westernmost border in the Battle of the Crossroads, Ares set forth as his next goal the complete eradication of the slave markets. But he discovered that fighting them was like trying to wipe out fleas—when he had smothered them in one place, they cropped up in another. And since Corona was the center for the buying and selling of slaves from across the Continent, if Henry had been taken there weeks ago to be sold, there would be no way on earth to discover in whose hands, or where, he might be now. Almost as bad, if he continued claiming to be Lystran royalty until someone believed him, the ransom that would be demanded of Ares for Henry's life would be exorbitant—possibly, impossible.

Thom then admitted, "You should know, Surchatain, that the

moment I heard Lazear's claims, I sent three scouts on to Corona posing as traders to attempt to trace the Chatain—all of whom know Henry and can identify him. Since we were already so far north, and time is of the essence, I felt that we would lose precious days coming back here to ask your leave before sending them."

Ares looked at him a long time, then studied the rug woven in brilliant colors that lay under his feet. Water dripping from his arms or his breeches made little round stains in the rug that gradually faded, being absorbed into the wood underneath. Finally, Ares cleared his throat and said, "You . . . did well, Thom. I cannot think of anything more sensible to do tonight. I . . . need to sleep on it, and let this Lazear have the night to think about what he will tell me. Have him fed bread and water, then I will hear him in the morning, after which we will discuss our course."

Thom looked relieved and gratified. "Excellent, Surchatain. In the morning." He and Rhode saluted and withdrew.

Ares turned slowly back to the doorway of the bedchamber where Nicole stood, clutching the dagging on the sleeves of her robe. Reading his thoughts by his set face and clenched fists, she whispered, "No."

His face promptly smoothed, and he leaned over to pick her up. "I will finish what I started with you, Lady," he announced.

"No, Ares," she pleaded, tears coming to her eyes.

"Oh, yes, I will," he said, carrying her to the bed, though he knew he was not addressing her true objection.

He laid her across the sturdy bed, opening her robe, and she gripped his arms, whispering, "Don't, Ares. Don't go. Send Thom, or Rhode—oh, my love, there are a thousand soldiers who could find Henry, but none of them can rule Lystra."

As he lowered himself to her, he murmured, "I have not made up my mind that I must go myself."

Exhaling in relief, she kissed him fervently. In his heart, he dismally acknowledged his sin of lying to her in order to give them both a pleasant night.

In the pitch blackness of the early morning, Ares opened his eyes, wide awake. He sighed, reaching over to feel Nicole beside him, and eased himself out of bed. For some reason, for the past few months he had been compelled to wake at least two hours before the first morning bells were rung at seven. He felt compelled to get up and pray.

The bed chamber was chilly, as the fire had burned almost completely down, so Ares put another log on before quietly exiting, closing the door behind him. In his breeches, he sat at the leaded-glass window in the receiving room and opened it. The cool air that rushed in helped sharpen his mind as he looked out over the rolling landscape. The window in this room faced west. He preferred an eastern view that would enable him to track the progress of sunrise throughout these early morning vigils, but logistics dictated this to be his prayer window. So he could appreciate sunrise only when it was an accomplished fact. At this moment, all was still dark.

As was his mind. Ares bowed his head, letting his uncertainty, frustration and fears roil in silent prayer. How was he to find Henry? Even if Ares did not consider his oath of protection binding—which he did—just the thought of what suffering the pampered child was enduring would compel Ares to search for him. But Nicole also was right—the governance of the province could not be left dangling for months or years while Ares indulged in a hopeless search—too many other lives would be affected.

Leaning on the windowsill, Ares pleaded for insight from the One who sees all. And as the sun rose beyond Ares' sight, golden threads of thought began to form ideas that he could act upon. He perceived that it might actually be possible to walk into the blind unknown with the confidence of an unfailing Guide.

With some light to read by, Ares reached over to the table for his little book. After Nicole had noted his propensity to copy down quotations and Scriptures that spoke to him, she had made for him a special book of blank pages. Then whenever he ran across some wise words that he wanted to remember, he had one place to copy them down and keep them all together. This little book was now almost full, crammed with writing that covered the front and back of three-quarters of the pages. (She had already ordered the making of a second book for him.) He carried his little book with him everywhere, and whenever he had a few spare moments, would open it up for contemplation.

Today he was absorbing this message: "Verily it is perilous for a soul not to seek to make any further progress. Get to thee meekness and charity, and if thou wilt, then travail and swink busily to have them. You shall have enough to do in getting of them." Ares agreed: attaining meekness and charity was the hardest task he had ever attempted.

After wrestling with the knowledge of his insufficiencies for a while, he looked up as the morning bells tolled seven. Given that sunrise had displayed itself in full glory across the sky, he knew that it was time to begin his day.

He dressed quietly, but forewent shaving till his bath later in the day. When a servant brought up breakfast of daryoles and sweet wine, Ares sat at his table to read over yesterday's correspondence while he ate the cheese tarts.

Just as he was finishing, the bedchamber door opened, and he looked in surprise at Nicole, fully attired in formal court dress, with Ursula behind her. Nicole rarely rose this early, and rarely wore full-court regalia, even at open audience. Furthermore, he had never noticed the maid's entering when he was at the window this morning.

"Good morning, Lady. To what do I owe this honor?" he asked, seating her with him. "Breakfast for the lady, Ursula," he instructed. She curtsied and left the room.

"Good morning, my lord," Nicole said airily, arranging herself at the table without looking directly at him. She feared letting slip the intense feelings she harbored over the request she was about to make. "I would ask your permission to sit in on the interrogation of the slave trader. I desire to hear for myself what he did with Henry."

Ares just looked at her. "While I do not doubt your interest or your abilities, Lady, he will think it the most pleasant and unusual inquisition in the world, to be questioned by a beautiful woman."

"I will be quiet. Please, Ares?" she asked pathetically.

"Regretfully, no," he said.

"Then let me go with you to find Henry," she blurted. She had not been fooled by his lie, after all.

"No," he whispered. She sprang up from the table to stand at the window in agitation.

Alone, he went down to the small room just off the great hall near the dais, and sent for the prisoner. At this time, the room contained only a few straight-backed chairs, a table, and some writing instruments. Ares settled himself in the chair behind the table and waited.

The first sentry who entered deposited a collection of items on the table in front of Ares. "Surchatain, the Commander invites you to examine the trader's possessions, all of which we removed from his person. He is being brought up from his cell."

"Very good," Ares said. The sentry saluted and left; Ares leaned forward to sift through the trader's belongings: a large pouch that contained at least fifty royals, gold necklaces, rings, and some small packets of spices, all very expensive. There were some tools of the trade, including a dirk in a sheath and a set of keys on a ring. Then there were haphazard items that had apparently caught the trader's fancy in the course of kidnapping people: an ivory toothpick, a small, gilded hand mirror, a tortoiseshell comb inlaid with mother-of-pearl, and—a hair ribbon embroidered with gold thread. The sight of this frayed, soiled ribbon sent a heart-stopping shock through Ares.

At that time, the sentry brought in a lumbering, nervous man with a pronounced tic of his left eye, obviously born of years of watching his back. Being scruffy and habitually unclean, he scratched at the scabs of old insect bites. He was dressed in tattered hose and coat that reeked of body odor and urine. Upon entering, he glanced sharply around the room, but seeing no instruments of torture, let out his breath—until his eye landed on Ares' scar.

Ares glanced at the sentry, nodding at the chair opposite him. With manifest disdain, the sentry shoved the trader into the chair and stood back. Still holding the ribbon, Ares leaned back, crossed his legs, and studied his guest silently for several long minutes. The trader had managed to survive in his profession of choice by sizing up every situation and responding exactly according to its dictates, so while Ares studied him, he studied Ares: the gaping purple scar, the severe black brocade, the tall, leonine build, the deep, inscrutable eyes. But what made the trader most uneasy was the deliberate way the Surchatain played with the girl's hair ribbon, as if he wanted to draw attention to it. Yet, it was probably the least costly of all the treasures on the table. Ares looked him in the eye, then looked at the ribbon, which he draped prominently over his long fingers. So the trader studied the ribbon, scratching himself in thought. This silent inquisition went on for probably a quarter hour.

Still without speaking, Ares leaned over to pick up the carved ivory toothpick. It was about five inches long, inlaid with lapis lazuli. The trader now focused his attention on that. Looping the ribbon around it, Ares fashioned it into a garrote while the trader watched. Then Ares stood, walked behind the other's chair and threw the gold-embroidered noose around his beefy neck, tightening it in one motion. The fellow jerked a startled hand to his throat where the garrote rested, snug but not uncomfortable.

Ares leaned down to breathe in his ear, "I am not going to waste my time listening to any lies. What is your name?"

"Your servant is Lazear, Lord Surchatain," he said shakily, his left eye blinking.

"Lie," Ares hissed, tightening the garrote. The man gasped, clawing at the ribbon. "Where do you keep camp?" Ares asked again.

"I keep on the move all the time because of the soldiers—but you can find me in Corona at the spring and fall fairs, Surchatain," Lazear averred in a tight, thick voice, hand ineffectually at his throat. He knew that struggling, that any movement at all, would worsen his situation.

"Another lie," Ares uttered, tightening the garrote again.

Lazear began to gurgle, his face growing deep red. "No, I swear!" he said in a choked voice. Though he had both hands on Ares' arms, he could not have prevented his strangling him to death.

"And what became of the boy you took this ribbon from?" Ares asked in a voiceless whisper.

"Sold him to Lord Morand of Hornbound!" Lazear choked out.

Ares released the tension on the garrote and Lazear fell face down on the table, gasping. Unwinding the ribbon from around his neck, Ares turned to the sentry standing against the wall. Although the soldier knew better than to praise his superior, he could not completely veil his admiration for a quick, clean, ultimately harmless interrogation. Ares instructed him, "Have him taken back to the dungeon. And summon Giles to take these goods to the treasury." He tossed the toothpick back down to the table, but kept the hair ribbon.

"Immediately, Surchatain," the sentry saluted.

On impulse, Ares paused over the table to take up the keyring as well. He turned into the great hall from the little room, stopping in the middle of the hall to think. *If* this Lazear was telling the truth, the situation had gone from possibly bad to the worst possible. Ares knew the name *Morand* from merchants' reports of the goings-on at Hornbound—he was a high-ranking nobleman in Ulm's court. Should Henry stay alive long enough for Morand to discover his identity, then a crippling ransom demand was sure to follow—either that, or a proposition to trade: Henry for Melva.

Still absorbed in thought, Ares crossed the echoing hall and exited into the foyer. Heading to the stairway, he was mildly startled to encounter Renée directly in his path. With studied carelessness, he brought the ribbon and keyring behind his back. "You are up unaccountably early this morning, Chataine."

She dispensed with her usual posturing. "I heard that Henry may have passed through the hands of the man captured yesterday, a slave trader. Is this so?"

Ares paused. He knew that several soldiers fed Renée information in hopes of sleeping with her, but if he ever found out who, it would cease forthwith. "Perhaps, Chataine. I am not sure."

She lifted her chin, and he noticed that she wore much less makeup today. "I will give whatever I own to free him. Everything, if need be."

"That is very gracious of you, Chataine. I hope it will not come to that." With a slight bow, he turned up the stairs, hiding his find in the front of his jacket. Privately, he added, *If it comes to that, what you had even before Nicole started robbing you would not be enough.*

He went to his apartments where Nicole sat at the window, waiting for him. She turned as he entered, and he sat beside her, placing the bulky keyring on the sill. She glanced at it, perceiving at once its significance: he would need it to unlock shackles. He took her hand to kiss it while she watched, pale, waiting to hear that he was going to leave on a long journey to risk his life for one runaway child. "The Lord helped me," Ares said quietly. "I found this among the trader's possessions." And he laid the hair ribbon across the keys.

"It is Melva's! She gave it to Henry," she gasped.

"Yes. So I knew that Henry had indeed fallen into his hands. The man says he sold him to Lord Morand of Hornbound."

"Hornbound!" Nicole breathed. "Oh, Ares, how can you walk into Hornbound and demand Henry's return?"

"That would be an admirably direct way of going about it," he admitted, looking out the window with a slight smile. "But, I don't know. . . . I am thinking it may be time to attack Ulm." Nicole stared hard at him. To his mild surprise, some color began to return to her face. "You approve of that plan?" he asked curiously.

"If it means that you can send your army," she said cautiously.

He leaned back thoughtfully against the window casing. "I will need to think on it. Pray for me," he murmured, and she leaned on his chest.

A while later, a sentry came to the door to report that Carmine had left for Nicole's Harbor with a small entourage of servants and soldiers—but not Renée. "Then he may accomplish something," Ares said hopefully. Before the sentry left, Ares instructed him to summon the Commander and his Second, as well as Lord Faguy and Counselor Vogelsong.

Shortly, these men arrived to sit with Ares and Nicole around the table in the Surchatain's receiving room while a pair of sentries stood outside the door. Drawing up his chair to the table, Ares told them, "When I examined the trader's possessions that the Commander had delivered, I found this among them—" he dropped the hair ribbon onto the table, but the men's blank faces compelled him to explain, "It was a gift from Melva to Henry."

Vogelsong paused. "A thousand pardons, Surchatain, but—are you sure? I never saw her treat him with any favor. She is older than he, you know, and seemed to regard his attentions as a nuisance."

"True, Counselor," Nicole said. "All the more reason for her to discourage him, gently. But I myself saw her give him this ribbon, which I had bought for her."

"So he *was* taken!" Faguy exclaimed in distress.

"Yes. And the trader told me that he had sold the boy to Lord Morand of Hornbound," Ares continued.

Thom leaned back pensively. "How likely is it that he is telling the truth?"

Ares sighed. "I have no way to judge that, but—in my bones I believe him."

"Do you intend to retrieve him?" Faguy asked.

"Yes," Ares answered, winding the ribbon around his wrist.

There was a short silence, then Rhode spoke: "Forgive me for asking, Surchatain, but—why? As the usurper's grandson, he can do you great harm, and frankly, has been nothing but trouble for years." Thom sat in silent agreement.

When the Surchatain leveled a gaze at someone, that person found it hard to focus on anything but the unnerving scar. Eyeing Rhode, Ares asked without rebuke, "How long do you think Henry can keep secret who he is?"

"He's already let it out, else we never would have known to look for him among the slave camps," Rhode answered.

"So, were it to become known to Ulm, how much do you think Henry could tell him about Westford?—our strengths, our weaknesses, our plans, our stores, our families . . . and Melva?" Ares asked.

Rhode's jaw went slack and Thom sat up, noting, "He would prove more valuable to Ulm than twenty spies in Westford."

"Quite so," Ares said. "For our own protection, we must rescue him. The only question is, how? By stealth, or outright attack?"

Thom rubbed his scratchy face. "I do not see how we can attack when we know so little about the city. From the merchants who do business there, we've gathered some worthwhile information about court life, but we know next to nothing about Hornbound's physical defenses or layout. It sits atop the Lone Mountain, so secluded and inaccessible that we've never been able to get spies into the city. The Qarqarian soldiers we've captured know nothing, being mercenaries, and even Chiacos, when he was hired as Melva's guide, was blindfolded whenever he was brought in or out. Of course, now that *he's* disappeared, he can't help us at all. . . . Melva herself was so young when she came to us that she could give us little useful information. We do know that Ulm has been regathering his army—again—though we never know how many he has until he's on the march. Blast those mines! With all the gold they produce, he can regroup no matter how many times we smash him."

"Again, I must betray my ignorance," said Vogelsong, who was undoubtedly the most well-read person in the room. "Roman's *Annals* clearly say that the gold of Qarqar was merely a legend, and the Polonti found none when they attacked Hornbound. Yet we have seen with our own eyes the products of their mines. How can this be?"

Ares said, "I believe the one copy of the Annotations is still in Carmine's chambers. But that volume explains it, Counselor: In Roman's time, the Qarqarians realized that their newly discovered gold made them vulnerable to plunderings, so they shrouded in it legend, claiming to have buried it in the graves of the Abode—then made sure that Roman's emissaries saw that there was, in fact, no gold buried there, and no evidence of their new wealth anywhere. The reports the emissaries brought back were taken at face value by Roman, whereas his Counselor, Lord Troyce, was able to discover the truth because he suspected the Qarqarians of lying."

"Where had they hidden the gold, then?" Vogelsong asked.

"No one knows; that knowledge died with Troyce. We suspect, however, that Lone Mountain is full of well-obscured hiding places," Ares said.

"Fascinating as this digression is," Thom said with a little bite, "it does not address how we might meet an army funded with their very real gold."

Ares looked off as he did whenever pondering difficulties. "There is the sticking point: Assuming we were successful in retrieving Henry, we would still have to contend with Ulm's mercenaries whenever he chose to deploy them against us."

"Even if we cannot get into the city, we can attack before they march onto Lystran soil," Rhode said stubbornly.

"How can we attack when we do not know how many he has?" Faguy objected. "Our own troops are taxed merely defending our borders." Since Ares' annexation of Calle Valley, Faguy considered himself thoroughly Lystran.

Ares leaned forward on his clasped hands. "The mines must be shut down."

"Ulm uses slave labor to work them," Faguy pointed out.

"Counselor, our map of the provinces bordering the Fastnesses." Ares nodded toward Vogelsong, who got up to select one map from the many housed in the honeycomb. This he spread on the table before Ares, and the others leaned forward. Surveying the map, Ares observed, "It is a straight shot of two days' ride from Corona to Hornbound. So the bulk of Qarqar's slaves must come by that road, eh?"

"Certainly, once they cross the border. The problem is that there are so many smaller camps that thrive in southern Qarqar, northern Lystra, and northern Scylla. Our friend Magnus has done a fair job of blocking the Pass to them, but they seem to find other ways around," Thom said, tracing routes on the map with his thumb.

Ares studied the map for several minutes. He then observed, "Ulm is quite familiar with Wolfen Road"—the route to Lystra between the Fastnesses and the Poison Greens.

"He's got an army marching down it once a month," Rhode quipped bitterly.

"But he only tried going around the western edge of the Poison Greens once, aiming to march down the Pervalley Highway," Ares continued, his gaze shifting to the western section of the map.

"We slapped him back roundly when he did, before he even got past the crossroads," Thom said. "He had not expected much resistance until he got to Crescent Hollow, and was unprepared for a defensive attack the moment he passed the Poison Greens."

"That was—three years ago," Ares said.

"Three years this August," Rhode clarified.

"Why hasn't he come that way again?" Ares asked.

No one replied until Vogelsong said tentatively, "I have read a few Qarqarian manuscripts that speak of the curse of the portal, Surchatain. And the portal apparently lies on that road."

Ares' scar throbbed visibly at his hearing something so sig-
nificant for the first time. "What is this portal?"

"That, I do not know," Vogelsong admitted. "Apparently, it is
a Qarqarian legend—"

"Another legend!" Faguy uttered.

"—One they fear considerably," Vogelsong finished.

Thom and Rhode glanced at each other. Thom said reluctantly,
"Again, there may be more truth to the legend than we allow. After
the battle, we heard some of the Qarqarian prisoners speak of it.
They blamed it for their defeat. So . . . Oswald said he was going
to see this portal. . . ."

"And never returned," Ares said in a gravelly voice. "I did not
know he had gone off to investigate a legend."

Thom added, "When his horse returned without him, we sent
searchers after him, but they did not venture far enough into
Qarqar to find anything resembling a doorway." Nor had they
found any clue as to what had happened to Oswald. So they had to
assume he was dead. And it had been almost three years since.

Ares straightened. "So here is the question we must address
first: should our advance, whether by few or many, take Wolfen
Road which is thick with Ulm's spies, or the northbound branch
of the Pervalley Highway, which his people fear?"

"We need to know what the portal is," Faguy said stubbornly.

"What difference does it make, if the Qarqarians fear it?"
Rhode scoffed.

"And what if it had something to do with Oswald's death?"
Faguy demanded. "Are you prepared to gamble your best men—
or yourself—on an unknown evil?" he asked Ares.

"I know something of the portal," Nicole said quietly, and they
looked at her in surprise.

"Enlighten us, Lady," Ares invited with a gesture.

"Do you remember the crippled silversmith who came to the
fair at the Harbor last fall? He had a great dog that pulled him
around on a chair fashioned with wheels," she told Ares.

His brows drew down. "I doubt I ever saw him, Lady. I left the
registration of the merchants to Giles."

"I chanced to visit with him for some time. Some of his wares
caught my eye—they had a most peculiar greenish glow—so I

stopped to look at them. They were of a cunning make like I had never seen before. I asked whence they came, and he gave me this rather contrived tale regarding a merchant in Eugenia. I then asked why they glowed as they did, and he seemed most surprised. He said, 'If you see that, then you would see the portal.' I had no notion what he was talking about, and gave it not another thought until today," she said.

"Did you buy anything of his? Did Renée?" Ares asked.

"I did not—something happened to occupy me elsewhere, and I never saw him again. I have not seen any of his wares in the palace, either," she replied.

"Surchatain . . . a greenish glow . . . does that remind you of what we saw in the Poison Greens?" Thom asked.

"But we cleansed the ritual place, and the green lights left," Rhode said anxiously.

"Does evil have only one doorway?" Vogelsong asked. There was a sober silence, then he added, "What if Oswald is not dead? What if he passed through this doorway unknowingly and cannot return without help?"

Ares rose abruptly and turned his back on them to stand at the window. This action, coming from someone so habitually restrained, amounted to a temper tantrum. As such, it caused the others to sit quietly while he faced the dilemma with his head bowed. A few of those present interpreted his reaction as an indication of his feelings for Oswald, but the most perceptive among them realized that it had more to do with Nicole. If the rescue party took the Pervalley Highway—as it appeared they must—then she must be among them. Someone must be able to identify the portal.

Minutes later, he turned from the window and reseated himself. Subdued, he said, "Whenever I would withhold anything from the Lord as too dear, He requires that very jewel from my clenched fist." Several faces looked back at him in puzzlement, but Vogelsong glanced at Nicole.

Ares eyed those seated around him. "I will lead a small party to scout the Pervalley Highway into Eugenia and Qarqar. If God allows, we will draw close enough to Hornbound to discover how to regain Henry and stop Ulm. Thom, you and Rhode select twenty of your best men—include Alphonso and Buford—have provisions packed and be ready to leave at daybreak tomorrow."

"Yes, Surchatain," Thom said as if waiting for some proviso.

"Faguy," Ares said, turning to him, "I leave you in charge of the financial dealings of the palace. I will prepare written instructions for Giles to report to you. See that the nobles honor the trade agreement with Scylla while I am gone."

"I understand, Surchatain."

"Vogelsong," Ares said, shifting. "You have the judicial responsibilities—I will leave written directives for you, as well. Do everything you can to help Carmine stay sober. Have Sophie and Bonnie guarded with utmost care."

"Of course, Surchatain."

Finally, Ares turned to Nicole. She waited patiently, saying nothing, but attentive. Eyes on her face, he uttered, "You all have your instructions. You are all dismissed—but the lady."

**4**

Thom and Rhode rose from their chairs and departed with hasty salutes; Faguy and Vogelsong insisted, as usual, on bowing before leaving the room. (They were among the administrators who had argued that bowing, rather than saluting, was the proper mode of showing respect to the Surchatain for those who had never been in the army. Ares allowed them to inflict their preference upon him because they were otherwise so sensible.)

When only the Surchatain and his wife remained in the room, he lowered himself to his knees in front of her, resting his head in her lap. "All the heavens conspire against me to see that you go on this mission, when I would for the world keep you safe at Westford."

She stroked the thick brown hair, with a few strands of grey at the temples, and bent to lay her arms over his broad back. "Then you must explain it to our darling Sophie. She will be in a rage of envy."

He raised up to regard her, and she brushed her lips against his. "I wish you to understand that you cannot hold me to my 'promise' on this journey, Lady. It will be a day and a half of hard travel to Crescent Hollow, and another two days before we reach the western edge of the Poison Greens. We shall have no privacy, nor comfortable quarters, nor feather mattresses for frolicking," he said almost resentfully.

"I understand, my lord," she whispered, so that he kissed her urgently.

He broke off to add, aggrieved, "Nor shall I feel compelled to satisfy you today, with all that must be accomplished before we leave."

"Certainly not, my lord," she said, eyes lowered. Groaning, he stood to heft her in the burdensome dress, and she smiled over his shoulder at the thoroughness of this particular rout: she won every point.

Outside in the corridor, Vogelsong paused to nod good day to Faguy before hastening across the landing toward the library. Faguy stopped at the head of the stairs to watch Renée leisurely ascend as if she had not been loitering there. But she betrayed her purpose by casting limpid blue eyes in the direction of the Surchatain's suite. "And here I meet dearest Faguy, straight from the war council. What have the men decided, darling?" she purred (ignoring the fact of Nicole's presence in the meeting).

"We shall all know that when the Surchatain announces his plans," Faguy said. He was much too clever to be coaxed into spilling premature news.

"You disappoint me," she uttered, tossing her head as she progressed away from him toward her quarters. And he watched her till she had entered her rooms, closing the door behind her.

Before daybreak the following morning, before the palace gates were opened to the waiting merchants, the scouting party gathered in the courtyard, lit with torches that reflected brokenly off the smooth, damp cobblestones. The party was taking only two carts to carry their supplies, for western Lystra was mostly barren rock, and when the roads became rough, anything with wheels must be left behind. The palace courtiers had been generally informed that the Surchatain and Surchataine were setting off to inspect the vineyards that had once been Calle Valley's before the annexation. Not even Giles, Carmine or Renée knew differently (despite her efforts to find out). The royal children had been told that Mother and Father were taking a much-needed trip together; Sophie asked when she would be old enough to go, and Bonnie asked if she would be allowed to wear makeup in their absence.

Nicole, with her unconventional good sense, had attired herself in the dull, functional clothes of a common laborer—even the pants. She had become a rather proficient horsewoman since the birth of the twins, but never could get past the fact that the men enjoyed such a singular advantage in not having to ride in bulky skirts. The palace gossips were duly scandalized when she first donned pants on one outing on horseback, but as she continued to wear them only when riding, the indignant whispers gradually lit on more interesting topics.

In the dark orange glow of the torchlight, Ares inspected his band: besides his wife, his Commander, and his Second, there were, as instructed, Lt. Alphonso, Lt. Buford, and eighteen other sturdy, competent men, including Captain Crager. Ares went down the line as they stood at attention. He took note of each face, inquiring the names of those he did not know. "Where is Paramore?" he asked Thom.

"Still in Nicole's Harbor, supervising the fleet, Surchatain," the Commander replied.

Ares paused. "Did I send him there?"

"Yes, Surchatain."

Ares looked irritated. Then he turned to inspect their arms and provisions. He personally carried two items of particular importance: Lazear's keyring and Melva's ribbon.

By the time Ares was satisfied with their state of readiness, early sunlight had broken over the towers of Westford. Ares addressed Nicole: "You have your choice, Lady: shall you ride on horseback or on a cart?"

Nicole considered her options. Neither would make the trip easy, but Ares' engineers had outfitted both carts with splendid suspensions that greatly improved their ride. She chose a cart. So Ares assisted her to sit on the cushioned seat beside the driver, Wirt. Then Ares mounted up, instructing his men with a wave to do the same. And the palace gates were opened for them to depart while the merchants waited, respectfully and impatiently, to the side of the road until they could enter the bailey and commence with palace business.

In the last few years, Ares had taken pains to straighten, widen and pave the road between Westford and Crescent Hollow, which was prudent, given the amount of traffic between the two cities. Because of this, what he remembered as a day and a half of travel time was reduced to one day, if the weather was clear. And the cost of these improvements was quickly recouped by the taxes collected from the resultant quadrupling of trade.

Therefore, Ares kept the group moving at a uniformly fast pace throughout the day, allowing for brief stops to rest and eat. He did not insult Nicole by continually inquiring after her state—he just assumed that if she needed to stop more frequently, she would tell him so. For her part, she would sooner have expired on the cushioned seat than demand special attention. He may have been forced to take her, but she would not let him regret it.

Once they passed the many acres of cultivated fields around Westford (the summer wheat being thick and green) they paused at a gate in the ancient hedgerow marking the end of the cultivation. A hundred paces beyond, the coppice crowded up close around the road.

While one soldier dismounted to open the gate, Ares nodded at the rest and drew his sword. They did likewise. Even so close to Westford, robbers—or slavers—were a possibility wherever there were good hiding places. Ares had ordered these trees cut back from the road more than once, but the woodsmen seemed always to have some excuse as to why it wasn't done. The traveling party advanced through the gate and waited for the man on foot to close it and remount. Then they spurred toward the dark road ahead in formation, Nicole's cart to the inside.

They crossed from bright sunlight into shadowy greenness. Even the air was denser, laden with odors of musty woodland. Shafts of light penetrated the tangled canopy of leaves to randomly illumine the undergrowth. Allowing for less headroom and more obstacles, the riders slowed to a gentle lope. Numerous eyes scanned the trees on either side.

Alphonso suddenly hissed a warning and reined up. For a man of his healthy girth, he could move quickly when he wished; so in a flash, he and two others had dismounted to part tangled bushes at the edge of the road, weapons raised. Alphonso then lowered his blade, bending to study their discovery more closely while the other two peered over his shoulder. Ares waited patiently astride his dancing horse.

Shaking his head, Alphonso left his find and came up to Ares' horse, a black gelding named Neruda. (Karst had been put out to stud after years of faithful service.) Crossing his arms over his chest, the lieutenant looked up and said, "Well, Surchatain, it's some poor soul that was stabbed and dragged into the bushes. The only clothes left on him are what were all bloodied and ruined, so I'd say he'd been robbed, as well."

Ares nodded shortly. "Remount." For a wounded man he would have delayed their trip to see to his needs, but a dead man could not be helped.

They continued down the shady road, where moss grew between the paving brick and water trickled across the low spots. Someone's horse skidded on a mossy patch, so they slowed yet again. In other places, tree roots were feeling their way across the road, causing the carts to bounce mightily over them. Ares muttered a reminder to himself to find responsible woodsmen somewhere, somehow, who would keep this road clear.

At this point the party came upon such a thick, tangled root mass invading the road that they were forced to stop and unpack an axe to hack it away before the carts could pass. When the axe was found, so was a stowaway on the second cart. Ares' page Ben, not having been invited, chose to come anyway. They were now too far from the palace for Ben to return safely alone, so he took his place as an official member of the party. Ares' chastisement of him was so brief as to be considered praise, which is how Ben received it.

They were not long in the coppice before it gave way to meadowlands, allowing view of the Poison Greens not far off. The road suffered less obstruction here, so, following a rest stop, they resumed their former brisk gallop. It was tiresome, to be sure, but Nicole understood Ares' desire for haste: with her in the party, he was determined to spend the night in Crescent Hollow. As it was, they might already have to travel after sunset to reach the city, and nighttime travel was dangerous even on paved roads, even in Lystra. So they pressed on through the warm afternoon. Bouncing in the sunshine made her sleepy, but when Wirt kindly offered to make her a bed in the back of the cart, she snapped awake. For her to show a lack of stamina so early in the journey would have Ares groaning.

The afternoon melted away into lengthening shadows. The riders blinked, shielding their eyes from the sun now in their faces. It lit up the paving bricks like eddies in a river of fire. Having the shadow of the vanguard to travel in, Nicole could appreciate the beauty of the blazing sky more than they. With the Poison Greens looming on their right hand, she watched the progressing sunset. The orange burned itself away to purple, then faded into a dark gray which collapsed into night. The party kept riding while the moon appeared over their shoulders to illumine the road.

Soon, the fields, orchards and vineyards surrounding Crescent Hollow came into view as black disturbances on the horizon. Wirt had to urge the weary carthorse on with the whip as well as words—"Hey, Butter; come on, 'at's my girl"—when the vanguard picked up speed. The carts began to lose ground to the faster horses, but the rearguard would not pass them. When Alphonso, bringing up the rear, whistled a warning, Ares (invisible to Nicole somewhere up ahead) made everyone slow down.

With stars glittering overhead, the party finally made the gates of Crescent Hollow. Ares raised the hilt of his sword to bang on the wood, calling up to the sentries, "I am Surchatain Ares! Open up!"

There was some indecisive scuffling above, as he could not be clearly seen in the shadows of the gate. "How many of you be there?" a sentry called suspiciously.

"There are two dozen of us—not enough to take Crescent Hollow. Take us in as prisoners," Ares suggested in mild exasperation. He should not have been surprised at a chilly reception, as he had not sent word ahead of his coming.

There was some discussion among the sentries, then another voice called from above, "Hold this!" and a lit torch was dropped over the gate. Ares caught it by the handle, looking up. His personal signature, the cleft in his face, showed prominently black in the wavering orange light of the torch. The crossbar was soon lifted, and the gates opened for the exhausted party to ride in. They were escorted down the main street to the palace, where the ornate iron gates (with brass fittings, courtesy of Renée) were opened to them.

The horses were stabled and water was brought for the party to wash up. Ares glanced around, then told the steward, "My wife requires a private room to bathe."

As Nicole removed her light cloak, the astonished steward extended a torch toward her. "Certainly, Surchatain. Hiya, you!" he summoned a soldier.

At that moment the administrator of Crescent Hollow appeared in the bailey in considerable surprise. He was rather portly, with curling black hair and beard around a cherubic face that belied the sharp intelligence which had garnered him this prestigious post. "My word, it *is* the Surchatain! To what do we owe this honor, sir?" He saluted with a special flourish that distinguished it from a soldier's salute and spared Ares the discomfort of receiving his bow.

"Good to see you, Roerich," Ares responded, offering his hand, which the other quickly clasped. "My wife desired a tour of the valley, and I decided this was as good a time as any to accommodate her."

Roerich then looked in greater surprise to see that, yes, the slender figure in pants was the Surchataine Nicole. To her he made no hesitation to bow, and smartly ordered her taken to the best guest quarters to bathe before dinner. There in the bailey with his men, Ares sponged away enough dirt and sweat to make himself presentable at table, then Roerich escorted the party into the keep, where hasty dishes were already appearing from the kitchen: persillade soup, smoked venison, peach wine, and oat cakes.

The administrator urged him to a seat at the head of the table; Ares stood behind it, asking generally, "So how goes it, Roerich? Does the lower garden still flood in the spring?"

"Not as badly, Surchatain; the retaining wall helps greatly," he replied, glancing at Ares' party. The hungry men stood like statues around their places at the table, looking at the wall. The sight was rather unsettling, given their nonresponse to the aromatic dishes continually filling the table.

But then Surchataine Nicole arrived in the keep after taking only moments to freshen up, still wearing the traveling clothes she had worn all day. Ares kissed her hand and seated her beside him, then the rest of the men sat in unison. Roerich was mildly impressed at their discipline in the small things.

Thanks to Renée's efforts (and a considerable portion of the wine tax) the keep in this castle was more refined and luxurious than the great hall at Westford, though smaller. The walls were plastered, set with decorative sconces for candles—certainly not nasty, smoking torches—and tapestries hung from ceiling to floor. The fireplace was lined with smooth pink marble imported from some great distance. The whole certainly reflected Renée, except for the lack of costly appointments. Roerich would not allow the temptation of a display of wealth.

While they ate, Ares made genial small talk with the administrator, asking after this or that, to which Roerich replied in careful detail. But when those trivial topics had been exhausted, and Ares fell silent, Roerich watched him and Nicole with sharp eyes. Finally, he ventured, "Surchatain, I must confess . . . as honored as I am by your visit, I am also rather mystified that a leisure tour of the Valley's vineyards should require not only yourself and the Surchataine, but your Commander, his Second, and numerous other high-ranking officers of your army."

Ares straightened, glancing at him, and Nicole kept her eyes on her plate. Ares had found Roerich trustworthy, else he never would have appointed him to a position requiring trust. In a reluctant stab in the general direction of truth, Ares admitted, "I am looking for a particular merchant who probably came this way, whom only the Surchataine can identify."

Roerich's curly black brows crept up. "His wares must be astonishing," he murmured, studying Ares. Then he hastened to add, "Forgive my curiosity, Surchatain, but it stems from my concerns over the disturbances spreading from the western border."

The whole scouting party looked up with an interest that the administrator did not miss. Ares asked, "Disturbances from what? Qarqarians?"

"In a manner of speaking," Roerich allowed. "Qarqarian renegades who dislike serving under Ulm will cross the border to operate independently, so to speak, robbing and plundering our villages. When we catch them—as we always do—they start blathering strange tales about the Road of Evanescere."

"The what? I have never heard of this," Ares said.

Roerich answered, "Excuse me. That is what the Qarqarians—and the Eugenians—call it. It is the northbound fork off the Pervalley Highway that runs through the corner of Eugenia toward Qarqar"—the road on which Oswald disappeared. "The Eugenians avoid it, as they do the Poison Greens, and indeed they have little need of it. But the Qarqarians have attempted many times to make use of it, each time meeting disaster. When those we question describe it, they babble about men, or animals, or whole carts being swallowed up by the road. Hence, the Road of Evanescere—the Road of Vanishing. But I trust that your tour will not carry you beyond Lystra's border, so you should not encounter anything untoward."

Ares studied Roerich while the party sat in attentive silence. "I would like to speak to one of these Qarqarians," Ares said.

Roerich looked troubled, stroking his curly beard with a beefy hand. "I do not know that any are left. They were obvious undesirables to begin with, and most intractable. Several died of unknown causes, another two escaped, and several we drove into the Poison Greens rather than keep them chained in prison. Let me see if any remain." The administrator beckoned to a manservant, who bent his ear for instructions before ambling off. Roerich turned back to the table to see Ares frowning down at his plate. "Is the venison unsatisfactory, Surchatain?" he asked in courtly alarm.

"Not at all," Ares said, picking up his fork but nonetheless glowering at his plate. He did not like receiving crucial information belatedly—in this case, years late.

Minutes later, the servant returned to indifferently explain that the Qarqarian in question seemed to have died in his cell while no one was looking. "The body's being taken out to be burned, along with his plunder," the servant reported.

Ares startled. "Burn nothing until I can see it," he said, rising from his seat.

The servant waved dismissively. "'Tis all junk; everything valuable was taken from him already."

Ares stopped, confounded. "Are you *arguing* with me?"

"Not if ye be getting all huffy about it," the servant groused. "This way." Following the servant, Ares glanced at Roerich, who was watching with subdued amusement. The scouting party rose as one to follow Ares and Nicole out through spacious, brightly lit corridors. Roerich accompanied them. As the servant led them through one door after another and down a flight of steps, the corridors became narrower, darker, and coarser.

"What is your name?" Ares asked, his voice echoing off the bare stone.

"Huysum, sir," he replied respectfully enough.

"Do you know who I am?" Ares asked.

"Aye, ye be the Surchatain, as any fool could tell, and I've heard often how yer lordship respects a man what speaks his mind and doesn't paint pretty pictures out of fear of ye," Huysum said easily. He took a torch from its sconce to lead the party into dark, wet, foul-smelling passageways. Glancing back at Nicole, Huysum observed, "The lady may find the sights ahead objectionable."

"The lady has as little fear of consequences as you do," Ares replied stiffly. Nicole was amused that he wasn't quite sure what to make of the presumptuous servant. Part of Ares' conflict lay in the fact that Huysum's accent pegged him to be from northern Scylla, where beloved Gretchen's ancestral roots ran deep.

The entourage met up with servants dragging stinking bundles; Huysum barked orders at them to display their gruesome burden on the muddy stone floor. Obediently, they spread out the corpse along with its pitiful possessions. Nicole gazed in pity at the recently deceased, then looked at his meager belongings and gasped.

Ares glanced at her sharply out of the corner of his eye. "Perhaps the sight *is* too much for the lady," he amended, withdrawing her by the elbow. Out of the others' hearing, he whispered, "What did you see?"

"The round shield with the black markings—it glows green," she whispered back.

Ares looked back at the pile on the floor. "I see the shield," he murmured. "But I see nothing green about it." Evidently no one else did, either. He came to stand over the questionable object, bending to pick it up. Nicole instinctively grabbed at his arm in warning. Turning the object over in his hands, he observed, "This is not a shield."

The others pressed forward to see for themselves. It was round, about fourteen inches in diameter, and silver in color. It had recessed insets, painted black, that resembled the spokes of a wheel. It had a curiously shaped rim, but no arm strap. Instead, the back side was impressed with a string of numbers. "What is that metal? It is not silver, nor tin, nor steel," Roerich observed.

Ares nodded in agreement. With his bare hands, he was able to bend the disk. "Coyle?" he inquired, turning. This man, an engineer, came up to take the object. Nicole cringed, not liking to see anyone handling it. She feared the effects of the faint, fluidic aura that clearly emanated from the disk. Then again, the merchant had handled similarly glowing wares easily enough. Then again— he was crippled. And why was this Qarqarian now dead?

"I've never seen this metal before," Coyle said, inspecting it. "It's light and malleable and soft. The edges here are for attachment. This piece attaches onto something else. It's only a part of something."

"How curious. Is this like the wares of the merchant you seek, Surchataine?" Roerich asked Nicole. He had apparently noticed her alarmed reaction.

"I had thought so at first, but it is actually nothing like what he had. He sold common household pewter, though of a clever design," she explained.

"I'd like to take it with us, Surchatain," Coyle said, reluctantly handing the disk back to him.

"No," Nicole objected anxiously.

Much to her relief, Ares tossed it back to the corpse. It landed on his chest, where it rested like a family crest. "I don't see why we'd need it. Roerich, I wish to make an early start tomorrow. Show us to quarters, if you will."

"Certainly, Surchatain."

Ares and Nicole were given the quarters reserved for visiting dignitaries. While certainly spacious and comfortable, it did not have the luxury of running water, so Nicole sent for two tubs to be filled—one for herself, of course, but another for her husband.

Following Dr. Wigzell's long-standing habit of washing his hands, she wanted Ares to bathe after handling the strange disk. He held his hands out and remarked, "You don't see any green, do you?"

"No, but that makes no difference. Please," she said, loosening his coat, and he complied.

While he relaxed in the warm water, she sent the servants away to bathe him herself. He closed his eyes to mere slits under the soapy sponge, murmuring, "Was the disk not at all like the merchant's other wares?"

"Other than the green aura, no, not a bit," she said, bringing up handfuls of water over his sinewy shoulders.

"Then the only connection may be that they both came through the portal," he said.

"That is all I can think to explain it," she admitted.

He closed his eyes, sinking lower into the warm water to groan, "What an inconvenience, when our most urgent task is to recover Henry. Why the Lord would put such an obstacle in our path, I cannot imagine—" He suddenly looked straight ahead as if startled. "Unless . . . He means for us to use it."

Nicole leaned on the edge of the tub in uneasy contemplation.

At the palace in Westford, Renée had just stepped from her own cushioned tub, and was now wrapped in a great, warm towel. But she stood fixed in place, hair dripping on her shoulders, hands clutching the towel, as she had also just received some stunning news from her maid, Eleanor. "Are you sure?" she hissed, white-faced, with no makeup at all.

"Yes, Chataine," Eleanor said tightly, shaking out the sheets and plumping the downy pillows on the canopied bed. "The Surchatain told him that if he'd stay sober a month, the divorce was his. That came straight from Merle herself"—the reigning authority on palace gossip.

Renée stared ahead in a daze, then snapped to. "Don't bother with that. Help me get dressed."

"Now, Chataine? This late?" Eleanor asked in dismay.

"Yes!" Renée insisted, rubbing her head fiercely with the towel. "Now, find me that soft lilac dress that I regretted buying— or did Nicole take that one?"

Eleanor ruffled expertly through the crammed wardrobe. "No, it's here. The Surchataine took the yellow with the great sash and the purple that Melva liked."

"Fine," groused Renée. "Leave the black and white in the bottom of the wardrobe for her to take next."

"The black and white!" Eleanor repeated in shock. "Not that one! You only wore it once, and you created such a stir in it!"

"Which is precisely why I won't wear it again. Now bring me the lilac."

Once Renée was hastily dressed in the demure lilac dress, she paused to pour herself a goblet of wine from the bottomless pitcher on the bedside table. Sipping it, she exited into the corridor and asked a sentry: "Where is my dear Counselor Carmine?"

The sentry bowed. "He is in Counselor Vogelsong's chambers, reporting on his trip to Nicole's Harbor, Chataine." Cup in hand, Renée turned down the corridor toward Vogelsong's chambers, and the sentry looked after her perceptively. She stopped in the middle of the corridor ten or twelve feet from Vogelsong's closed door, and there she waited. For almost a quarter of an hour she stood patiently waiting, watching his door.

At last it opened, and she began sauntering down the corridor as if en route from somewhere to somewhere else. Carmine appeared from Vogelsong's chambers looking drained, irritable, and in dire need of a drink. Her action of raising the goblet to her lips immediately drew his full attention. "Why, Carmine! Working so late? It's been far too long since we enjoyed each other's company. Come share a pitcher with me. I promise to make it only one."

Sweat sprang out on his forehead and he licked his dry lips, watching her toy with the goblet of wine. But ten feet behind her stood the sentry, fixing Carmine with an anxious, stern look of warning. Weak and wavering, Carmine took his eyes off Renée to regard the sentry, and he could almost swear he heard Ares utter, *Your life hangs on your obedience.*

At Carmine's glance over her shoulder, Renée turned around, but saw no one. So she urged, "Come, dear Carmine, what is the debate? Come drink with me." In her impatience, she allowed a tiny note of petulance to creep into her voice.

And he heard it. Slight as it was, it was enough to alert him to her purpose and arm him against it. Bowing, he said, "Forgive me, Chataine, I am very tired. The Surchatain has saddled me with a lengthy list of responsibilities during his absence which I cannot hope to accomplish without adequate rest. Excuse me, Chataine. Sleep well." He retreated to his own quarters and firmly shut the door.

Aloof and composed, Renée returned to her apartments. Once behind the closed door, she flung the goblet against the far wall, splattering its contents all over the white plaster, and threw herself onto the brocade loveseat to weep bitterly.

# 5

**B**efore daybreak the following morning, the scouting party was ready to resume their journey on the Pervalley Highway toward Eugenia. Roerich had strongly desired to send along a bodyguard, which Ares declined, so the administrator had instead laden them with additional supplies. It was a splendid morning, clear and cool, but the soldiers—experienced travelers, all—eyed the red-tinted sky with suspicion. Meanwhile, Nicole was regarding the cart with equal misgivings. She felt as though she had only climbed down from the seat an hour ago. However, knowing that riding horseback would be worse, she allowed Wirt to assist her into the cart once again.

They made good time for the first few hours of this leg of the journey. Nicole, having never been west of Crescent Hollow in her life, was eager to actually see the legendary vineyards that provided so much joy across the Continent (and income to Westford's coffers). As they progressed into the Valley, the road dipped lower and lower, until around one bend there appeared on either hand acres of grapevines that hung heavy and luxuriant for miles around. Hundreds of workers labored in the rows, removing basal shoots, picking leaves away from the ripening grapes, and working the green tendrils through the trellis supports to allow sunlight to penetrate to the precious clusters. Wirt, who worked in the vineyards when he wasn't required for soldiering, gave her a running commentary on the crop, with the information that it took years for a vine to mature to good bearing capacity, and that cold, wet weather during fruit set could make the grapes shatter—that is, fall from the cluster. And once set, the crops required constant vigilance against mildew, birds, and fire, any of which could wipe out a whole year's produce.

Fascinated, Nicole strained to get a closer look from the wagon seat, and so drew the attention of one of the many armed guards—Ares' men—who were assigned to protect this valuable enterprise. Ares was in too much haste on this journey to stop and make himself known. But since the unidentified party showed no inclination to wreak mischief, the vineyard soldiers allowed them to pass without hindrance.

They rode through field after field, some with green grapes, some with red, and Nicole almost wished they really were touring the Valley so that she could take the time to learn more about the beautiful crop. At one point, Ares did allow them to stop so that she could get a closer look and pick a few grapes. But the grapes she ventured to sample were not ripe—they were so sour that she spat them out again. Ares smiled, and they continued on.

The sheer size of these fields, and the enormous amounts of fruit they contained, so filled her senses that she did not notice Wirt's sudden silence, or his upturned face and deepening scowl. Finally perceiving the overall darkening of the landscape, she looked up at dark grey clouds merging over the sun. Ares called a halt so they could unpack heavy, waterproof cloaks. Nicole overheard some discussion as to whether they should go ahead and make camp here for the evening. But as the ground around was low-lying and damp already, and so much potential daylight remained, the vote was unanimous to continue on while they could, meanwhile watching for a more suitable place to camp.

Wirt assisted her down from the cart, then she watched in surprise as he turned up the seat, raised a hinged extension from it, and locked it into place. He relocated the seat cushion to rest in the cart bottom under this extension before finding cloaks for the both of them. Once she had donned one, he guided her to sit under the cart seat extension—an innovation of Coyle's, she was sure. Moments later, when great drops of rain began falling and the party resumed travel, she alone was completely protected from the downpour. As a matter of fact, she found the width of the space ample for her to curl up and go to sleep in relative comfort, though she had to allow for a rope knotted through a large eyescrew in the floorboard.

She must have dozed in the bumpy, bouncy cart for hours—she did not know how long—for when she awoke, all was dark. They were still moving, but at a much slower pace than before. Rain was coming down in miserable, drenching sheets. Though she was dry, for the most part, there was one tiny gap in the cloak which had allowed a puddle to form at her feet. Nicole belatedly tightened the cloak to close the hole, then leaned around the seat extension to see what she might.

It was much too dark—she could see nothing but occasional glints from the falling drops. Over the pelting of the rain, she could hear the whistling of the wind, the horses' grunting and plodding, the creaking of wheels and slapping of wet leather, and the indistinct voices of the men as they attempted to navigate the invisible road. Nicole discerned that they were trying to locate the safest route to shelter against a cluster of rocks at the base of the Poison Greens—at this time a formless darkness in the surrounding darkness.

In the midst of this, there was a sudden flash of lightning and shuddering crack of thunder. Tired, jittery Butter, the horse pulling Nicole's cart, reared in panic, and she felt the right side of the cart lift. The alarmed shouts of the men did nothing to stabilize the horse, who flipped in an ungainly sprawl over the shoulder of the road, taking the cart with her.

The instant Nicole felt the cart upending, she gripped the rope that was knotted to the floorboard and curled around it to prevent being thrown. Then the whole cart went wheels up and crashed atop her. The thud of its landing splintered the seat extension, which now became a floor between her and the mud beneath, while the floorboard of the cart became a roof. But the seat itself formed a sturdy wall that prevented her being crushed. Beyond her little house, she heard piercing voices, the screams of the horse, and the stubborn turning of the wheels in the rain.

"Nicole! Nicole!" She heard Ares' cries, and felt the cart tip up as he endeavored to raise it off her. Then she heard Thom's voice, loud but calm, ordering hands to this side of the cart to right it. Before she could catch her breath to speak, she felt her world upended again, as with a mighty hoist and lurch the men restored the cart to an upright position in a depression just off the road.

Ares threw himself blindly into the cart, knocking away muddy, cracked wood, to feel for her body. "Oh, my Lord . . . mighty Jesus . . . Nicole. . . ." His voice was a broken prayer.

"I'm all right," she gasped. "Where is Wirt?"

"Nicole!" He found her arms, feeling along them for broken bones.

"I am not hurt!" she insisted. "Ares, what of Wirt?"

Gripping her, he turned to pass along her inquiry. Someone of the party replied that Wirt had gotten a faceful of mud when he jumped free of the cart, but was otherwise unhurt. Butter they were endeavoring to calm, as she, too, had no apparent injury.

Ares lifted Nicole out of the remains of the cart to convince himself that she was not hurt. She was leaning on his shoulder, allowing him to feel her meticulously for wounds, when something caught her eye. She turned to peer through the rain and the dark. "What is that?" she murmured.

He did not hear her. "Be still, my love, and tell me where it hurts. You will begin to feel the pain when the shock wears off," he said anxiously.

"Ares, I am not hurt," she said, pulling away from him slightly. "What is that?" She pointed off in the distance.

Only then did he look up; Thom, beside him, did likewise. "That is the western edge of the Poison Greens. We are near the border of Eugenia," Ares replied. His hood had slipped off his head, and the water poured down his hair and face into the neck opening of his cloak.

Unheeding, she stared through the slackening rain. "I see the mountains. But the green glow is not coming from them—it comes from somewhere to the left of them."

"That is where the Road of Vanishing lies," Thom said, squinting through the rain. "But I see nothing."

A quick poll was taken of the other men, none of whom saw

the glow. Ares asked her to describe it. "It is very faint, like early sunrise. But it is green," she said. "It comes from somewhere beside the mountains, and fades before reaching half their height. It is a small spot."

By this time the rain had abated, but the cloud cover was still heavy. Soaked through and unnerved by the near loss of Nicole—their seer—the men elected to stop where they were rather than risk another disaster with the carts in taking them over unknown terrain to theoretical shelter. So they hunkered down in their cloaks beside their horses, and Ares made a bed for Nicole as best he could underneath the cart. In this way, they managed a few hours of uneasy rest before dawn.

Despite the discomfort of wet ground for a bed, Nicole managed to sleep rather late into the morning—she woke only when the men began to effect repairs on the cart above her. Blinking, she climbed out from under the cart to watch Coyle tap boards into place. Then she looked around the green, rolling countryside, smelling the sweetness of late spring after a good rain. Wirt was soothing Butter with handfuls of grass while he examined the scratches on her side. "Are you both well this morning, Wirt?" Nicole asked, seeing his bruised cheek. He was a long, lean fellow, and as she should have guessed, quite agile.

He bowed self-consciously. "Aye, Surchataine, thank you."

Nicole reached out to stroke the cream-colored mare. "Why do you call her Butter? Because of her color?"

"Because she's as soft as," Wirt said wryly. "Don't know why Coyle insisted on bringing her."

The engineer did not even look up from his work to reply, "I had no say in choosing the horses, an' if I had, I would not have brought such a nervous creature. Somebody brought her because he loves her."

"I won't have anyone second-guessing my decisions," Ares said irritably, coming up to place a hand defensively at Nicole's back. He, like the others, had removed his coat and loosened his shirt to dry somewhat in the morning air. She opened her mouth to correct his mistaken assumption when he asked in a low voice, "What do you see this morning, Lady?"

Nicole took in the fresh morning around her. They were by

now out of the wine country, and the road ran through pleasant meadowlands full of purple spiderwort and pink touch-me-not. Nicole looked past the meadow and the bordering forest toward the Poison Greens in the distance. "Nothing," she murmured in disappointment. "I see nothing of the green, probably because of the light. The glow I saw last night was so faint that the sunlight must obscure it—at least from this distance."

Ares followed her gaze with troubled eyes. "Then we must wait until we come upon it for you to see what you will. Barring disaster, we will reach it today."

Nicole was not frightened. Being the only one with the gift of sight among this group gave her a sense of responsibility great enough to outweigh the trepidation. And she never forgot that their ultimate purpose was to recover Henry safe and whole.

She became aware of a delicious, sizzling aroma, and she turned to see Sacco, the second-youngest of the group, tending a skillet over a low fire. When he saw her turn toward him, he heaped a portion of the contents onto a plate, which Ben (definitely the youngest and smallest) brought to Nicole with a bow. Another soldier showed her to a seat on tack waiting to be loaded, and a fourth brought her a cup of wine to go with the fried bread, sausage and onions. Resting the plate on her knees, she lifted the first morsel to her husband: "Eat with me, Ares."

He bent to take an obligatory bite before explaining, "I have already eaten, Lady, and have much to see to at present. We will set out when you are finished—but please take your time." His urging her to linger over breakfast was somewhat perfunctory, as his hands were restlessly working the leather pack he held, in order to make it a tighter, neater bundle. So Nicole ate quickly and attended to morning necessities as discreetly as she could with all the men standing around. She briefly wished she had brought a maid, but—Ursula would have been useless in these circumstances.

Coyle had managed such seamless repairs to the cart seat that Nicole could not tell where it had been broken. When she was seated beside Wirt once more, the party started off toward Eugenia with the sun at their backs and a pleasant breeze in their faces.

The closer they got to the border, the more sparse were the

meadow grasses, and the more rocky the soil. Gorse began to dominate, encroaching on the road and irritating the horses. An hour's ride through increasingly rocky terrain brought them to the border, marked by a lone stone post and the sudden appearance of forest.

Entering the woods, dominated by hardy chestnut, elm, and hickory, the party had ridden barely a half-mile before they encountered the fateful fork in the clearing. Here, the main part of the Pervalley Highway continued west while a branch of it curved northward. Another, newer road had been cleared through the trees southward from this point, which Ares knew extended all the way to the Green Lady—the mountain range along the coast. There were no signs or markers at this division of the road, but here is where, three years ago, Ares' army had met the invading Qarqarians and cut them down before they ever set foot on Lystran soil. It was known in the history books as the Battle of the Crossroads. All those who had been present at that battle relived it now as the woods sighed for the dead.

The group peered silently into the ominous clearing. On horseback, Ares drew alongside the cart to murmur, "What do you see, Lady?"

"Nothing, my lord," she said, shaking her head.

"Then we advance," he said, turning Neruda's head toward the northern fork. Wirt urged Butter on, and the rest of the party instinctively fell behind them. The one who had the sight must be given room to see. Tense and watchful, they rode on.

The forest thinned as they approached the western edge of the Poison Greens; the road, which had been wide enough for four to ride abreast, gradually narrowed. It was not paved, only hard-packed dirt, but at least it had been smooth and even at the intersection. The farther north they rode, the more uneven it became. Ares periodically glanced at her with the unvoiced question. As much as she strained to see, however, she discerned no green glow.

They continued north along the deteriorating road, increasingly full of pits and rocks. The Poison Greens rose starkly off their right hand, and the trees gave way to scrub brush. When the cart axles began creaking loudly in warning, Ares gave orders for several of the men to stay behind with the conveyances. Ben, to his disappointment, was one of those left with the gear. But since Ares had not intended to bring him at all, the boy had to accept whatever duties were offered him at this point. They retreated to a more comfortable place to wait on the edge of the forest, and Nicole was given a horse on which to proceed with Ares, Thom, and the remainder of the party. Thus they rode on.

For another hour they rode over roughening terrain, but the men kept their eyes on Nicole, watching for the slightest indication that she saw something. She didn't, and became agitated over the possibility that she might miss the portal in the daylight—or already had. When they stopped to rest toward noon, Ares attempted to reassure her by pointing out, "If you had missed it, one or other of us would have found it by falling through it and disappearing. So we keep looking."

The road began to climb from this point, and the day became warm. They were guiding the horses around another outcropping of rock when Thom observed, "At this point, I see nothing left of the road."

They stopped to look around. It certainly appeared that the road had petered out—vanished. They were standing directionless but for the sun. "Is this why it's called the Road of Vanishing?" someone muttered.

"Let me look beyond the rocks ahead," Crager offered, nodding to a formidable obstruction that would have blocked the road, had it continued. While the others waited, he rode forward as far as he could, then dismounted to climb over the rocks and scan all around. He clambered back down, remounted, and returned brimming with news.

"There is a gorge that drops straight down for a hundred feet just past those rocks. We cannot ride further this way. No army could have marched from Qarqar this way. The closest way around I can see would be to cut back and go through the Poison Greens, about five miles east of us," he reported.

Nicole turned her horse in distress. "I have missed it. Somewhere along the way, I have missed it."

Thom leaned over to whisper to Ares, "But we saw a whole army advance from somewhere along this point to the fork in the road. How then did they come? Could a whole army march through this portal?"

Ares shook his head mutely, indicating that he did not know. Since there seemed nothing else to do, they backtracked slowly along their course while Nicole looked intently all around. Fearing that she might strain herself to uselessness, Ares offered, "Perhaps we should wait till nightfall. It could be that you can see it only at night."

"But I saw the merchant's wares glow plainly in the daylight," she protested, as if the inability to see the portal now was her fault. She was anxious not to let him down in this matter, since it was the whole reason he brought her against his wishes.

They retraced their steps clear to the point at which they had left the carts, and still Nicole saw nothing. By now it was late afternoon, and she was in such a state of flustered anxiety that Ares decreed there would be no more searching today. They found a suitable place to camp against the gentle foothills of the Poison Greens, and the men set to pitching the tents and lighting the fires that they wished they'd had last night.

Dismayed and weary, Nicole sat against a twisted old scrub oak. She ineffectively wiped at the road grime under her shirt collar, and passed a hand over her sweating forehead. One of the men brought her a skin of water, and she poured a little on the edge of her cloak to wipe her face and hands. Sighing, she leaned back against the tree to watch the bustle of camp-making.

Several forest birds, mostly finches and wrens, as well as one curious cuckoo, were also intrigued by the process of making camp, particularly the shoveling (that unearthed various insects) and the unpacking (that revealed the bread). Nicole half-smiled, watching the braver birds swoop over the heads of the men to get a closer look before returning to their perches on the hillside. She idly watched them all line up rather comically on a curved ledge on the western face of the hill.

That was the first thing that caught her attention—the rounded shape of the rock ledge. It did not look like a natural formation. Scrutinizing it, she realized that what appeared to be a half-moon shape was actually circular, the upper part being more defined than the lower. It was, in fact, a circular rim carved in the rock face, with the crude beginnings of bas-relief embellishments all around it. The diameter of the circle was about fifteen feet.

The bottom of the circular rim looked to be resting on a shelf, or a threshold, not five feet off the ground. And from either end of this threshold there extended out and down to level ground what could have been steps, so broad and flat that a horse could ascend and descend them with ease. The whole edifice gave the impression of being the beginnings of an ancient stone temple that was never finished. On first glance, it was not apparent to be a carving at all.

As she was studying this curious structure, trying to make sense of it, the sun dipped below the trees behind her, and the hillside was cast into shadow. That is when she finally saw faintly glowing green lines vertically splitting the center of the circle. To her eyes, the lines looked exactly like light seeping between the slight gap of double doors that were closed on a brightly lit room. Only this light—besides being green—was an undulating, almost *living* kind of light.

"Ares," she murmured.

s Nicole sat staring at the hillside, Ares glanced at her. Though too far away to hear her, he turned to see for himself what held her rapt. The bustle of camp-making gradually stilled as the soldiers watched the Surchatain take a long look at the rock face, then toss down his pack and walk over to kneel in front of his wife. "What do you see, Lady?" he asked. Thom and Rhode drew forward to hear, being careful not to block her line of vision.

"The portal," she replied. "I see the green outlines of doors that are closed. It's there in the side of the hill."

Thom turned to look. "From what I have heard, the carvings are the beginnings of a tunnel, or a cave, that someone thought to dig out many years ago. The work was abandoned before much progress could be made. We do not know why."

"The portal sits within that circle," she insisted. She was so surprised to find what she had been looking for that Ares had trotted over to the hillside steps and advanced up them before she realized what he was doing. Several of the men followed him, and as he approached the doors, horror sprang up in her throat. "Ares! No!"

He placed his hands on the hillside rock and pushed. Nothing happened, as would normally be expected when a mere man pushed on a mountain. He moved his hands all over the solid rock face, feeling nothing but rock, and Nicole leaped up from her seat to run toward him. "Ares, don't! Please!"

"Are you certain it's here?" he asked, turning. Thom and Rhode were also feeling along the rock inside the circle.

"Yes! But the doors are closed. I can see glints of green light coming through the cracks. Oh, Ares, do be careful. I can't lose you through those doors, should they open unexpectedly," she said anxiously.

Puzzling over this, Ares scrutinized the bare rock. "I still see nothing," he muttered.

"Nor I. How do you suppose we get it open?" Thom asked.

"She saw the glow from a distance last night—the doors must have been open then. We wait," Ares decided, withdrawing back down the steps. Most of the other men had to satisfy their curiosity by poking and prying around the rock before they, too, gave up to wait.

"Ares," she said, grasping his hand, "if—or when—those doors open, promise me you won't try to enter."

He looked down on her, perturbed. "Then how shall we find out what is beyond?" he asked. "Don't tell me: you want to send Thom."

"I will go, Surchatain," Thom said quickly.

"We will discuss this when the opportunity arises to do something," Ares said, gently withdrawing his hand from her stubborn grasp. "Are my hands green?" he asked almost teasingly.

"No," she said, glancing aside guiltily, for he had caught her scrutinizing them.

Two of the men who had been left behind with the carts returned from hunting with their reward: the carcass of a stag, which was quickly dressed and set to roast over the fire. Buoyed by a hearty meal of fresh roasted venison, smoked vegetables, and mellow Valley wine, the traveling party enjoyed the descent of evening, especially as there was not a trace of rain in the air. With great self-discipline, they kept their eyes off the Surchataine, who had not the self-discipline to keep from glancing at the maddening portal once every few seconds.

The moon rose and Thom gave orders for the men to bed down for the evening, and still the portal had not cracked. Nicole, almost beside herself with weariness, could not bring herself to lie down until Ares wrapped his arms around her, obscuring the portal from her view. "When it opens, if it opens, you will know; but I can't have you wear yourself out watching it," he said. She balked for form's sake, but fell right to sleep.

In the dead of night, tucked in Ares' arms, Nicole flinched at a bright light in her face. With a murmur of protest, she rolled over, hiding her face. But the light persisted, so she raised up, blinking. The hillside was aglow with green light that poured from between the pillars. "Ares. Ares!" He startled up. "It's open," she whispered. "Can you see it? How bright it is!"

He stared at the hillside, then shook his head. "I see nothing. But I will see more than that soon." Tossing aside the blanket that covered them both, he got up.

Nicole grabbed his arm. "Ares, don't! Please."

Though exasperated, he took care to be gentle. "Nicole. You were given the ability to see this portal for a reason. It was placed before us for a reason. I believe it to be an opportunity to rescue Henry, and perhaps many others. How can I let fear prevent me from using what the Lord has sent us? That won't do."

Chastised, she released his arm. But she noted, "It may just as well be a temptation. How do we know that it is not evil, and that using it will not result in evil?"

"What warning have we had against it?" Ares countered, and the men began stirring, waking up. "A mountain pass is neither good nor evil—that depends on who passes through it. For all I can see, this is no different. That it is supernatural does not make it evil. The Lord is Master of the supernatural."

"I understand," she murmured, not convinced by his arguments as much as by his determination.

Several torches were lit from the smoldering campfire; carrying one, Thom approached Ares and Nicole. "Is it open?" he asked, glancing between them.

"Yes," she answered glumly.

Thom's blue eyes glinted with excitement. "Let me pass through with you, Surchatain."

"Let us test it out, first," Ares said, with a conciliatory glance at his wife.

He took one torch and led them up the steps to the portal. Nicole followed to the foot of the steps, though she could hardly bear to see his face bathed in the bright green light that illumined his scar to its depth. He passed the torch over the rock face, but saw nothing different than what he had seen earlier. What he and the others did note was the instability directly in front of the rock. There seemed to be invisible currents that roiled from the portal, tending to throw them off balance. Ares looked down at Nicole. "Do you see what is making these waves?"

"All I see are streams of light," she said, barely able to look up. "It is like—looking into a vast river of light that flows with great force. It is most fearsome."

He put out a hand to touch the hillside, and his hand disappeared into the rock. Several men murmured exclamations, but Nicole saw his hand extending through the portal into the river.

Ares quickly pulled his hand back, then glanced at her. "Is my hand green?"

"Yes," she said stonily, giving no outlet to the fear welling up in her.

Ares worked his hand, clenching and unclenching it. "I feel nothing." Deliberately, he extended his hand again. The other men saw him thrusting his arm up to the elbow into the side of the hill. "What do you see, Lady?" he asked her.

Eyes on his arm, she replied, "You have put your hand through the open portal into the stream of light."

"Can you see my hand?" he asked, wiggling his fingers.

"Yes," she said.

"What else is there?" he asked.

"That, I cannot tell," she replied. "The light is overwhelming."

Thom interrupted to ask, "Which way are the doors standing open? In or out?"

Nicole studied the round hillside carvings. "I—cannot say. They are not opened out toward us, but whether they open inward, I cannot see. The light is too bright."

Ares withdrew his hand again, shifting to keep his balance in the invisible waves. Then he extended the flaming torch past the threshold. The men saw the light disappear into the earth. "Do you see the torch still?" he asked her.

"Yes, but the torchlight is very feeble in the green," she replied.

With no warning, Ares leaned over and stuck his head through the opening. Nicole gasped and Thom grasped the back of his belt, to pull him out if necessary. Ares turned a little this way and that, then stepped back out of the green hole, inhaling. "Well. It's very dark. I could see nothing. The torch barely glowed at all, and illumined nothing. I also felt nothing."

Ben pushed forward. "Surchatain, let me go have a look. Tie a rope around me so that you can pull me out, and I will go see where it leads."

Ares looked down at him in some surprise. "That is rather a good idea. Bring rope," he instructed someone nearby, who sprinted back to the campground to fetch it.

Handing off the torch, Ares took the rope and tied it around his own waist while Nicole looked off with tears in her eyes. He extended the other end of the rope to Thom. "As Ben said, I will have a look around. Give me slack if I pull on it. If you see reason to pull me back, tug once. I will tug twice if I wish to stay."

"And I will tug once more, hard, if you need to come out," Thom said.

"Someone should go with you, Surchatain," Rhode argued. "We always send scouts in pairs."

Ares hesitated. "Next time." He leaned down to kiss his wife on her bowed forehead, then, taking the torch, he turned and plunged into the rock. Thom twisted the end of the rope around his fist, and Rhode assisted with the slack. Then they watched it disappear inch by inch into the earth.

Inside the portal, Ares fell forward onto nothing. The lack of support under his feet made him flail, losing hold of the torch. But when he realized he was not falling, he stilled. The torch hung listlessly in dead air, untouched, and the rope stretched straight back from his waist. He strained to see in utter darkness, but it was futile—as he had noted earlier, the torch illumined nothing. He reached his hands around him and felt nothing. But he was whole and breathing. "Hello?" he called, just to hear his voice. It fell dead on his own ears as if from hundreds of miles away.

He then determined to see how much forward movement was possible. Some experimentation demonstrated that making swimming motions seemed to advance him, as he felt intermittent tension on the rope. He stopped abruptly and looked around, realizing that the torch was no longer to be seen. That made him pause, but the full implications of it did not strike him right away. He was focused on getting through the blackness to somewhere— only, he could not determine what direction he was going. In the back of his mind was the firm hope that he could find his way to Hornbound. He could only pray that the portal itself had limited dimensions, like a corridor. He was also very glad for his tether to the outside world. Without it, he would be hopelessly lost. Once he had passed over the threshold, there was no indication at all where the opening was, but for the rope.

Ares reasoned that as the rope, stretched out behind him, indicated the way back, then to move away from it must indicate he was going forward. So he energetically worked his arms and legs to propel himself away from his anchor. He could not tell that he was making any progress at all despite the steady tension on the rope. He did not feel the strong currents inside the portal as he had at the door, and wondered if that meant he was being carried along with them.

Suddenly he was stumbling onto solid ground. The sensation was so disorienting that he fell flat on his face. Raising himself from the cool earth, he stood there for a few moments to realign his senses.

It was still nighttime. He was standing in a lightly wooded area, and there was light from a first-quarter moon, as there should have been. The moon was high and small, as at midnight—about when he entered the portal. The rope was still attached to his waist. Looking behind him, he saw it stretched taut for about five feet before disappearing into thin air. So, this was the other end of the portal. He had made it through. But to where? The trees that surrounded him were firs and larches, with a scrubby willow in the mix. It was also rather cooler here than at the Road whence he had departed. All this hinted at a higher, more northerly location.

Looking all around, he discerned that there was a road not far ahead of him. He started toward it, then stopped. There was nothing at this spot to indicate where the portal stood other than the rope stretched out in midair. But without knowing the length of the corridor, he dare not risk wandering beyond the reach of the rope. So Ares untied it from around his waist and retied it securely to the base of a fir sapling. After marking the spot well, he made quietly for the side of the road.

Peering through the brush, he waited until he was sure that the road was deserted. It curved back into the night in one direction, but in the other direction, it seemed to terminate at something large and lighted. Ares marked the place he left the woods, then stepped cautiously onto the road to follow it to its end.

He had not gone far when he saw a great fortress looming ahead in the night, several hundred yards past the line of trees. It had spiked towers lit with torches, and even at this distance, he could discern the movements of watchmen on the walls. It was surrounded by a wide, black moat.

Although Ares could see nothing beyond the near side of the fortress, he instinctively knew that there was a city behind it, sharing the protection of its walls. A fortress this size required fields, flocks, commerce and manpower to sustain it, and that meant a city. Glancing up at the moon again, he ascertained that its illumined side was on the east. Therefore, the fortress ahead of him faced south.

Despite the fact that he had never seen this fortress before, a definite suspicion—or hope—arose in his mind as to which it was. But he must make sure. He crept down the road to the very edge of the trees, straining to see what he might. He exhaled in frustration—he was too far away to see the standards at night. Either he would have to get much closer or wait until daylight to see more. But he could not afford to take that much time on this solo trip—he would have to return with the entire party.

Turning back down the road, he mulled over the possibility of getting horses and carts, not to mention Nicole, through the black void of the portal. It did not seem feasible. But if they were to use it at all, they must bring at least the horses. Then he contemplated how Ulm might have managed to get a whole army through the portal, as apparently he had, in order for Ares to meet them at the Crossroads.

But his thoughts took a different turn when an unexpected gift came galloping down the road toward him and the city. A lone rider was a few hundred yards away from completing his mission, whatever that was—and Ares' experience told him that the man was a messenger. Just from the heaviness of the hoofbeats, Ares could tell that both horse and man were bone-tired, looking forward to bed and board at the end of a long, dangerous road. Well, they had almost made it.

Stopping a horse in midgallop without injury to oneself was a nice feat; the timing was crucial. And Ares must do it before they broke through the cover of trees. Crouching beside the road, he waited until the horse was barely ten feet away, then he sprang up, waving his hands in the horse's face with a sharp, "Hiya!"

The horse reared in fright; the messenger lost his seat and landed on his back in the road. Scrambling beside him, Ares pulled him up by his cloak, demanding, "Where are you going?"

"Huh—I—I—" The fellow could not catch his breath.

Glancing back at the horse, which had regained its footing and resumed a wild run, riderless, for the fortress, Ares urgently shook the man. "What is the city ahead?"

"Hornbound!" he gasped. "I—I carry no money! Only a message from Weygand!"—the capital city of Eugenia.

Ares yanked the man's message pouch from his shoulder and stood, again looking toward the fortress. The horse had been spotted; any moment now armed scouts would storm the woods to look for its rider. Leaving him in the middle of the road, Ares darted into the woods at his marked turnoff to return to the portal.

Only, he was mistaken. The point that he entered the woods was not, in fact, the place that he had marked, but he did not realize this until he had wasted precious minutes looking for the sapling that anchored the rope. By then the messenger had recovered enough to run from the woods shouting at the top of his voice; already the wrenching sounds of the drawbridge lowering were echoing through the trees.

Coolly, Ares ran back onto the road to search for the turnoff marks. While soldiers stormed over the drawbridge, Ares walked down the road toward the fortress with his head down, intently searching the brush in the faint light of the moon. When he could hear the thudding of hoofbeats coming in his direction, he finally found the marked turnoff and plunged once more off the road.

This time, he walked carefully and quietly, retracing his steps exactly to the sapling. As he went, he looped the messenger's pouch securely over his neck and left shoulder. Then he spied the short length of rope tied to the supple tree, and the sight flooded him with relief. While searchers began noisily combing the woods forty feet away, Ares untied his lifeline from the tree and knotted it around his waist more hastily than he should have. Then he followed the rope to its apparent end, where the waves drew him back through the portal.

Once more he was engulfed in the disconcerting blackness. He began pulling himself back toward what was presumably the other mouth of the portal. But as he pulled on the rope, Thom (or whoever held the other end) let it out, apparently assuming that he needed the slack. Lengths of rope began floating uselessly around Ares, now stranded and drifting.

He stopped all extraneous movement to think about this situation. He had left Thom a signal for not wanting to be pulled back, but he had left no signal for wanting to be pulled back. Well then, Ares decided, he must cross back as he had crossed over. After coiling the extra rope lengthwise from palm to elbow so that he could determine its direction of origin, he began swimming that way. He marked his progress by additional coils of the rope, which he slung over his right shoulder when it became too unwieldy to hold.

Along the way he paused—something had reached him. A sound? A ripple? A movement? He neither saw nor heard anything, but . . . he had the sudden, uncomfortable sensation that something else was with him in the portal. He thought about the torch, and wondered what had become of it. He wondered what the capacity of the portal was—how large was it? Then he wondered what, or who else, had found its way in when the doors were open. Had any of the searchers from Hornbound stumbled into the portal after him?

Senses straining, he resumed his ghostlike trek. Suddenly a face—wild, intense, angry—appeared so close to his own that Ares lost his hold on the rope, and it was yanked from his hands. "A way out!" the voice screamed in his face, though the words could barely be heard. "Give it!" And the interloper began pulling violently on Ares' lifeline.

The coiled rope was torn from his shoulder, raking his flesh. And when the man saw that it was tied to Ares' waist, he began clawing at the loose knots.

But by then, Ares had regained enough presence of mind to fight back. He rammed the heel of his right hand up into the man's nose, then with his left struck him in the throat. Effectively immobilized, his attacker began drifting away. But then Ares looked down and saw his end of the lifeline, unknotted from his waist, also drifting away into darkness.

He lunged after it as more and more of the coiled rope disappeared from view. Focusing with all his might on the last visible six inches, Ares stretched himself taut and caught hold of it with one hand. He made sure his grip was firm before cautiously pulling it toward himself—or himself to it. Hand over hand he went up the rope until he had ten feet of it floating around him, then he wrapped it three or four times around his left wrist before passing it around his back, preparatory to retying it.

Suddenly he was stumbling onto solid ground again. Numerous hands caught him, and he looked in surprise at Thom, Rhode and Crager grasping him. It was still deep night here, the carved portal being illumined by four torches lashed to poles set in the ground close by the steps. "Surchatain! We thought we'd lost you," Crager gasped. Thom looked too stricken to speak. And Nicole, very pale, was sitting in a heap at the base of the hill. Crager trotted down the steps to touch her shoulder and tell her that they had retrieved her husband, whole. She weakly looked up.

It took a moment for Ares to catch his breath. "How long has it been?" he finally asked.

"Not but—an hour," Rhode guessed. "But, toward the end, the rope began swaying and jerking, then fell loose. We . . . thought you were gone."

"I have seen the fortress of Hornbound," Ares said, calmly

tossing the rope aside. "The portal leads to a concealed point just outside the walls."

"That's three days' travel in this terrain," Thom said, glassy-eyed.

"But we can get there in moments," Ares said. "Only, it is rather difficult. . . ." He looked down at Nicole at the foot of the steps, and a shadow of doubt began to cross his mind.

She watched him, still unable to speak, then her face changed. Her eyes widened in fresh horror and her mouth fell open. In the split second before he turned to discover what she might be seeing in the portal behind him, he wondered whether he shouldn't have heeded her concerns after all.

Finally she found her voice to cry, "It's closing! The portal is closing!"

Several things happened almost too quickly to see. The three of them—Ares, Rhode, and Thom—were standing close to the threshold at the top of the steps. As Nicole cried out, there was an intense, invisible (to them) stirring, a sudden airless whoosh. Thom jumped back and Rhode fell in, disappearing bodily into the hillside. Ares, knowing what was beyond, shot out an arm to catch him. Then the portal doors closed. Ares' arm was locked in solid rock and Rhode was nowhere to be seen.

# 7

ith a wretched cry, Nicole sprang up the steps on all fours. Crager almost tripped over her getting to the top of the steps before her. Thom had jumped forward, slamming himself ineffectively against the hillside. He did this again and again until Ares ordered, "Stop! I have him."

They stilled in breathless hope. Thom asked, "Are you whole, Surchatain? Are you in pain?"

"No—yes—" Ares said, then explained, "I am all right. My arm is stuck, but I am holding onto Rhode. I caught his sleeve, and he is now holding my arm with both hands, just as he should." Nicole collapsed at his feet, and he looked down to reassure her, "I am whole." But he could not sit or move more than a few inches one way or the other. His right arm was buried almost up to the shoulder in rock. As if the sight weren't distressing enough, Nicole was almost nauseated by the intense green aura that surrounded him, overwhelming the torch light. But that did not prevent her from clinging to his legs.

The others stood around dumbly, wondering what to do. Then Ben came up with a skin of wine, which Ares received appreciatively. Thom ventured to ask, "You . . . saw Hornbound, Surchatain? Are you sure?"

"Yes. Take this." He began working the pouch (which no one

had noticed before now) off his left shoulder. "I took it from the messenger, who said it was a letter from Weygand to Hornbound. Read it to me."

Thom opened the pouch and removed the solitary letter. While Crager held up the torch, Thom broke the seal on the parchment and unfolded the packet. Other men gathered on the steps to listen as he began to read: "'To the Honorable, Majestic and Benevolent Surchatain Ulm, Ruler of Qarqar, from your Humble Servant and Ally Surchatain Klar of Eugenia: Greetings.

"'We have studied at length the proposal your majesty graciously sent for our united efforts against the vicious tyrant Ares of Lystra, and your plan pleases us greatly. Your good council may certainly count on Eugenia's quick and obedient response to the best of our ability, decimated as we are with the plague that has spread throughout the province. Please do not let this scourge deter you from sending your troops at once to unite with ours. Victory to the Realm of the Sun!' And it is sealed with Klar's signet," Thom related.

"Fire and ice," Alphonso muttered under his breath, along with several choice epithets directed at Klar.

"Then Klar has betrayed us. How shall we fight Eugenia *and* Qarqar?" Buford asked.

Crager looked confused. "Plague? I've heard no word of this from our scouts."

Thom replied to Crager, "There is no plague."

Ares nodded, resting his hip against the hillside. "Our treaty with Eugenia stands. Klar is unwilling to incur Ulm's wrath by refusing an alliance, as he does not have the strength to fight him. So he is putting him off with a lie. The problem is, we need Ulm to receive this letter. I should not have robbed the messenger. He told me what I needed to know," Ares added in bitter reflection.

He raised his head. "I need two volunteers to carry this letter back to Klar at Weygand so that he can resend it to Ulm." From where they were now, this would require less than a day's travel. A pair of men immediately stepped forward, whom Ares instructed to deliver the letter to Klar with apologies, and assure him that his messenger was unhurt. They were not, however, to explain the circumstances whereby the letter fell into Lystran hands—"Decide between yourselves on a likely story which he cannot refute, that leaves us innocent as children in the matter. And . . . stay and have a look around in Weygand for a few days, then come back to this place. If we are not here, return straightway to Westford."

"Surchatain," they saluted. After packing supplies, the two volunteers set off on horseback with the letter at once.

Ares remained trapped in the hillside. He craned his neck to see the moon—judging from its proximity to the horizon, there was only an hour or two left before sunrise. "Have the men bed back down, Thom. They can't do me any good standing around." So Thom gave orders, and most of the men reluctantly returned to their bedrolls. Ben sat on the steps next to Nicole, and Thom and Crager remained standing beside Ares.

Morning crept up, pink and glowing, and Ares saw no reason not to open the western window in his mind and sit at the sill in prayer. The moment he did, however, troubling thoughts about the portal, and Hornbound, came to him that he did not wish to entertain. So he shut the window again.

Out of sheer weariness, Nicole fell asleep against his leg, and Ben lay down beside her. Thom ordered Crager to bed so that he could relieve him later. In the misty dawn, Thom leaned against the rock to keep Ares company, lest he fall asleep and lose hold of Rhode. "What was it like in there, Surchatain?" he asked.

In a low voice, Ares told him everything about swimming through the black void, the companion portal in the wood, the fortress of Hornbound, and his return through the void, including the fight for the rope. Thom absorbed it all with admirable restraint up till that point, when he asked quietly, "Do you still have hold of my Second in Command, Surchatain?"

"Yes. Better, I can feel that he has tied his arm to mine with his belt. He will be safe until the portal opens again," Ares replied.

Thom glanced down at Nicole, slumbering on Ares' leg (now stiff). "Do we have any way of knowing when that might be?"

"No. At least, I do not," Ares replied. He did not voice his fear that it opened at the same time every night. If so, he would be standing here for a long time yet.

They were quiet for a while, watching the early fog burn away. As the portal faced west, with the sun ascending over the

Poison Greens behind them, Ares stood in the chill of the hillside's shadow for hours, but he declined offers of a blanket. Every now and then Thom would glance at his arm, and Ares would nod, "He is still there." Sacco, the camp cook, arose to start distributing a late breakfast of bread, cheese, and dried fruit. Ares ate, and Nicole woke to eat at his feet.

For several hours more, while the sun tracked its course over the Poison Greens, Ares stood pinned to the hillside. The June sun climbed to its apex to beat down on him, as there was no shade. Coyle rigged up a tarp on stilts to cover him, but it had to be shifted so often that Ares finally waved it away.

Meanwhile, the men busied themselves tending the horses, cleaning gear, or foraging for water, kindling, meat, greens, and ripe berries. Crager relieved Thom so that the Commander could snatch a few hours' rest, but Nicole left the rock only for a necessary trip into the woods. When she returned, she sat as before at his leg. There was no need for her to watch the rock; when the portal did open, they would know it. And, she said nothing.

Her silence convicted him more than anything else. "Nicole," he finally said, and she looked up. "I . . . may have been . . . wrong to ignore your counsel about the portal. When I said I had no warning against it, I was discounting the warning you were trying to give me. I did not ask the Lord for discernment before I entered; I just assumed it was there for my use. But . . . you may have been correct in pointing out that everything that crosses our path is not necessarily useful to us. There are also traps set in our path. The Lord gave you alone the sight to see this trap, and He also gave you a healthy fear of it. It was foolish of me not to listen to you."

"Oh, Ares." She stood to wrap her arms around him. "At least you are out. And you are not so green anymore. It is fading."

"Then we are grateful for small encouragements," he smiled at her.

Crager tried to pretend that he did not hear all this. But then he looked up in sudden alarm. "Surchatain," he ventured, "once the portal opens again, we may expect the same disturbance that sucked the Second in. Should we not take measures to prevent your falling in with him?"

Nicole drew a quick breath and Ares said, "You are right." He called for the rope so that it could be retied around his waist and tied off to the closest cart. By this time, Thom had awakened, and came over to see that all was secure.

As Ares tested the knots around his waist, he paused. "Thom— how much of the rope did you feed to me while I was in the portal? Can you guess how much rope you played out?"

Thom and Crager studied each other. "I'd say about forty feet, at most," Thom said, and Crager nodded.

"Forty feet! Are you sure?" Ares exclaimed.

"Well, that may be on the high side. This rope's but sixty feet long, and we had ample to spare," Thom pointed out.

"Forty feet," Ares mused, still disbelieving.

"Are you . . . sure it was Hornbound you saw, Surchatain?" Crager asked dubiously.

"You saw the letter," Ares gestured. "That was Klar's seal, and the messenger was definitely nearing a fortress which fit what we know of Hornbound, down to the spiked towers and drawbridge."

"But what you saw of the walls does not match what I have heard. The fortress you saw may have been a waystation for the messenger. I don't see how we can know for sure it was Hornbound, as little as we know about it," Thom said in frustration.

One of the men who had come close to unpack supplies from the cart heard Thom, and turned around. "Excuse me, Commander—Surchatain. I—thought that's why you selected me for this mission."

They turned to look at him. "Miers," Thom said. "What do you mean?"

"Well, sir, I'm one of the Qarqarians you took prisoner after the Battle of Crescent Hollow"—five years ago. "You gave us the choice of prison, digging the waterway, or joining the army, so I joined," Miers said.

Thom looked mildly flustered. "I didn't know that's where you came from. All I knew was that you could track anything."

"Thank you, Commander. But I was a lieutenant in the Qar-qarian army before Ulm assassinated Melva's father, Surchatain Shryoc. I have seen the city from the inside," Miers said.

Ares seized on this. "Then let me describe to you what I saw, and you tell me if it fits. Do not hesitate to say so if what I describe to you is not Hornbound." The man nodded deferentially, and Ares related every detail he could remember of what he witnessed beyond the portal.

When he had finished, Miers said, "There is no doubt that you saw Hornbound, Surchatain, and that from within the city walls."

"No, no," Ares shook his head. "The drawbridge was before me. I was outside the walls."

"You were outside the fortress, but within the city walls," Miers corrected him. "The woods you were in are the Surchatain's private hunting grounds within the city compound, which covers perhaps twenty square miles of pasture, woodland, and fields, besides the city itself, atop the Lone Mountain. The outer wall, which is ten feet thick, completely encircles the mountaintop below the city. At the base of the mountain are the mines. The city is reinforced thus to protect it not only from invasion, but slave uprisings. Hornbound has never been taken except by treachery from within. Its walls are unbreachable."

Ares exhaled. "The portal put me within striking distance of the fortress. If I had even a small army . . ." he trailed off, glancing at Nicole, who lowered her eyes in dismay. But rather than say anything more to upset her, he looked toward the western sky and began to pray.

The day wore on. Thom and Ares pumped Miers for any more information he might have about Hornbound, but he knew little more than what he had already told them. It seemed that even lieutenants in the Qarqarian army were not much trusted. One curious detail that Miers did relay to them was Ulm's elaboration on the role of executioner. As Miers described it, executioners, whether hangmen, axemen, or torchmen, were drawn from the most elite ranks of the army. When Ulm decided that someone should die, he would hand-select the executioner, dress him up in black robes and black mask, then send him to that person's house to bring the condemned to the fortress for a summary judgment. And death was meted out for any offense against the Surchatain—including criticism spoken in private.

"It kept the nobles of the city properly terrified," Miers related. "No one dared speak above a whisper against Ulm. As a matter of fact, we heard rumors that he himself played executioner at times, whenever he took the crime personally."

"Shryoc might still be alive had he employed some of that suspicion toward his own Counselor," Thom noted.

"How would he guess that Ulm was conspiring against him? But people change . . ." Ares murmured, thinking of Carmine.

In Westford at that moment, Carmine had just returned to his quarters after a difficult session with Vogelsong. It seemed to Carmine that the former amanuensis was enjoying too much his elevation in status—he had far more responsibility than such a young man should bear. And to be named a Counselor! Carmine pursed his lips in disapproval, looking down at his shaking hands. He wanted a drink very badly. Very badly indeed. Why, he—

With a start, Carmine spotted the golden pitcher and cup on his bedside table. What was that doing here? Curiously, he went over to look in the pitcher, and the bouquet of sweet Valley wine engulfed him, causing his knees to buckle. He sat heavily in the chair, gripping the goblet to fill it from the pitcher. "It is a gift from God," he sighed.

*From whom?* the thought crossed his mind. The urge to drink without thinking about it was fierce—almost smothering. But Renée's chalk-whitened face flashed before his eyes, and he paused at her familiar, contemptuous smile. She wanted him drunk—his drunkenness was her security. As long as he was a sotted wretch, she was in control. He knew why she relished Ares' taking one responsibility after another away from him: because when he was "incapacitated," his wife could legally step in and make decisions for him, although she had never been certified in the Law, had never even read it. His drinking had made him her toy, her patsy, once again. Only this time he stood to lose more than his manhood. Ares had warned him.

Carmine deliberately placed the filled goblet on the table. Turning his back on it, he went to the door to summon his servant. The man was a long time coming, and Carmine sat on the brocade bench to wait, staring at the golden pitcher from across the room. When the servant finally came, escorted by the guard who fetched him, Carmine waved the guard in with him and pointed to the table: "What is that doing here?"

The servant glanced at the refreshment and disavowed any knowledge of how it got there. "You are dismissed," Carmine said. "Forever. You are to leave the palace and never come back." He gestured to the guard to make this command a certainty.

Sulking, the man was taken away. Carmine then sent orders for another manservant to be sent up. When the new one arrived, Carmine inquired his name. "Your servant is Hauffe, Lord Counselor," the man said with a bow.

Carmine told him, "Hauffe, I require a new personal attendant. I shall reward you amply if you prove faithful, and I will banish you if you betray me. Do you see the wine service on the table? I want it removed. No wine, ale, or beer is ever to be brought into these quarters. And if you listen to anyone who beguiles you with different words, it will be your undoing. Have I made myself clear?"

"Yes, Counselor." Hauffe bowed again with remarkable composure.

"Then attend to your duties," Carmine said, and the wine was speedily removed.

When the servant had left, Carmine sank back into the brocade seat. "I have a newly dangerous enemy," he mused. And he began to ponder what he should do about her.

On the Road of Vanishing in Eugenia, the men made themselves as useful as possible, but there was only so much they could do while their Surchatain hung between worlds. Ares worked his arm every now and then just to confirm that there was no getting it free of the rock. At the same time, he reassured his anxious wife that the blood flow was not constricted; he retained feeling and the use of the hand and fingers he could not see. "I am suffering more discomfort from the belt Rhode has wrapped around my arm," he said, wincing. "He seems to be moving around a lot. I fear he is trying to explore."

Coyle rigged a high seat of crates and a saddle for Ares to sit on, and by late afternoon he was dozing against the hillside. But since there was no place to lay his head, he jerked awake again after a fitful nap. Nicole stood close to his shoulder so that at least he could rest his cheek on the top of her head. That gave him a few minutes' more sleep. Then with bleary eyes, he watched the sun set below the trees, counting the hours until midnight—the presumed time of the doors' opening.

With the coming of evening, the men secured torches on either side of the portal so that they could see what they were doing when the time came to act. Although very hungry by now, Ares declined dinner. He would not allow anyone, especially Nicole, to clean him up after an involuntary evacuation.

They waited, growing drowsy. Upon further thought, Ares decided that the doors opened last night sometime around midnight. So he probably had a four-hour wait from here.

He raised his head, and Thom looked at him. A spasm of discomfort crossed Ares' face. "Surchatain, what is it?" Thom could see Ares' body jerking slightly from the movement of his trapped arm.

"Something's happening," Ares said, wincing. "Rhode is thrashing about. Ungh!" He grunted in pain as his arm was twisted. Lowering his head, he gripped what he could feel of Rhode on the other side.

Ares let out a gasp, and Nicole stood fearfully. They could see his body reacting to the violence beyond the closed door. Ares clenched his teeth and flexed his hidden arm as far as he could, to prevent its breaking.

Nicole let out a sudden cry and fell back, covering her face, but they did not need her to tell them that the portal was opening. All at once Ares tumbled backward off the threshold with Rhode in his arms. Thom and Crager were careful to jump free of the turbulence at the mouth of the open doorway.

Ares fell down the steps and rolled in the dirt with Rhode, holding on to him. This required unexpected effort, as Rhode was shouting and struggling to get up. Ares shouted over him, "Stop! What is it? You almost break my arm and now—what are you doing?" The other men ran over to assist however they could.

"Surchatain! Let me up! Let me back in there!" Rhode exclaimed.

"Why?" Ares shouted.

"Oswald is in there!" Rhode cried, and they all froze.

After a stricken silence, during which Rhode, groaning, looked back to the portal, Ares whispered, "Oswald?"

"Yes! Among others, mostly Qarqarians. But I saw him and talked to him. That day three years ago he came up this road looking for the portal, and saw the green light of its opening. He looked in and fell. He had no idea that it has been three years, but—he cannot find his way out. He said that every time the portal opens, the bright light blinds him and he cannot see where the opening is. I had him hold on to me so that he could come out with me, but when the—the turmoil began right before the portal opened, a Qarqarian came up and began wrestling me for hold on your arm, to get out. I had to fight him off. But in doing so I lost Oswald," Rhode gulped.

Ares listened with his mouth hanging open, rubbing his sore arm, and Rhode looked back to the portal. "Is it still open? I must go back, Surchatain. I must retrieve Oswald."

Ares turned to the steps. "I will go."

Vehement objections were raised on all sides. By proximity, Thom's voice prevailed: "Surchatain. You've had nothing to eat and no sleep the whole time you were trapped in the portal. Your arm is injured. We must send someone who is fresh."

Nicole added softly, "Ares, I beg you to send someone else."

He glanced at her and dropped his head. Then he inhaled thoughtfully. "So . . . Oswald could see the green light, Rhode?"

"Yes. That's how he found the portal. But from the inside, he said the light makes it impossible to see your way out," Rhode said.

"Couldn't he just—feel his way out?" Crager asked.

Rhode turned to him. "When you are inside, there is nothing to feel. Even if you think you are laying your hand on the rock, you feel nothing. It is all a void, but for the green light."

"Did you see the light?" Ares asked him.

"No. Oswald told me that it shimmers throughout, but moments before the doors open, it begins building until it blazes. Then it begins fading, and the doors shut. I saw none of this. Only he could see it," Rhode replied.

"Are you saying that the light begins fading before the doors close?" Ares asked thoughtfully.

"Yes, that is what Oswald told me," Rhode replied.

Ares turned to scrutinize the hillside again. "Yes, we must get him out. And we may not have much time before the doors close again."

"Surchatain, send me," Rhode said, in a voice low with urgency.

"But you've been in there for so long—aren't you tired?" Ares asked.

"No. I feel as though it's been only moments. Please, Surchatain—I had my hands on him!" Rhode pleaded.

Ares glanced at Thom, then looked past him to Crager. "Coyle!" Ares called.

The engineer appeared at his side instantly. "Surchatain?"

"We need you to quickly rig up halters for Crager and Rhode. They will go in together to look for Oswald," Ares instructed.

Coyle got to work by torchlight. It took only minutes for him to modify the carthorse harnesses into sturdy halters that buckled around the chests of the two men, freeing their hands. Coyle included a strap to attach them to each other, and a belt for Oswald. When Rhode and Crager were outfitted, the rope was fastened at two points on the halters. Then they eagerly ascended the steps and leapt into the rock. Buford and Alphonso made themselves anchors of the rope.

Ares ate and drank, then sat wearily under a tree with Nicole to watch the torchlit portal at a distance. "Wake me if anything happens," he murmured, and lay down with his head in her lap.

While Ares slept, Thom divided the men into shifts to hold the rope and keep watch over the portal throughout the night. He positioned himself close by Alphonso and Buford, who stood off the steps about five feet away from the door (and the treacherous turbulence). Buford, a large man, had the very end of the rope knotted to his belt, while Alphonso, in front of him, let inches of spare rope slip through his hands as it was required by Oswald's rescuers.

For the next several hours, Alphonso fed rope steadily into the portal. After checking to see that Ares was still sleeping comfortably, Thom returned to Alphonso to ask, "How far out are they now?"—for this time, they had been marking the length of the rope they played out.

"Just over thirty feet, Commander," Alphonso replied. "And

I hope they're closing in on the rascal, for that's half the length right there—" He broke off at the sudden windless uprising. The hillside became solid rock once again, this time with a length of rope dangling from it.

Thom, Buford, and Alphonso stood there staring at the place in the hillside where the rope sprouted like an errant vine. Although Alphonso could feed no more of it through, neither did it appear to be severed. Gradually, Thom let out his breath. "Well, if they stay in their harnesses, they're secure until it opens again. But—blast! The thing opens for a while, then shuts again for hours, and seems to go by no schedule at all."

Buford looked back to where Ares and Nicole were soundly sleeping. "Should we wake him, Commander?"

Thom shook his head. "No. Let him sleep. It's only a few hours till sunrise, anyway, and he'll wake then. See, both of you, there's no use your standing there for the next ten hours till the blasted thing opens again. Tie off the rope securely to the cart there. Go ahead and bed down, but stay close by in case it opens again." These orders were carried out. Before long, the whole camp was peacefully slumbering, save two who stood sentry.

Those two were reliable men, too well trained to sleep on duty, but watching a rope is not the most stimulating predawn activity. So they kept themselves alert by talking together, or scanning the nearby forest, or keeping the fire burning warmly, and only occasionally glanced at the rope spanning the barren ground between the hillside and the cart. So they may be excused for not noticing the first tiny twitching of the rope in warning.

The coming of sunrise cast the hillside face in a dark shadow, which is the other reason the sentries did not notice the rope shuddering upon invisible waves. Nor did Nicole, sleeping with her face turned away from the portal, waken when it opened. While the sentries talked quietly and the others slept, something on the other end of the rope caused it to twist and yank against the knots on the cartwheel. Again and again the rope was stretched taut, but the knots held.

At last, one of the sentries looked over and raised a shout; at the same moment, two figures were propelled through the portal to roll on the ground beside the cart: Rhode and Oswald.

# 8

The sentries ran forward to assist the two who had returned, shouting to rouse the camp. For some time there was chaos as Oswald was shaken and hugged and passed from hand to hand to be studied and marveled at. After scrutinizing the big man with his curly head and reddish beard, Thom concluded that he looked just the same as he had three years ago, down to the scratch on his cheek that he'd gotten in horseplay with some Green recruits.

The soldiers went quiet, parting for Ares to step through. Bleary-eyed, he regarded the newly found Second without saying anything at first. Then he reached out his hand. "Welcome back, Oswald."

"Thank you, Surchatain, to be sure," Oswald said, happily grasping Ares' hand in both bear paws. Nicole came up to put her arms around him despite the strong green glow, but he went down on his knees to receive her welcome.

Less welcoming, Ares turned to Rhode as he was being unbuckled from his harness. "How did you lose Crager?"

"Well, Surchatain," Rhode said faintly, "I'm . . . not sure he's lost, sir."

"Explain yourself," Ares said.

Rhode relayed haltingly, "We . . . we were floating in the portal, calling for Oswald, just . . . hoping he could hear us. And Crager said he wondered how big the portal was—if there were branches that Oswald could have gotten lost in. And I said, if there were, we couldn't find them, because we had less than sixty feet of rope to carry us. And he said, well, if the Surchatain got to Hornbound on less than sixty feet, then maybe we could get farther than we thought . . . like, say, to Westford.

"'Westford!' said I. But then, Surchatain, we . . . landed upon solid ground, and looked around, and Crager said, 'Tear me to pieces if this isn't the Surchataine's orchard!' And I looked, and it seemed to me it was, because there were the pear trees afore us all in bloom. And at my feet was the Surchataine's planting of bistort. . . ." Rhode hesitantly stuck his hand in his jacket and withdrew a spike of flesh-colored flowers, only slightly crushed.

Nicole gasped, reaching for the stalk, which Rhode laid in her palm. "I knew that she had searched all over for roots to plant, as it had become so scarce, and Dr. Savary uses it. I also know of nowhere else that it's grown near pear trees, and the west wall, and the globed lights along the path," Rhode swallowed.

Ares patiently repeated, "Where is Crager?"

"Well, Surchatain, when we saw where we were, he got out of his harness and volunteered to run into the palace and grab someone. He said, 'Think of it, sir! We can send messengers back and forth in the blink of an eye.' I said, 'Hurry, then, and I'll stand at this end of the portal.' But while he was gone, I felt that rushing sensation, and fell back inside the portal. The door to Westford must have closed," Rhode shrugged.

"When I was inside again, I knew I had better see to what we had set out for, and started calling for the Second Oswald, and by God's grace somehow he heard me, and came. So I put the harness on him, and then the light flared up—though I didn't see it, the Second had to shut his eyes against the brightness. When he confirmed that the door was open, we began pulling ourselves forward on the rope, and fell through," Rhode finished.

There was an awed silence. Ares looked toward the portal. "Is it still open?"

"Yes," Oswald and Nicole answered at the same time.

Deliberately, Ares turned his back on it. "Then let it stay open or closed as it will for a while. We must think and pray about what to do from here. Sacco—what of breakfast?"

"Coming right along, Surchatain," the young man said, hastening toward the campfire.

As morning brightened into day, the men sat around the fire and ate, relentlessly quizzing Oswald about his strange tenure in the portal. He was somewhat hungry, as there was nothing that he could see to eat or drink in the void. But then, he thought he had been there for only an hour or two. Yes, he had seen others, and had tried to hail one or two, but no one seemed to be able to hear him. Either that, or no one was interested in anything other than getting out.

"It seemed to me, Surchatain," Oswald related, "that there was no way to get out unless you had a connection with someone on the outside. I never saw anyone else enter nor leave."

"But you saw the portal open from time to time?" Ares asked while Sacco handed Oswald a platter of squabs and mushrooms braised in butter.

"Yes, Surchatain," Oswald said, reaching up for the platter. "As it is open now. The light blinds one."

Most of the men glanced toward the maddening rock face that looked no different than any other hill at any other time. Nicole did not turn to look; she could almost feel the waves of green light. She was firmly ambivalent about Oswald's ability to see it. On the one hand, it took a great burden off her to share the sight; on the other hand, it meant that Ares could send her back to Westford at any time. She caressed the stem of bistort thoughtfully.

"How many times did you see it open?" Ares asked Oswald.

He squinted over his plate as if counting shadows. "How many times . . . ? Surchatain, I fear I cannot tell you. When I think back on it, it seems that it was always open."

"But," Rhode protested, "you said the light blazed up when it opened, and faded when it closed."

Oswald nodded. "That's how I saw it then. But now I can't say whether it blazed up when I turned toward it and faded when I turned away. Inside, you've no sense of orientation."

"No, you don't," Ares agreed. "Nor of time, nor space. . . ."

"Well, we know that it's *not* open all the time," Rhode said.

Ares looked again toward the hillside. "Not from the outside," he said quietly.

Following, Ares decided to climb to the top of the hill that housed the portal, and do it alone. So Michaud, the expert climber of the group, equipped him with boot spikes, gloves and rope, pointing out the most advantageous route to the top, which could be seen from the camp. Ares shed his coat, as the day had grown warm, and they watched him make his way up the rocky slope.

The men hunted, foraged, and finished a lean-to (sturdier than a tent) for Nicole and Ares before improving upon their own shelters. In the twenty-four hours that they had been here, they had seen no one else. This did not surprise them, as they were, for all practical purposes, at a dead end. But they kept an eye on their Surchatain as he reached the top of the hill. He sat, facing away from them to the east. His head was bowed at first, then he raised his face and looked all around. Nicole watched the dark brown hair, barely visible at this distance, lifted in the light wind.

A few hours later, in late afternoon, he finally began to descend. Thom was irritated that he chose to do so without the rope, as he apparently wanted to keep it free for the portal. But whatever he had wrestled with on the hilltop had apparently been settled for good or ill, as he climbed down with an air of resolution. The last five feet he jumped, landing nimbly on his feet beside the right portal steps.

"Surchatain," Thom greeted him indifferently, gesturing to his boot, and Ares lifted his heel for Thom to assist him out of the climbing spikes. Nicole approached, harboring a vague dread to hear what he may have decided to do.

"Is it still open?" Ares asked, nodding toward the invisible doorway.

Nicole nodded. Thom, darkly cheerful, explained, "That's because we haven't tried to use it yet." He handed the boot spikes and rope off to Michaud as Ares turned to Nicole, taking her hands.

He raised them to his lips, and she dully regarded the stubble of beard that framed his scar. Now that she knew what was coming, she steeled herself to accept it gracefully: He was going to send her back.

"You have been of invaluable service to me," he began, and she lowered her head. "Without your sight, we would never have found the portal, and never recovered Oswald. But now that we have him, I cannot risk your life further." He was quiet for a moment, and she looked at him curiously. With that decided, what was he struggling over now?

He continued, "At the same time, I cannot dismiss the use of the portal, even though it is dangerous. As far as I can see, it is our only chance to assault Hornbound and recover Henry. This time, Lady, I would have you know that I have been seeking a word from the Lord on whether to use it or not. I . . . have not received clear permission or denial. It is almost as if . . . the choice is mine whether to make use of it or not. But if I do, and anything goes awry, I must live with the consequences." Others began gathering around them to listen.

"There is only one way I can see to determine whether it may help us retrieve Henry," Ares said. "My love . . . will you go with me through the portal to Westford?"

Nicole regarded him while the others stood in stricken silence. She contemplated what he asked: Step into the void, the green, that she feared more than death itself? What if she were lost? What if the doors closed forever? But if Ares was with her. . . . "I will go anywhere you bid me, my lord," she replied.

He pressed her hands to his scar in a gesture of humility, of genuine deference to her. "Then let us prepare," he said softly.

They ate and cleaned themselves up a bit. Ares made sure he had on his belt the two items he had taken from Lazear—the slaver's keyring and Melva's hair ribbon—though those items had not left his person since he had set out from Westford. He donned his coat and placed Nicole's cloak around her shoulders, as it was getting cool (even though Westford would be balmy right now).

Then, in early twilight, Ares called for the harnesses to fasten on himself and her. While they were being outfitted, he explained, "I have developed some theories about this portal that may or may not bear out. First, this end appears to be the entry with any number of exits, depending upon where one wishes to go. It is obvious that it closes from the outside, but I believe it is always open from the inside, if one has a link to the outside. I was not hindered in exiting by the rope—neither were Rhode, Crager, or Oswald. But the rope is crucial." This point troubled Thom: then how had Ulm brought his army through? But he chose not to interrupt, and Ares continued:

"Therefore, I propose that the Surchataine and I return to Westford through the portal, establishing the rope link. Then I will begin sending men and arms back through—even horses, if we are able. Once we have enough men on this side, we will enter for Hornbound," Ares finished.

"Surchatain—do you suppose it is possible to go straight from Westford to Hornbound?" Thom asked.

Ares paused. "I don't know. We may try." He turned to Nicole. "Are you ready, Lady?"

"Yes," she said, trembling.

As he took her hand, a number of other hands took up the rope that was fastened to their harnesses. He told Thom, "It seems best to tie off this end to the cart. If we get through, I will tie off the other end on that side. If all goes well, you will see others come through. If you see nothing for several days, you had best send a messenger back to Westford—the long way. Do not come through the portal if you receive no word."

"Yes, Surchatain," Thom said, glancing at Nicole, then glancing down. "God speed."

Ares faced the portal. "Is it still open?"

"Yes, my lord," Nicole answered.

"Then come." With the rope trailing, he escorted her up the side steps. Then, tightening his grip on her hand, he let himself fall into the opening, taking her with him.

With Thom supervising, Rhode and Alphonso began feeding the rope into the hillside after them. The men did this for only a few minutes before sensing the airless shudder. Rhode uttered an angry cry as the portal clamped shut, throwing them backwards. "Blast!" Thom gasped. "They've only—how much rope?"

"We were able to feed out less than twenty feet before it locked up on us, Commander," Alphonso said, agitated. "I swear that this monster has a mind to taunt us."

Thom glared at the placid hillside. "Then we shall find a way to tame it."

The men stood around studying the rudimentary carvings in rock—all they could see of the invisible portal. Even Oswald could only just detect the glimmerings through the closed door. Then Rhode murmured, "Commander, I wonder . . . I can't help but wonder why whoever began work on this fine entryway, with the carvings and all, gave it up. . . ."

At that time, the dinner hour had just commenced in Westford. Contrary to expectation, it was not any livelier with the ruling couple absent. Since, by Renée's decree, no children were presented to the table in the absence of the Surchatain and Surchataine, it was actually much quieter. Some preferred it that way; some did not. However, the fact that it was quieter did not make it dull.

Carmine had used the time since finding the wine in his room yesterday to prepare carefully for tonight. Clean and healthy-looking, he was very nearly back to his old impressive self. He made witty conversation with Lady Vivian (Renée's mother), who was thrilled at the attention. He heaped praise on Counselor Vogelsong and Doctor Savary for various competencies he had observed during the day. He even threw a bone or two to Giles, seated next to him. (The one consolation Giles received—and Carmine, for that matter—for Vogelsong's being named Counselor was that both Giles and Carmine retained their seats above Vogelsong at the table. Ares had privately conferred with the young upstart on the matter, making him to understand that honors aplenty would come his way if he would be gracious in this, to which Vogelsong quickly agreed.)

The one person Carmine did not acknowledge during dinner, it seemed, was Renée, sitting directly across from him. Yet he so brilliantly guided the conversation on topics of which she was ignorant that she could not say anything without interrupting with a wholly new topic—which she was quite prepared to do. But even as she opened her mouth to speak, Carmine looked at her and said, "My dear Renée, how especially lovely you look tonight. I've no clue why the servants laugh at ladies who use chalk when it looks so fetching on you."

Hearing one of her own kind of rapierlike insults directed

at her, from him, rendered her speechless. So her husband courteously filled the void: "And you have been so marvelously helpful on the apportionment council in my stead that I almost regret reclaiming the seat from you. But how can decisions be made when everyone is staring at you?" he laughed lightly, and her eyes widened.

"Yes, I am a poor substitute for such attention," he murmured humorously, without a shade of a sneer, despite the abundance of unflattering attention that had been focused on him during his long period of incapacitation. No one else remarked on his observation, and most were staring at their plates. Carmine resumed seamlessly, "I hope you will be pleased to know, dear Chataine, that Giles and I have been discussing how you can help us in other ways. We propose a change in your allowance that both befits your station and provides amply for your needs."

Renée almost stopped breathing, as a glance at Giles' beaming face confirmed her worst fears. The horn of plenty was being withdrawn, and without Ares to restore it, whom could she turn to? She looked over to Vogelsong, who had his face down in his headcheese (made from hog's head and tongue). Although he did not particularly care for headcheese, smothering himself with it was preferable to facing her, especially when Carmine noted, "Counselor Vogelsong has offered his support and gratitude for your cooperation in this new endeavor, Chataine, and I myself thank you from the bottom of my heart. I thank you so much, in fact, that I have taken pains to send up a small gift to your chambers."

When, after dinner, Renée hastened to her chambers, she found on her bedside table the same pitcher and goblet, filled with wine, that had graced Carmine's quarters yesterday. His point was obvious: that she should recognize the set. Picking up the goblet, Renée took a delicate sip and murmured tightly, "I shall repay you for this gift, dear husband."

Inside the portal, Nicole gripped Ares' sleeve, closing her eyes tight against the nauseating waves of green light. It seemed to buffet her, bully her, as if she were a bird in a cage attended by a large, hungry cat. Only when Ares put his arm around her waist, holding her clawed hand gently in his, did she realize he was speaking to her. Upon discovering that she could not understand his speech without looking at him, she barely opened her eyes.

The green waves illumined his face in the most ghastly glow, making him look as evil and unnatural a specter as any in her nightmares. She could scarcely stand to look at him as he asked, "Lady, are you all right?"

"Yes, my lord," she gasped. "The light is—is everywhere."

"What do you see?" he asked.

Clutching him, she forced herself to look around. "Waves of light. Oh! They're everywhere! What strange people! Ares, they're going out by the rope!"

He quickly looked over his shoulder at the point that the rope terminated in the darkness, but saw no one. "I don't. . . . Lady, what do you mean? Whom do you see?"

"Oh, Ares! There must be hundreds of them leaving by way of the rope! They don't look friendly. Will they attack Thom and the others? What if they have to let go of the rope to fight?" she asked disjointedly.

Uneasy, Ares peered again into the unyielding blackness. "Describe them, if you will, Lady."

Her voice hollow in his ears, she replied, "They are mostly soldiers—they look Qarqarian. Oh! Many of them look to be badly wounded. I wonder how they can walk at all on the outside, wounded as they are. . . ."

Ares was thinking hard. Neither he nor Rhode had seen anyone but the individuals who attacked them. Oswald had seen others, but no one leaving. Then again, he'd had no rope. Had there been rope providing an escape, then Oswald should have seen them. But . . . while Ares himself had been in the portal on the rope, no one had used it to leave—

*That he could see.* Dread dropped like a leaden ball in his stomach. She had sight, evidently, for more than just the light. "Lady . . . can you hail them?" he asked.

"No! Oh, Ares, let us leave, please! If we are going to Westford, then let us go!" she pleaded.

"We shall," he assured her, feeling the strong need to get her to safety. "We are going to Westford now." Checking the direction of the rope behind them, he faced away from it and instructed her, "Do this—move your arms and legs as if you were swimming." Nicole began swimming most earnestly, but he saw that, in relation to himself, she was moving not at all. So he began swimming, and found himself keeping pace with her nicely.

Calmly, he said, "Just—think of Westford. We are going to Westford." She nodded, squeezing her eyes shut and swimming as if she would cross the Sea to Westford.

All at once he was falling over her, and they landed tangled up together in some underbrush. The world here was also on the verge of twilight, with long shadows cast by the trees around them. After shaking off the residual disorientation, Ares sat up and looked at a fir sapling, the familiarity of which caused his bones to freeze. Woodenly, he gazed around the wood of firs and larches, with the road running through it.

Nicole murmured, "Where are we? Oh, this is not the orchard!" she added in irritation, as if their driver had not been paying attention. "Ares, I do not know these woods. And it's so cold! Where are we?"

He stood, peering through the trees toward the road ahead. He cleared his throat, but his voice was still gravelly as he said, "We are in Hornbound."

9

Nicole pressed close to him. "Hornbound! Are you sure?" she whispered.

"Oh, yes," he nodded, sick to his stomach. He stood, assisting her up.

"Well then, I suppose we had best go back," she said mildly, turning on the rope.

"I agree, Lady." But even as he said it, they felt the soundless rush of something closing in their faces: the door. The rope hung taut in midair as before. They were stranded outside the portal, in Hornbound, until such time that it reopened.

"How rude!" Nicole exclaimed.

Despite the gravity of their predicament, Ares raised an eyebrow in amusement. "Rude, Lady?"

"It need not laugh at us like that," she said angrily.

"Laugh . . . ?"

"Did you not hear it? That mocking laughter," she said.

In light of recent events, this new and unwelcome information altered Ares' impression of the portal considerably. All along he had been treating it as an impersonal phenomenon, like a mountain pass, a corridor, or a real wooden door. He had entertained no thoughts of a Doorman. "Ah. I see," he murmured.

Inhaling, he turned to regard the woods and the road, which

appeared deserted. Behind him, he looked to where the end of their lifeline hung magically suspended in midair about four feet off the ground. Fortunately, when they had fallen through, they had brought about fourteen feet of rope with them. So the first thing Ares did was to maneuver Nicole, still attached to harness and rope, to a relatively sheltered place beneath the scrub willow.

Then he unfastened himself from the harness and quietly gathered brush, which he built up under the suspended rope end to camouflage it. He covered the trailing rope with forest debris, and added brush and branches to Nicole's shelter to completely obscure her. That done, he crouched beside her.

Peering between willow branches, he could just barely see her green eyes fixed on him in the waning light. "My lord, what of you?" she whispered.

He sighed, making himself comfortable beside her. "I will wait here with you for the portal to reopen—hopefully, it will sometime tonight. But . . . we are in the Surchatain's hunting grounds. If anyone decides to make use of it, we are likely to be discovered. In that case, I intend to lead them on a chase they will not soon forget—away from you."

She closed her eyes, shivering. "No."

"You can do it," he urged. "Just pull yourself back through on the rope. Then you can alert Thom to . . ." he trailed off.

"To what?" She leaned toward him, dislocating branches.

He carefully rearranged them to cover her. "Tell Thom to go back to Westford the long way and gather the army, then march on Hornbound—the long way. We have retrieved Oswald; that is enough. We shall not give our Doorman any more entertainment," he said dryly. "I shall attempt to open the lower gates of Hornbound from the inside for Thom," he added to cheer her.

She was quiet for a time while small nocturnal creatures came out from hiding to resume their evening hunt. Branches rustled overhead, and a stately owl looked down on them imperiously. "But if it opens while you are here, you will go back with me," she said.

"Certainly." Ares shifted to a drier spot on the thatch beneath him. "But if it opens when we are separated, you must go back without me."

"Oh!" She expelled a breath in exasperation, or dread, and reached a hand through the branches. He intercepted the small fingers and kissed them. "Once you told me that you were taking me back to Westford, I . . . I'm ashamed to tell you that the first thing I thought of was how nice it would be to have a hot bath and wash my hair!" she whispered. He laughed in a low voice. "It seems that I have been no use to you in rescuing Henry," she added dismally.

"No. You performed beyond my wildest hopes," he insisted. "You saw what no one else could see, and heard what no one else could hear, and kept warning me when I would not listen. I see now that the Lord would not give me further instructions about the portal because I would not listen to what He was trying to tell me through you: that it was not for our use. But somehow or other, I was determined to make it so. Now there is no telling what I have unleashed on the countryside."

She shook her head slowly, unseen to him behind the willow screen. "No. You were right to see it through. Had you not ruled out for yourself the possibility of using the portal, you would have wondered forever if you could have, and resented me for preventing you. The Lord can see to those—creatures that escaped. Ares, do you think they were the ghosts of those who died in the portal?"

"I do not know, and I decline to speculate, since I have proven myself singularly ill-informed about the portal, or. . . ." He looked up, listening. Then he raised up enough to peer over the willow bush. Although she did not hear anything, and could not see what he was looking for, she knew to be absolutely still.

Some moments later she heard it: the agitated conversation of two men coming up the road: ". . . they'll be partridge on the table. Partridge! The man'll send us out for peacocks and baboons next, and if we don't produce 'em, we'll be meat for the hounds' next dinner."

"Aye, don't you worry. Bloody will find whatever's good for the table—oho! He's caught wind o' something! There he goes!" And Nicole heard a deep, lustful barking that grew louder by the second.

Ares sprang up from beside her hiding place and leaped out

onto the road to be seen by the two wardens, one of whom carried a lantern, and their mastiff. Then he dove into the woods on the other side, running directly away from Nicole, the rope, and the portal. After the first startled instant, the dog was bounding after him, barking furiously, while the wardens ran behind, shouting. With a constricted heart, Nicole listened as the din faded, then suddenly ceased.

Brushing aside branches, she raised up out of her hiding place, still hearing nothing. They had caught him. With trembling fingers, she began unbuckling her harness. There was no use waiting here to be captured at their leisure. She would not let him be taken alone.

The sudden burst of green light almost knocked her off her feet, and she covered her face from the awful, yawning hole in front of her, looming like an open grave. "No," she gasped. "Oh, no! Ares!"

But he would not be coming; he was otherwise engaged. And before the hound caught scent of her, too, or the portal closed back up, she had scant moments to decide whether to obey him or defy him. Not fearing capture nearly as much as the horrible green void, she hung suspended in the agony of irrevocable choice. Go back without him or stay?

The image was brought to her mind of the grief and disappointment in his face when they brought her to join him in his fate. This sight decided her course. So, closing her eyes and biting her mouth, she picked up the rope and jumped into the light. She felt the waves suck her in, and then she was floating alone in the void, gripping the thick rope with weak, wet palms.

She could hardly bear to open her eyes, as the light assailed her fiercely. She could feel it menacing, taunting, buffeting her—*What if you can't get out?* She thought of Ares, and what he might be suffering right now; she thought of Bonnie and Sophie without father or mother, dependent on the questionable goodwill of other aspirants to the throne. Now, at all costs, she must be strong.

Blind and shaking, Nicole hauled herself hand over hand on the rope. As much as she slipped, she could not gauge her progress, but it seemed that she toiled on that rope for hours. When her palms began burning, she chanced at last to open her eyes just to see if they were bleeding, but the sight of the wraiths streaming out along the rope ahead of her caused her to squeeze her eyes shut again, choking back a cry.

Suddenly she was falling. She glimpsed rocky ground coming up to meet her and someone's arms intervening to catch her. Staggering upright, she looked into Thom's alarmed face, painted orange in the torchlight. "Surchataine! Where is the Surchatain? What has happened?"

"Oh, Thom." She clutched his arms, trying to stand on her own, but she couldn't—her legs were like water. Ben brought her a skin of wine, and someone else sat her on the hillside steps.

No one interfered while she took a long drink and composed herself. Then she looked up at Ares' Commander and uttered, "The portal is evil, Thom. There is an evil power behind it. Tell me—when we were inside, did you see anyone else come out by the rope?"

"Anyone else?" Thom frowned. "No. No one." He looked around in case any of the men might have something different to say, but everyone else was shaking his head.

"Then they must be ghosts. I saw many of them—perhaps hundreds—fleeing the portal by means of the rope. They were all green, and they looked . . . unnatural," she said weakly.

"But what of the Surchatain, Lady?" Oswald asked tenderly.

"Oh!" Her eyes filled with tears. "The portal took us to Hornbound, then shut up. Ares hid me in the woods, but the woodsmen came by with their hound, which smelled us right away. So Ares drew them away from me, and got caught himself."

Thom looked up stonily at the portal. "Then we must go retrieve him."

"Yes, but—while we were waiting, Ares instructed that, if he was taken, you were to go the long way back to Westford, gather the army, and assault Hornbound," she said.

This elicited such an animated response that she startled. The men around her were hurrahing, pumping their fists, even jumping in excitement. Thom, following Ares' example, looked grimly satisfied. Nicole was surprised at this outburst only because she did not know how long and how earnestly the officers had desired to pursue this very course.

"Then that is what we will do," Thom said, with a cool lift of the brow. "Rest while we break camp, Surchataine. We are leaving tonight."

In Ares' absence, Ben attended Nicole while the rest of the men made the camp disappear. In less than an hour, the shelters were dismantled, the gear packed, and the campfires scattered so that by the time they were done, the ground was just as it had been, looking as if nothing more foreign than a summer thunderstorm had visited the area. Wirt made ready her cart, and then they were off. Oswald rode Neruda, Ares' horse.

As they passed the portal for the last time, Thom nodded toward it. "Pray tell, is it open, Surchataine?"

"Yes," she said, turning her face away.

In a sudden fit of anger, Rhode hurled a lit torch toward it. "Shut your gaping mouth, you demon!" The torch disappeared into the rock.

Nicole startled. "It has closed!"

"Then stay that way," Rhode growled, and they passed on.

The next two days were an endless blur to Nicole as Thom drove the scouting party in merciless haste to Westford, allowing only the briefest stops for rest. They did not stop for rain or dark; they did not stop in Crescent Hollow. Nicole was fitfully sleeping in the cartbed when they finally passed over the southern Passage to Westford, and only dimly recollected being escorted up to the Surchatain's chambers. Try as she might, Ursula could not rouse her for a bath until the following morning.

As for Thom, the moment they arrived, he summoned Vogelsong, Faguy, Giles, and the rest of his officers to meet with the scouting party for a war council. Captain Crager was also found to attend—as they had hoped, he had indeed been deposited by the portal at Westford. Before sunrise the next morning, messengers were riding out of the palace gates with summonses for all off-duty soldiers to report at once.

In Hornbound, moments before Nicole made her decision to re-enter the portal, Ares was tearing blindly through the woodland with the barking, frothing mastiff close behind. He knew he had no chance to escape; he was determined only to lead them as far as possible from Nicole's hiding place. Feeling the animal nipping at his pant leg, trying to get a good firm hold, Ares shot out an arm to swing himself around a vine-laden stump and gain a precious second or two. But then the mastiff managed to sink his teeth into his boot, bringing him down with a heavy thud in the soft earth. Prostrate, Ares lay very still under the drooling jaws, to not provoke him to rip into flesh.

Shortly, the wardens arrived, full of praise for Bloody and wrath at the intruder. When they jerked him to his feet, Ares tried to keep his face down, vainly hoping to obscure his signature scar. If Henry was a boon to Ulm's interrogators, what would they make of the Lystran Surchatain? Lazear's keyring jingled on Ares' belt, but the wardens were making too much noise themselves to hear it and neglected to strip off his coat to see it.

"Curse these slaves! This must be the one that waylaid Klar's messenger! Scum!" one warden shouted, striking Ares again and again in the face while the mastiff barked excitedly. Ares did not fight back.

The other, calmer man held up his lantern. "Who'd you steal the clothes from, villain? Ho, that's a nasty scar," he observed. Ares still kept his head down as much as possible while blood trickled from the scar down his neck. "Hold up, Herzl; you'll want him conscious when we take him in, or I'll not be helping you drag his carcass down to the dungeon." Again he paused, surveying Ares by the light of the lantern. "Faith, he's the soundest mine slave I ever saw, or a new one. Did you escape the traders at the mines, man? And thought you'd do best coming up the mountain?" he asked curiously.

Even if Ares were inclined to answer, Herzl was too enraged to listen (and thus learn anything). "You want me to walk him into sup with the genteel council?" he cried, taking one last shot at Ares before stopping to catch his breath. Anger provided only so much energy to someone who sat around and drank as much as this man did, and tonight's punching bag was resilient and sturdy. "D'you know what you cost me, transgressing in my woods? No, I'll not leave so much as an arm or a leg for the council to inspect," he spat.

With that promise, he began shoving Ares toward the fortress drawbridge while the mastiff followed, biting at his leg and licking the blood that came.

The other man followed with a shade of anxiety, gaining control of the dog. "Down, Bloody! Heel. Good boy. Herzl, wait—think, man! If he's the one who did rob the messenger, the council wants to know. Where's the pouch? Where's he been hiding? They'll want to know, an' if we don't produce him in shape to answer questions, it will be the worse for us."

"They won't ever know," Herzl breathed, then stopped to turn on his younger companion. "They won't know, will they, Laymon?" It was a pointed threat.

Lowering his lantern, Laymon capitulated, "No, Herzl. They won't ever know."

"On your hands and knees, slave. Walk like the dog you are." Herzl shoved Ares down to all fours, then removed the collar from the dog to strap it tightly around Ares' neck and lead him with the leash. The wardens exited the woods, approaching the fortress by the main road, leading Ares by the leash while he scrambled on hands and knees. In this manner, they crossed the drawbridge over the moat in full view of the sentries, who laughed or turned their backs on the wardens with their prize. "Caught us a runaway slave!" Herzl shouted to them repeatedly. "A runaway slave."

The two men then walked Ares toward a round corner tower, keeping the lantern away from him while they waved to the guards at the crenelation. The mastiff, pleased to be freed of the leash, trotted happily alongside Laymon in anticipation of reward. So as far as the guards could tell, the wardens were returning from the woods with a large dog and wounded prey. "Runaway slave!" Herzl called up to them. Ares was getting the distinct idea that some specific and most disagreeable punishment was meted out to runaway slaves. The frenzied barking of many dogs grew louder at their advance.

They approached an enclosure of iron bars set against the fortress, and Laymon began fumbling with the keys at his belt. Numerous hungry dogs, smelling blood, pressed their bared fangs against the bars in welcome of a late dinner. Bloody grew too excited to wait, sensing that he'd better get a mouthful while he could. He attempted to sink his teeth into Ares' shoulder, though succeeded only in ripping his coat. By now, Ares had apprehended both the plan and that he had moments to avert it.

Laymon turned the key in the lock and Herzl glanced back over his shoulder. In that instant, Ares flipped onto his back, yanking the leash from Herzl's hand and knocking Laymon against the enclosure. He dropped the lantern, which crashed to the ground and went out.

In the darkness and confusion of Herzl's cursing and Laymon's fumbling, Ares wrapped the leash swiftly around the dog's neck and pulled it tight. In the space of a minute the beast went limp. Meanwhile, Laymon finally got the gate open a crack, to his misfortune. Ares shoved him into the pen, then unwound the leash from the unconscious dog's neck and tossed the animal in after him. Laymon screamed; Herzl, blind, shouted, "What? Lay—" before he found himself falling into the pen after him.

Amid the clawing and snarling and desperate cries, Ares slammed the barred gate shut again, turning the key in the lock before removing it. Wiping the blood from his face so that he could see, Ares glanced around the shadowy darkness, pocketed the keyring, and jumped up to begin scaling the fenced enclosure.

# 10

**a**res gained the top of the pen, which was also barred, and looked down on the wriggling shapes of the dogs clustered around the wardens, whose cries were growing weaker. Although no one came in response to the tumult (as the animals' taste for raw flesh and blood had apparently been nurtured), Ares knew that he needed to get somewhere else quickly. He unstrapped the dog collar from around his neck, dropping it and the leash into the pen below. Then he looked up.

From the top of the enclosure, he was able to grasp protrusions of stone in the fortress wall to climb to a lower-level parapet on the southeastern tower (that closest to the pen). This he dragged himself over, gasping. The bites in his right calf were not deep, but painful, and impeded his movement. Crouching in the shadow of the parapet, he looked up and down the catwalk, but saw no one. As he began to get up, he caught the glimmer of an advancing light. There was nowhere to run without being detected, so he threw himself back down and flattened himself horizontally against the four-foot-high wall, lying on his right side.

A guard with a torch ambled lazily up the catwalk toward him. Ares braced himself to spring, but then another guard making his rounds from the opposite direction hailed the first, and they stopped in the catwalk not three feet from his face. Every muscle tense with the effort, he lay perfectly still in the deep shadow of the parapet. The guards held their torches up to check in doorways or illumine faces; they did not think to lower the lights to look at their feet.

"Whoa, scoundrel, what say you?" one demanded.

Though his heart constricted, Ares did not flinch and the other guard replied, "If I don't get leave from watch duty I may hang myself from boredom. What're we patrolling for night and day? Who's going to storm the fortress of Hornbound?"

"Ah, you're nought but a complainer, Shahn. Pull your duty and better posts will come," the other assured him.

"Like what? Guarding the Lady Rejane, perhaps?" Shahn proposed, a leer in his voice.

"Um. So we all wish—before she's hanged, anyway. Don't overly concern yourself; I just looked in on her, and she's well, she's well. Make your circuit," the elder instructed, and they parted in opposite directions.

When they were out of sight, Ares let down with a groan. He must get off the catwalk—it would be patrolled all night, and he was sure to be spotted sooner or later. Warily, he rolled to his feet, limped across the catwalk and began to inspect the entryways to the fortress along this level.

He opened one door and peered down into a winding stairwell. That was no good—if he couldn't see where it led or who was coming up, he'd do just as well to go in by the front doors. He shut that door and moved north along the parapet, past the tower to the eastern wall, watching for torchlight from either direction.

The next avenue of entry (in the eastern wall) was a set of double doors leading into a loft overlooking what appeared to be the audience hall, brightly lit, filled with elaborately dressed bodies. Ares hastily shut that door again—while it was good to know that this is where the great hall was, announcing himself at this time would be somewhat premature.

He moved with increased urgency along the exterior wall, lit by bracketed torches. This random door-opening was going to get him caught unless he promptly found a secluded area to hide and plan his movements. Approaching the northeastern tower, he paused, seeing movement on the parapet. So he quickly turned to retrace his steps to the southeastern tower. He came upon a recessed door in the tower, locked. Glancing warily over his shoulder, he started to move on, then reconsidered: to continue in this direction would take him back to the front of the fortress, but a locked door was more likely to lead to a private room, and maybe . . . he had the key. He shifted against the wall, glancing down the catwalk either way as he brought up the warden's keyring.

There were only four keys on the ring, of varying sizes; two he eliminated by their size alone (too large), and the third he tried. It turned reluctantly in the lock, and he eased the door open an inch to peer in. Unlike the other doors, this one opened out, preventing his getting a clear view of the whole room. It was a bedchamber, apparently, dimly lit by dying embers in the fireplace. Seeing no movement in the room at the door's opening, Ares slipped inside, closing the door behind him.

When he turned around, he was mildly startled to see a young woman eyeing him indifferently from a padded bench. She was clearly a lady of rank, judging from her dress and surroundings, but her demeanor was listless and her voice hollow as she said: "Whatever you wish to do to me, you have only a few hours, for in the morning I'm to be taken out and hanged." She was very pale and almost gaunt, with large, beautiful eyes that were gray and unfocused.

"Lady Rejane?" he hazarded.

She sat up a little in vague curiosity. "Who are you?"

He tentatively took a chair across from her, and she looked down at his bleeding leg. "I am not here to harm you," he said.

"Really?" she replied as if it did not matter one way or another. She stood, crossing the room to a wash basin where she wet a long, narrow hand towel, wrung it out, then brought it over and knelt in front of him. She gingerly rolled up his ripped, soiled pant leg to begin delicately cleaning dried blood from the bite marks. "Tell me more," she said.

He nodded toward a bottle of wine on a side table. "May I have a drink?"

She rose from her ministrations to fetch the bottle and hand it to him. He took a swig, then took the bloodied towel from her hand and doused it with wine. This he applied to his wounds, grimacing. Watching, she asked, "Do you have a name?"

He looked up at her standing in front of him. "Ares."

She showed no reaction other than to pose, "So, Ares—what do you want?"

He tied the small towel firmly around the wounds on his calf, then leaned back. "I want to kill Ulm."

For the first time, some color rose in her face. She resumed her seat on the bench to languidly inform him, "I am sorry that I cannot help you there."

"Oh, but I believe you can. Why are you slated to die?" he asked.

"Because he is tired of me," she said, looking off vacantly.

Ares made several lightning connections: Ulm's mistress was a young relative of the ruler of Eugenia—"Then you are Klar's niece?"

"Grandniece," she corrected, but her eyes focused on him intently now. "Who *are* you?"

He leaned forward, elbows on his knees, clasping his hands. Smiling, he said, "I am someone who *needs* to kill Ulm."

With an ironic answering smile, she rose to reclaim the bottle from him and fill a goblet. This she lifted in a toast to him: "Then I salute you, Ares of Needs. But I still do not know how I might help you."

"Tell me what the protocol is for a hanging," he said.

Her face lost what little color it had. "At sunrise, I will be taken to make my confession and receive absolution. Then the Executioner will escort me to the gallows in the courtyard and march me up the steps for the entertainment of young and old. My lord Ulm has promised the rope shall be tied so that the drop breaks my neck, and I do not strangle to death," she said softly. He regarded her without reply, and she withdrew a small silk handkerchief from her sleeve. This she dipped in her goblet of wine, then applied gently to the blood caked on his scar.

Ares drew back. Touching his scar was a gesture of intimacy that no one but Nicole had even attempted, before tonight. "Does it hurt?" she asked.

"Yes," he mouthed. Stirring, he said, "Tell me how to get to this room from the inside of the fortress."

She paused, then pointed behind him. "You must go out the way you came, then go left until you come to the double doors, and there take the left corridor. You will pass the stairwell, then go to the door past the window of the sun."

"Then I will return shortly." He left her chambers by the outside door, leaving it unlocked behind him. Then he skulked along the wall to a shadowy corner and waited.

As he expected, lazy Shahn soon came back around on his rounds. Inattentive as he was, he never saw the blow that rendered him suddenly unconscious, but he bounced off the stone wall and fell directly into the intruder's waiting arms. Ares quickly stamped out his torch, then dragged him to Lady Rejane's door, glancing anxiously down the catwalk for Shahn's superior to come around the corner. Shouldering the door open, Ares dragged the guard inside.

Rejane stepped around him to close the door, then watched in rising hope and astonishment as Ares stripped the guard's hood, mantle, mail and linen undergarments from him. Neither did she turn away while Ares bound and gagged the naked man tightly with silken cords from the lady's bedding. Then he scooted the unconscious Shahn underneath her bed. "I would rather take him down to the dungeon, but it would waste valuable time, and someone might recognize him," he muttered.

With no modesty whatsoever, Ares removed his own clothes to don Shahn's, taking care to tie Melva's ribbon around his neck, concealed under the linen shift. Then he stood, adjusting the mail, which fit him tolerably well, considering that he was a bit bigger than its previous wearer. He put on the belt with the guard's sword and scabbard, resting it comfortably on his left hip. The two sets of keys—Lazear's and the warden's—hung from the belt, as they should. Then he fit the helmet on his head, gazing down at her from under its brim.

"You appear most formidable, Ares of Needs," she murmured. The cheek guards of the helmet covered the still-tender scar with steel, but his eyes were visible.

"The door past the window of the sun? I shall return," he said, wadding up his Lystran clothes into a tight bundle. This time, he locked the outer door after leaving.

In guard mode, he strode confidently down the catwalk, pausing only to toss the bundle of clothes over the edge of the crenelation into the moat below. He proceeded to the double doors, where numerous sentries were coming and going. Having received his orders (so it appeared) he did not dally to converse, but entered and turned down the left corridor, lit by candles in golden sconces along the walls. He found the stairwell, then came upon a large, stained-glass window. It depicted the bearded face in the sun that he recognized as the emblem of Qarqar before Ulm had ascended the throne. As the glass was bright yellow, with peripheral reds and oranges, Ares could well imagine how brilliantly it must blaze in early morning light. This was the window of the sun.

Moving on to the door immediately past it, he brought out the same key that had opened the outer door to this room. Thus he gained access to the waiting Lady Rejane, now on the point of believing that her life might be saved after all. Closing the door, he turned to her and said, "Now, where is the priest who will give you absolution?"

Her newfound hope collapsed. "There is no priest. My lord Ulm will perform that function," she said with a sardonic edge.

He scowled. "That will not do. I must get you to a safe place where I can retrieve you after—*I* have made my peace with Ulm."

"There is a secret passage," she said, her gray eyes glinting.

"Excellent! Where does it lead?" he asked.

"From the Surchatain's quarters to many points in the fortress."

"And outside? Does it have an exit?" he pressed.

"Yes, of course," she said.

"Is Ulm in his quarters now?" he asked.

She hesitated. "As far as I know. But he is either in conference or . . . entertaining. He is never alone."

"Leave that to me. How do I enter the secret passage from his quarters?"

She whispered, "In his bedchamber, there is wainscoting imprinted with a row of reverse images of the emblem of the sun. You must get his signet and insert it in the imprint that is fourth from the edge toward the bed—"

"Which wall?" he interrupted.

"That behind the bed. The room is round," she said impatiently.

"Where do I start counting on a round wall?" he asked slowly, to make her understand.

"Ah. From where the wainscoting begins to the left of the bed. You match up the emblem on his signet with the one on the wall and turn it to the right," she said, demonstrating as if turning a key in a lock. "The wall will open."

He looked off, visualizing the scene. "Where does he keep the signet?"

"He has it on his person at all times."

"Excellent," Ares murmured, smiling slightly. He looked down on her again, and she began to tremble. "Now. Where is the closest point that you can enter the passage?" he asked.

She looked off as if searching through the fortress. "My quarters, but—I cannot get there without being seen. Everyone knows I am confined for execution. I cannot go anywhere without being stopped."

He looked distinctly amused. "How can you have been mistress to the Surchatain and learned so little of authority? Where are your chambers?"

"Down the staircase to the corridor on your right. The door is marked with my name. Or at least, it was," she murmured.

"From there, where is Ulm's quarters?" he asked.

"Back up the stairs to the floor above us. His is the only suite on the topmost floor of the tower, and guards are always posted at the landing," she said as if to emphasize the impossibility of gaining access to it.

"Perfect," he mused, contemplating the plan that unfolded in his mind. "Now, I am going to escort you to your chambers. Forgive my rough handling. Once there, you must enter the secret passage and find your way to the Surchatain's quarters. Wait for me in the passage outside his bedchamber. Can you do that?"

"Yes, but—it will not succeed should you speak to anyone. Your accent betrays you as a southerner," she said anxiously.

His brows elevated slightly. That she took care to point out a flaw like that told him she was fully engaged in his plan. And, what she said was true—native Qarqarians spoke in heavy, stilted syllables, but Ulm employed so many mercenaries from around the Continent, Ares' accent would not be held against him. Still, in connection with his face. . . . "Is that better? If I speak thus, will I pass muster?" he asked, mimicking Qarqarian tones.

She drew back slightly in surprise. "That's very good," she acknowledged.

"And you yourself still speak like a Eugenian," he observed. Then he paused, as something else came to mind. "What does Ulm look like?"

"He is—not as large as you. He has dark hair that curls on his shoulders, and he is clean-shaven. And he always wears gold robes that are cut like a priest's. He imagines himself a priest of the sun," she said.

"I see," he murmured. "Come, Lady—the hour grows late."

As soon as they had stepped outside the room, he seized her upper arm and began dragging her roughly down the stairwell. She gasped in surprise, holding her brocade skirts up so that she could match his fast pace without stumbling. Those they passed on the stairs hastened to get out of the way, assuming that he had official reason to be removing her elsewhere.

Coming off the stairs, he turned with her into the right-hand corridor, and she nodded surreptitiously at the door of her chambers. He opened it, tossed her inside, and closed the door to turn back up the stairs.

He had swiftly mounted the first flight of stairs when the realization of a fatal flaw in his plan stopped him cold. In order for it to work, Nicole must already be back through the portal to camp. If the portal had not yet opened, or if she could not bring herself to reenter alone, then for him to proceed on this course would mean her death, and his defeat. Furthermore, if she returned only for Thom to attempt to come after him by means of the portal, then he, and any he brought, would die as well. And Westford would be left virtually defenseless.

Cold sweat broke out on Ares' forehead under the cold steel of the helmet. What should he do? What could he do? Out of habit, he opened the west window in his mind to plead for insight, and, astoundingly—it came. The conviction that she was indeed back at camp came upon him so strongly as to drive him up a step or two. But still he hesitated: *I have been wrong so often before— how can I know that this is true? That it is not simply what I desire to be true?*

Glancing aside in his distress, he glimpsed the window of the sun off the stairwell, blazing with golden light. Ares frowned, craning his neck for a better look. Yes, the window was lit as though the early morning sun were behind it. But—sunrise was still hours away. It was pitch black outside; of that he was certain. But—still the window blazed, and no one but himself happened to be right there to see it.

This was his sign, he realized. This was the light he had prayed for so often—when he needed it most, it came. With renewed purpose, he lifted his face to the stairs to take them two at a time.

It was evident when he had reached Ulm's suite—the two guards at the door, attired in golden livery, were staring down at him in mild contempt. As he drew up to them, he was careful to use his Qarqarian voice to say, "I must speak to the Surchatain. The portal has been breached!"

"What?" one gasped, and the other stared.

"The portal, man! The Lystrans are making use of the portal to enter the hunting woods. I must warn the Surchatain!" Ares insisted.

The guards flung open the door, and Ares glimpsed figures seated around a room appointed with such luxuries as to make Renée fierce with envy, were she to see it. When the people in the room turned indignantly toward the source of the interruption, Ares' gaze fastened on the man in the center wearing the golden robe. "Pardon, Surchatain Ulm," one guard said, properly restrained. "This sentry has an urgent message for you."

All eyes turned to Ares. In the instant before Ulm nodded at him to speak, Ares surveyed the number and type of persons attending the Surchatain: three high-ranking military officers, a high administrator, and two female consorts. Given permission to speak, Ares gave the Qarqarian form of salute that he had observed for years. "Forgive me, Surchatain. I just came off duty on the southeastern tower, where an intruder attempted an escalade. He tried to kill me, but I subdued him, and forced him to speak. He gave his name as Rhode [a name Ulm would know]; he is an officer with the Lystran army. They have found the portal on the Road of Vanishing, and taken it to a point in the hunting woods here. The other intruder who accosted the messenger from Klar was one of them—they have discovered that they can go back and forth through the portal by means of a rope to a camp on the road."

Ulm exploded, "Where is this man Rhode?"

"Surchatain, he attempted to escape me by climbing back over the wall, and he fell into the moat below," Ares said regretfully. He was divinely covered in his ignorance here, for he did not realize that the moat was close enough to the fortress for a body to drop into it only at the southeastern tower. "But there will be others. They are going to attempt to bring their army through. Tonight."

Ulm rounded on his officers. "Go! Stop them! Comb the woods until you find the mouth of the portal!"

The room cleared but for the women, and Ares looked at Ulm. Bowing this time, Ares said, "There is one more thing, Surchatain. I removed a token from the intruder that you must see. But—it must be for your eyes alone."

Ulm snapped his fingers at the women, who obediently slipped out of the chambers after the officers. Then Ulm and his nemesis were alone.

# 11

"Well, what is this token?" Ulm asked, appropriately curious.

"It is this." Ares loosened the purple and gold hair ribbon from around his neck and extended it to Ulm.

Taking it in hand, he studied it with an irritated frown. While Ulm was thus preoccupied, Ares stole a hand back to quietly bolt the door. Waving the ribbon, Ulm declared, "This means nothing to me."

"Oh, but it should, my lord Ulm." Ares then removed his helmet, exposing his scar. "It belongs to the rightful ruler of Qarqar, the Chataine Melva, whose father you murdered in attaining the throne." He dropped all hint of a Qarqarian accent.

Ulm stared at him with bloodshot eyes while the situation became clearer to him. "You are the intruder," he said in a low voice. "And by your scar, I take you to be Ares of Lystra."

"Tonight, to you, I am avenger of the murdered. Make your peace with God, Ulm," Ares said, reaching for the sword on his hip.

Ulm opened his mouth to cry out as he attempted to dash past Ares to the door. Ares clapped one hand over his mouth, using the other to seize his long black hair and drag him into the bedchamber. Ulm twisted in his hands, trying to bite and scratch, as Ares kicked the bedchamber door shut. "For all your treachery, you fight like a girl," Ares noted wryly.

But Ulm was not done. This bedchamber was not just for sleeping, but a laboratory where he experimented with oddities he discovered on many trips through the portal. Ares glimpsed long tables crowded with containers, some of which had contents that oozed and hissed. Ulm managed to quickly reach over to one of these tables and grab a lead flask preparatory to throwing its contents on the intruder. Just as quickly, Ares knocked the bottom of the flask so that its contents splashed up on himself and Ulm. While the liquid (which had a greenish glow that Ares could not see) splattered on his shoulder, it caught Ulm full in the face.

Ares looked down in surprise at the shoulder plate of his chain mail sizzling under the mysterious liquid. But that did not occupy him for long, as Ulm began screaming, covering his face with his hands. He crashed into the table, reaching blindly toward a row of flasks, crying, "Pour it on me!"

Ares looked bemusedly over the table. One of these must be the antidote to the strange poison, but he did not know which, and he dare not touch anything unknown of this lot. But Ulm made it all moot when, in his agony, he knocked over the table, causing all of its contents to crash in a bubbling mass on the floor. Ares looked back at him, now writhing on a leopard-skin rug, and saw to his horror that Ulm's face was a mass of blood and bone. His eyes stared wide in their lidless sockets, and his exposed facial muscles twitched under the corrosive effect of the poison. Ares drew back in revulsion while Ulm thrashed, gurgled, and choked to death on his own blood.

Glancing down at his own shoulder plate that was still dissolving, Ares stepped around Ulm's body to take a ewer from an ornate washstand and pour water over his shoulder. That seemed to slow the poison, which had created pits and gouges in the steel, but had not eaten through. Careful to lean forward so that the runoff dripped away from him, Ares emptied the rest of the pitcher over his mail.

By now the mingled contents of the overturned flasks were producing disagreeable odors that quickly turned noxious. Eyes watering, Ares bent over Ulm to search through his bloody gold robes. Feeling the signet ring on a chain, Ares snapped it off. Then, realizing that he might yet need his disguise, he hurried back to the receiving chamber to retrieve the helmet he had dropped there. The sentries were already pounding at the locked outer door.

Ares tucked the helmet under arm and ran back into the bedchamber. He locked himself in with the stifling fumes and went to the back wall. Kneeling in front of the wainscoting, he eyed the recessed rosettes and counted—one, two, three, four. Coughing, he inserted the signet into the fourth rosette and turned. There was a gentle heave, and a four-foot portion of the wainscoting separated from the wall. Ares pulled it out like a hinged bin, peering into a passageway that was faintly lit. He climbed through the opening, pulling the trap door closed behind him by means of a chain attached to its back side. Then he looked up at Lady Rejane, who stood waiting with a candle in one hand, a jewel box in the other, and a dark cloak covering her elegant dress.

Ares stood, taking deep breaths of the musty air in the narrow stone passageway. As he placed Ulm's signet ring on his finger, he croaked, "Lead us out, Lady, if you will." The poisonous fumes seemed to lodge in his throat, seeping down to his lungs.

She stared at the blood on his hands as she covered her face delicately from the odors escaping the bedchamber. "What have you done?"

"I have created something of a stir, and we need to be leaving," he replied. They spoke in low voices, almost a whisper, lest they be heard through the walls.

She turned, and Ares' brows drew down at her hesitation. She asked, "Where are you taking me?"

"Ultimately, I will return you to Klar. But for now, I need you to direct me to the house of Lord Morand," he said.

She faced him in sudden decisiveness. "I will show you to Lord Morand's house *after* you find my lover. I do not wish to return to my lord Klar—I want to be with my lover."

"So that is why you were condemned to die," he noted ironically, then spit out a mouthful of phlegm. "Who is your lover?"

"He is a soldier—his name is Pares," she said defiantly.

"What unit is he in?" Ares asked.

"I . . . do not know," she admitted.

Ares groaned. "Has he any rank? Anything distinguishing that may help me find him?"

"He is young and very handsome," she said, blushing.

Ares sighed in exasperation. "Very well, I will find your pretty soldier. But we must get you to a safe place to wait until I do. Is there any place close by where I can hide you?"

She thought for a moment while Ares shifted impatiently, stifling a cough. The fumes were drifting through the cracks in the wall. Then she offered, "There is a garden cottage where my lord Ulm used to keep his mistresses. I suppose he shall not be needing it now."

"Lead on, Lady," he urged.

So she took him down a dark, narrow, winding stairway which branched at the bottom two ways. She led him down the right-hand branch, taking another candle from one of the many sconces along the wall. At various points along the way Ares saw peepholes to the rooms they passed, and stopped briefly to look and listen. After one such stop, he advised her, "They have found Ulm's body. Who else knows about this passage?"

"I daresay no one. He killed anyone who knew his secrets once they fell out of favor," she said. Ares nodded.

They passed several doors placed so ingeniously that no one on the outside could have guessed what they were. Then Lady Rejane stopped at a small, round-topped door, tilting her candle toward it. "This one," she said. "Push. It's hard to open."

Ares placed his shoulder against the door and heaved. It cracked open several inches, and he saw a mass of ivy covering it on the outside. Before opening it further, he peered out to make sure that no one was nearby. The door was in a wall of a garden that appeared deserted. So he cautiously broke away enough ivy to step out and look around, standing in a bed of fairy slippers.

A little white garden house with a clay tile roof sat a few feet away, its shuttered windows closed. Following him out of the passageway, Rejane whispered, "You need the signet to open the cottage door, as well." He nodded.

When he had satisfied himself that there was no one in the garden, he advanced to the door of the cottage, where his fingers found the recessed rosette in the darkness. Inserting the signet and turning it produced the sound of a latch being lifted on the other side. Ares opened the door and Rejane leaned in beside him. Taking her candle, he quickly canvassed the two rooms of the cottage. "All right. It is empty," he said, snuffing her candle.

When she protested, he hushed her. "No lights! Stay here; stay quiet, and I will bring your Pares to you." That quieted her, and she withdrew to the downy, pillowed bed.

Ares exited into the garden, locking the door behind him, and sighed tiredly. Sunrise would be upon them soon, and he ached to rest, but he dare not until he had located her lover. "Young and handsome," he muttered contemptuously, bringing the helmet up over his head. He himself had been young once, but never pretty. . . . Yet Nicole loved him anyway. He had to stop and close his eyes to subdue the sudden uprush of longing for her. Then he opened his eyes to focus on his next mission.

He located the northern gate of the garden, which was on the other side of a small brook. After crossing the arched footbridge, Ares knelt beside the brook to wash the dried blood off his hands and drink, as his thirst was raging. He had a sour taste in his mouth from the fumes in Ulm's chambers. He stood, feeling weak and tired, then exited through the garden gate.

Here, he found himself on a narrow terrace at the rear of the fortress, facing the enclosing stone wall. A footpath ran along the inside of the wall, which enclosed the entire compound, as far as he could tell. Curious, he climbed the wall to see what was beyond.

He had to grip the stones to keep his balance at the sight. Below him, at the very foot of the wall, lay a sheer rock cliff of several hundred feet. In the distance, at the foot of the cliffs, he could barely make out houses and buildings, roads and fields. This, no doubt, was Hornbound proper—but he could not go there yet.

Climbing back down the inside of the stone wall, he turned eastward to trot along the path toward the front gates. The moat began where the mountain top ended, giving an intruder the option of scaling vertical rock or swimming foul water to get to the fortress. (This moat was used as a sewer, as most moats were). But from the garden gate, Ares was able to pass in between the fortress proper and the enclosing wall. As he went, he could hear the moat lap against the stones on the outside.

With his pulse throbbing in his ears, he came around the southeastern tower, passing the dog pen. It stood open and empty—no dogs, no wardens. Ares suspected that the dogs were being used to patrol the woods, and that the wardens had been taken to have their wounds tended . . . or be buried. He eyed the guards at the drawbridge, but did not want to approach them—they knew too much. Possibly, they would recognize him, should he have to remove his helmet.

Then he saw three soldiers exiting the front doors of the fortress who appeared to be of insufficient rank to question him. So he approached, saluting, and they stopped to look at him. Careful to assume his Qarqarian voice, he said, "I have orders to bring one Pares, but I am new, and I do not know where he is stationed or what he looks like."

"Pares?" The three looked at each other. "Wait—I know him," said one. "He is standing watch outside the great hall tonight."

"Ah. Good." As Ares turned away, one of the three looked at him intently, even suspiciously.

"Wait!" the man called. Reluctantly, Ares turned. It would not do to get caught at this point. "Didn't they teach you to salute on leaving?" the soldier demanded. Agreeably, Ares repeated the salute, whereupon the three fell over each other laughing. "These recruits are so stupid," the man sneered. Ares sheepishly raised his hands and hurried off.

He ran up the broad steps leading into the fortress and cut through the wide foyer toward the great hall. There was a general tumult within, as ladies were herded upstairs to presumably safer quarters and messengers darted through crowds to deliver orders. Ares barely glanced at the luxurious furnishings he passed—the tapestries and golden candelabra and finely carved wall capitals and corbels—none of which was any use to Ulm now. The urgency with which troops passed Ares on their way out informed him that his warning about the portal had been heeded.

He came to the entrance of the great hall, standing open and empty. He looked between the two guards stationed there and said, "Pares."

The one on the left said, "That is me."

"Come quickly. You are summoned," Ares ordered.

The guard hesitated. "I cannot leave my post. Who summons me?"

The scarred old warrior drew up to the young man in the fancy tabard with his delicate features and curly blond hair, and Ares breathed in his face, "You are *summoned*. Come with me *at once*."

Intimidated, Pares acquiesced to follow. Ares led him away with a tight smile: had Pares done the correct thing and refused to leave his post until he knew who summoned him, Ares' efforts on behalf of Lady Rejane would have been for nothing. The only name Ares knew to give him was Commander Nexo, and odds were that Nexo was not even in the fortress tonight.

Ares took him down the front steps at a fast trot and they ran around the perimeter of the fortress toward the garden in the back. Those they passed assumed they were on some urgent task, as Ares' demeanor discouraged questions. But all the while he was watching to make sure he was not observed when he opened the garden's east gate. At this point, Pares finally challenged him: "What is this? Where are you taking me?"

"To the Lady Rejane. Lower your voice," Ares uttered. The young man became quiet and submissive.

As they came to the cottage, Ares leaned on the door, feeling suddenly light-headed. Sweating profusely, he thrust his hand with the signet into the rosette and turned. The door creaked opened into the dark room. Pares leaned in around him, whispering, "Rejane?"

"Oh!" They heard the feminine exclamation an instant before she threw herself onto her lover. Pares embraced her, kissing her passionately.

Ares sank down to the bed, removing the suddenly unbearably heavy helmet. "We must wait here," he groaned. "We must wait, and rest. . . ." He fell backwards on the bed in a dead faint. And there he lay, unconscious of anything more around him.

When he awoke, it was late afternoon. He raised up, groggy and disoriented. His face, throat and eyes were burning; his head throbbed with fever. Lady Rejane and her lover were gone.

Groaning, he staggered up to shuck off the heavy mail—the linen shift beneath it was soaked with sweat. Dragging himself into the next room, he seized the silver ewer from the washstand and drank all the water in it, dousing himself in the process. Then he fell back onto the bed, unconscious again.

For the next two days, Ares was not cognizant of anything other than being extremely ill. While Thom was driving the scouting party in furious haste back to Westford, and the Qarqarian soldiers scoured the woods for trespassers, Ares lay suffering on the downy bed in Ulm's love cottage.

The morning after their arrival in Westford, Nicole woke refreshed and cheerful—right up to the moment she looked over to Ares' side of the bed and saw that it had not been slept in. She raised up, and the memory of the sudden silence in the hunting woods assailed her. Ares had not slept beside her last night because he was captive at Hornbound. She flung herself down, weeping, then realized she was cold—her teeth were chattering. The window in the receiving room must be open, as Ares had last left it. Still weeping, she drew her robe around her and went into the next room to close the glass panes.

On the windowsill, she found Ares' little book. She was mildly surprised that he had not taken it with him—he usually took it everywhere. It was lying open at what must have been an important quotation, as it was boxed in and set apart on the page. Reading what was written, Nicole unconsciously sank down on the window seat. It said, "I will never fail you nor forsake you." These were God's words, she knew. Ares had evidently mulled over these words a long time, drawing lines and curlicues around them, smudging the ink.

*I will never fail you nor forsake you.* Then it was not by mistake, or evil impulse, that the portal took them to Hornbound instead of Westford. Yes, it could have been intended for evil by whatever malevolent being controlled the portal, but He who would never fail Ares nor forsake him had allowed it to happen for His own purposes. Ares was His agent in Hornbound . . . there to deliver Henry.

The thought calmed her utterly, so that minutes later, she

was able to rise and summon Ursula to assist her in her first proper bath in over a week. Following that, clean, dressed, and composed, Nicole summoned her daughters. When the sentry regretfully told her that the Surchatain had ordered them not to be disturbed in their lessons, Nicole condescended to wait another half hour until they were dismissed. At that time, the girls were told that their mother was waiting for them, and they rushed to her receiving room.

Nicole sank to her knees to gather them in, one on each side, as they clamored for her attention with kisses and complaints. "You were gone for so long! You should not leave us for that long!" Sophie chided indignantly.

"I am sorry, dearest. But never fear; your mother has discovered she's not the adventurer she thought," Nicole consoled her.

"Is Papa back, too?" Sophie asked plaintively.

Nicole smoothed her ponytail. "No, not yet. He had to travel farther than I. Commander Thom is going to fetch him."

Bonnie vented, "It's not fair that when you and Papa leave, Aunt Renée should leave me alone, too. I've had no one to play with but children!"

Nicole looked at her in surprise. "Aunt Renée has not played with you all week?"

"No!" she said, wounded, and Sophie nodded confirmation.

"Why, dearest?" Nicole asked.

"I don't know." Having secured her mother's sympathy, Bonnie allowed her large green eyes to well up with tears.

Sophie told her mother in grown-up tones, "Kara says that she's been too busy tormenting her dear husband."

"Really," Nicole said mildly. "Well. We shall have a special dinner tonight to celebrate my return, at least. Please run tell Georges what you would like to have for dinner."

"Hooray!" The girls took each other's hand to run downstairs.

Perturbed, Nicole stood. She felt it incumbent on her to do something, but did not know what. While she was pondering this, the sentry knocked on her door to inform her that Counselor Carmine was requesting an audience. "Show him in," she said.

Carmine entered, bowing. "Forgive my intrusion, Lady."

"You are not intruding at all, Carmine. How goes it?" she asked.

"Quite well, Surchataine. I have been able to expel a number of vagrants from Nicole's Harbor and post warnings as to the activities that will not be tolerated. But then, our young Counselor Vogelsong has all my reports, and may wish to apprise you of them along with other various and sundry goings-on of which I am ignorant. For instance, I was most surprised to see your party, minus the Surchatain, return in such heat from what was supposedly a pleasure trip, and now I notice of my own accord that off-duty soldiers are reporting in droves. What few rumors I have chanced to overhear specifically mention Hornbound as the object of our aggression. Dear Lady—will you enlighten me?" He looked pathetic, pleading, and painfully sober.

Nicole sighed, glancing away. She shared Ares' desire to see Carmine whole and useful again, and she did not agree with Thom's keeping him in the dark about the purpose of their trip. But she did not want to undermine Thom or say anything that might further endanger her husband. Still, the only way for Carmine to prove himself was for him to be given the opportunity.

She turned to him. "Yes, Carmine. Thom is attacking Hornbound. The truth is . . . Ares was separated from us, and, I believe, wound up in Hornbound—"

"Separated from you! How? Where?" Carmine asked.

"We had gotten as far as the Road of Vanishing in Eugenia," she admitted.

"He did not attempt to use the portal, did he?" Carmine asked in alarm.

Nicole felt faint. "What do you know of the portal?"

"I have known several merchants who traveled through it to secure odd and interesting wares to sell. Few can see the green hallmark it leaves, which clings to whatever it touches, and clings to metallic substances indefinitely. It is common knowledge that Ulm used it to bring his army from Hornbound to the Crossroads. But it is a trap, a grave. For every time a man enters the portal, it takes five years off his life. And everyone who enters it dies of violence or wasting illness."

# 12

t Nicole's bloodless face, Carmine repeated, "Please do not tell me that the Surchatain used the portal to travel to Hornbound."

"I have a request of you, Carmine," she said levelly. "Please go tell the Commander everything you know about the portal. Tell him I asked that you be apprised of our actions at this time."

"Thank you, Surchataine," he said, bowing deeply. "I shall endeavor to prove myself an asset to you." He departed, and Nicole sank to the floor in a heap of damask and silk. She bent her face to the floor, knowing nothing but the wrenching pain in her heart. No prayers could penetrate the wall of despair that enclosed her; no words could escape but a guttural sob.

A sudden disturbance at the window of the receiving room startled her. Quickly looking up, she saw a dove flutter down to the window sill and alight on Ares' little book. Evidently not liking its unsteady perch, it fluttered up again, knocking the book face up onto the floor in front of Nicole. Stubbornly, the pages remained open at the simple declaration that Ares had been studying, now illumined by a shaft of bright morning light: "I will never fail you nor forsake you."

As the words shimmered in the light, she was presented with the choice of accepting them at face value and receiving their solace or dismissing them as ancient, irrelevant text and clinging to her visions of death and bereavement. Nicole slowly sat up, staring at the passage. Then she picked up the book and read through it from beginning to end—every word, every thought, every pen scratch that Ares thought so important as to carry around until it became a part of him.

He believed it. That is how he could venture into unknown dangers in the first place: even were he so gravely mistaken that his actions cost him his life, in the end, he would not be forsaken. And to this day, he had not been. If he believed it so, then she would believe it, too.

There was a knock on her door, and the sentry called that the Commander desired an audience. Nicole stood, clutching the book. She smoothed her dress and said, "Enter."

Thom strode in, dark circles under his eyes, as he had evidently not slept for several days. Sweaty and grimy from the week of travel, he kept his distance as he went down on one knee. "Surchataine, I have received this—report from Carmine regarding the portal, as you directed. But I will tell you frankly that I do not believe it. It is nothing but an old wives' tale, and Carmine of all people should know not to pay attention to such prattle."

She was considering the fact that the legend of the portal itself was an old wives' tale, but Thom had other issues on his mind: "We have sent scouts to patrol Wolfen Road, and have amassed over eight thousand of our standing army already. We will set out tomorrow morning and be at Hornbound within three days," he promised.

Nicole listened to him, fingering the little book. "I shall not interfere with your commanding the army as you see best, Thom. But this I require: since you have done so much in so short a time, you must now go to your quarters and rest with Deirdre until the morrow." He started to protest, but she overrode him: "It will do you no good to reach Hornbound with men too exhausted to fight, and yourself too exhausted to think. Ares knew to rest when he needed it."

He did not miss how she spoke of her husband in the past tense. Lowering his eyes, he saw the book that she gripped. "We will retrieve him, Surchataine. Him and Henry."

"I trust that you will, Thom," she said. "Go rest now." Bowing stiffly, he turned away.

Without Nicole's knowledge, Thom went straight to the chambers of Counselor Vogelsong, interrupting him in his study. Thom looked so dark and angry that Vogelsong trembled slightly upon greeting him: "Commander! This is rather a surprise. How may I serve you?"

"You were the one who mentioned the legends you had heard about the portal," Thom opened, glancing around impatiently.

"Yes, I—"

"I want you to learn more. I want you to find out everything you can about it, and I especially want you to close it!" Thom snapped. "The Second Rhode, whom I am leaving in command of the standing army here, will tell you all we experienced on the Road of Vanishing, as will Captain Crager."

"Certainly, Commander. And you will be . . . ?"

"Leveling a mountain," Thom uttered, turning out, and Vogelsong stared after him.

For some minutes after Thom had left Nicole, she held Ares' little book, caressing it, almost feeling the warmth of his touch on it. Holding it to her chest, she thought about something else that needed to be done. So she said, "Guard." The sentry outside her door opened it immediately. "Have sent up to me a bottle of the best wine, with two goblets. And summon Merle, if you will."

He paused as if unsure of his hearing. "Wine, Surchataine?" Nicole never drank in her chambers.

"Yes. With two large goblets."

"Forgive me, but—and—the laundress, Surchataine?"

"Yes."

The wine made it up to her chambers first. As Nicole was filling one large golden goblet from the bottle, Merle was announced to her. The laundress came in fearfully, bowing prodigiously, as she did not know what to expect.

Nicole held out the goblet to her. "Good morning, Merle. Would you care for some refreshment?"

"Well—thank you, Lady—Surchataine, I mean. That would be lovely," Merle said, reaching hesitantly for the goblet.

"Sit," Nicole invited as she poured a goblet for herself. In wonder, Merle sat on the edge of a plush but restrained settee. After a long draft from the goblet, she settled back, a little more at ease. Taking a perfunctory sip, Nicole said, "I invited you here because I need your help, Merle."

"Yes, Lady?" Merle said, offering her goblet for a refill, which Nicole supplied.

"Yes. I need to know exactly what has been going on between Carmine and Renée while I have been gone," Nicole said.

"Oh, well," Merle said, relaxing in the familiar terrain of gossip. "Quite a bit, actually. I hardly know where to start."

"Start a week ago, the day I left with the Surchatain," Nicole advised.

So, continually supplied with refreshment, Merle relayed in detail every jab and counterjab between the Chataine and the Counselor—Carmine's efforts to stay sober and Renée's efforts to thwart him; Renée's efforts to maintain her standard of luxury and Carmine's efforts to thwart her.

After a twenty-minute recitation, Nicole was brought fully up to date. "Thank you, Merle. That is all I need to know," she said, standing, and Merle looked up in surprise at the early end of their confidential sharing. "Please take the rest of the bottle as my thanks for your cooperation," Nicole added, extending it to her. Satisfied, Merle bowed and betook herself back to the laundry pit with her reward.

Nicole paced for a few minutes, pressing the little book to her chest. Then once again she called, "Guard." He leaned in the doorway. "Summon the Chataine Renée, please." He nodded quickly and withdrew.

Some minutes later he returned in distinct agitation. "Surchataine, the Chataine regrets that she hasn't time to welcome you home properly, but she will do so at dinner."

Nicole barely lifted her chin. "Where is she?"

"In her chambers, Surchataine."

"Come," she ordered. Taking the book, Nicole exited her quarters and walked swiftly down the corridor with the guard trailing her. Arriving at Renée's door, she drew up and told him, "Announce me, please."

The guard rapped on the door and called, "Chataine, the Surchataine Nicole desires an audience."

"Enter," Renée said lightly from within. The guard opened the door for Nicole, and she nodded at him to wait outside. He shut the door, but the shadow of his feet was clearly seen underneath, toes facing the door. Renée's receiving room, though still luxurious, was conspicuously missing the most expensive, frivolous appointments, due to Giles' new power to confiscate.

Renée was sitting at her gilded vanity, applying makeup. Watching her, Nicole contemplated the best choice of words. She did not wish to confront her or humiliate her, as they both remembered Nicole's lowly estate before she came to the palace. But Renée could no longer be allowed to destroy Ares' officials for her own amusement. The loss that had already been incurred due to her years of torturing Carmine was inestimable. If only he had been able to come to them before they left with what he knew of the portal—!

"Dearest," Nicole said, standing behind her to look at her reflection in the mirror, "Bonnie was quite put out that you have not played with her all this past week."

"I've been so busy," Renée shrugged, touching up the coloring on her lips.

"So I've heard," Nicole murmured. Heart sinking, she watched Renée fussing with her face and hair. *What can I say to her to make her understand?* Renée needed to hear the truth, to see how damaging her self-centeredness had become, but—Nicole did not have it in her to blurt out such harsh words to someone she loved. For in spite of everything, Nicole did love her. She knew what good Renée was capable of, and only wished to elicit this higher agenda. If Renée could only hear—

Nicole paused as a perfectly horrid idea came into her head. Cautiously, she turned it over in her mind, as she turned over the little book in her hands, offering the idea to the Lord for His approval or rejection. As she seemed to receive blanket permission, she ventured, "Chataine, I have a rather unpleasant dilemma. I need your help." Renée look disinterested, so Nicole added, "It concerns you."

Renée's eyes flicked up. Nicole began pacing behind her,

tapping the book for emphasis. "I believe the servants' talking has gotten entirely out of hand. For instance, I have been hearing some outlandish things about you that cannot be true. So I have a mind to punish them for this despicable talk. The problem is, I need to sort out what is true from what is false—and that I cannot do. I need for you to hear what I am hearing. Then you can tell me what form of punishment you think is appropriate."

Renée watched her in the mirror, then looked away, torn. On the one hand, she was eager to punish anyone spreading tales about her, but on the other hand, she was not anxious to know what they were saying. Seeing her hesitate, Nicole emphasized, "If I do not do something, the problem will only worsen. Will you help me?"

"I . . . suppose I could," Renée said. How bad could it be?

"Wonderful," Nicole exhaled. "Come with me, then, dearest."

With the guard in tow, Nicole led Renée back to the Surchataine's suite, where she hid Renée behind a large hanging tapestry in the receiving room. Then Nicole sent for Merle again, as well as another bottle of wine.

Merle responded to this second summons with vague feelings of guilt and uneasiness, as she had already finished off the first bottle. But as she had already finished off the first bottle, she was a little too drunk to care. Nicole offered her a seat and another goblet, which Merle lifted in a toast to the remarkable generosity of the Surchataine. "Merle, you were so helpful earlier that I have just a few more questions for you. Please remember that when I ask you to tell me what you have heard, I want you to tell me just what you have heard—not what you think yourself. Do you understand?" Nicole said.

"Certainly, Lady. You have my word," Merle said, slightly flushed from these unexpected confidences. Renée, behind the tapestry, was positioned to hear everything.

"Very good. Now, I need you to tell me what you have heard about the Chataine Renée—aside from what we discussed earlier," Nicole said.

"Oh! Who has the time?" Merle exclaimed. "I hardly know where to begin." Nicole started to tell her to start anywhere, but Merle plunged ahead: "First, they think it awful the way she's trying to snare the Surchatain, when she could have had him years ago, but he was only Commander then, and not Ruler, but the shameless way she's been trying to lure him to bed with her, and usurp my lady—"

"That's not true!" Renée cried, flinging the tapestry to one side. Merle went white, dropping the goblet, and Renée pounced on her: "You shall be horsewhipped for such lies!"

"Guard!" Nicole called, and he ran into the room. He paused in confusion, for Renée was screaming at Merle, who was blubbering apologies, yet the Surchataine said nothing right away.

Nicole was shattered from the shock of hearing how Renée's actions appeared to others, which was far uglier than she guessed. In her naiveté, Nicole had always assumed that everyone else knew the history behind Ares and Renée's relationship—how he had suffered tolerantly for years as her patsy, her pet. But that former relationship, whether anyone remembered it or not, was clearly inappropriate now.

Moreover, Renée's attempts to preserve that relationship was destructive—not just to Ares' reputation and credibility, but to Renée herself, because she had come to believe that if she could treat *him* that way, then everyone else was fair game. And Nicole had passively stood by and let it continue without a murmur of protest.

White with anger, Nicole told the guard, "Escort Merle back to her duties. She is not to be disciplined in any way. Tell Georges he is to prepare a special dinner for her and ten select friends in appreciation from the Surchataine."

"Thank you, Lady!" Merle sobbed, and the guard led her out.

Renée turned on Nicole in fury. "What are you doing? You lure me here to hear outrageous gossip, and then when you hear it, you act as though it were true!"

Shaking, Nicole replied, "I know it is not true, only because you know that Ares will not yield to you. But still you play with him and tease him—this I have seen myself. I have seen how you entice my own daughter to defy me, making her think you are her special friend—then when I am not here to be goaded by your interference, you ignore her. And I have seen what you have done to Carmine, who could not escape you!"

"What are you talking about? Carmine drank of his own choice!" Renée sputtered.

"Today, I give him a new choice," Nicole said. "I give him permission to divorce you today."

"But . . . Ares said a month," Renée said weakly.

"Ares is not here. I am here. And I am sick of watching you play with people as if they had no more sensibility than a block of wood. That must cease, Chataine, or you will find yourself among a whole new set of patsies who may not play as willingly," Nicole said coldly. "Guard!" The new man at the door sprang into the room, and she gestured to Renée. "You may escort the Chataine back to her quarters. And send Counselor Carmine up to me."

"Yes, Surchataine," he said, turning toward Renée. She, in turn, gazed at Nicole with what was intended to be contempt, except for the unintended fear in her eyes.

Dinner that evening was so unusual that it was talked about for weeks. Merle, presiding over her own table in the kitchen, regaled her friends with an embellished retelling of the Surchataine's confrontation with the Chataine. The wine flowed so freely that no one at Merle's table noticed that everyone passing through the kitchen helped himself to the chicken roasted in honey and stuffed with pine nuts—fare intended for her guests alone.

Meanwhile, in accordance with the special menu that Nicole had promised her daughters, the kitchen produced crullers, raspberry fritters, honey bread and milk. (When Georges had alerted Nicole to the rather unbalanced menu, she approved the addition of meat pies with scallions, and, of course, wine for the adults.) Bonnie and Sophie gloried in the honor of sitting on either side of Nicole at the head of the table, until they expressed the desire to be excused to eat with their friends, which was granted.

Carmine was in restrained high spirits, having been officially awarded his divorce from Renée (as everyone knew minutes after Nicole had stamped the divorce decree with the Surchatain's signet). While he was much too savvy a politician to revel in it, or even mention it, his scintillating repartee at the table alerted one and all to the fact that Counselor Carmine was back as a player to be reckoned with.

But the most astonishing feature of the dinner was Renée herself. Early in the afternoon, she had requested permission to absent herself from the table for the evening, which Nicole denied. So Renée had appeared, sitting in her usual place across from Carmine. She was dressed sumptuously, but sedately, and wore not a particle of makeup on her face. When addressed, she responded politely, even intelligently, but made no effort to draw attention to herself—indeed, she may have been stinging by the number of studious sidelong glances that were directed toward her without any effort on her part at all. Finally, when Giles, in ghastly bad taste, offered a toast to Carmine on new beginnings, Renée gamely lifted her goblet, smiled and drank as if her future was just as rosy, or her life not shattered.

That morning Ares woke, turning his head to blearily study his surroundings. Where was he? . . . Oh, yes, he groaned. Ulm's love cottage. He felt unutterably weak, but the fever had left him. With concerted effort, he raised himself to sit on the damp, downy mattress and look around. The cottage was lit by narrow shafts of morning sunlight that exploited every crack in the closed shutters—enough for him to see the table with covered dishes that stood beneath one window.

Grunting with the effort, he stood and stumbled over to the table to uncover the dishes. There he found an assortment of cheeses, fruit and dessert breads. Sinking to his knees in front of the table, he ate all he could comfortably hold. Then he dragged himself back to the bed and spread out upon it again.

It was dark when he awoke a second time, but now he felt somewhat stronger. He sat up, listening and thinking. He had no idea how long he had been laying here—judging from the new length of his beard, he guessed days—but however long, he thought it curious that he had not been found yet. Surely after Ulm's death, they would have realized that there was an imposter about. And did the Lady Rejane and her soldier-lover escape? Ares believed so—else, under torture, they would have revealed his presence in the cottage.

Ares slipped from the bed and dropped to the floor to creep from window to window and peer out through the slits in the shutters. He saw not a soul—no one on guard. That was rather unnerving, given his ignorance of what may have transpired in the time that he was unconscious. Well. For now, he quietly unlatched the door and crept out on hands and knees. There was a dense cloud cover tonight, which made it very dark in the garden. He saw torches at points along the parapet of the fortress and in a window here or there, but nothing came close to lighting his surroundings.

So he was safely able to slip to the brook and quietly submerge in the cool water, still wearing the linen smock. Careful to make no noise, not a ripple, he bathed, feeling greatly refreshed in washing off the dirt, sweat, blood and residual odors from Ulm's chambers. It felt so good to lounge in the gently flowing brook that he lingered, letting the cool water rinse every pore and crevice, especially his scar. While he soaked, he listened to the gentle hum of a hidden pump. The brook was artificially created, obviously, as it rose up from the ground just inside one wall of the garden and disappeared back into the earth at the rear wall. How such a thing was managed, he could not guess.

The banging of the garden gate startled him out of his repose, but he lay like a crocodile, only his upper face free of the water, as he watched two soldiers with torches advance to the cottage. One was saying, "We checked it already; it was locked, and only the Surchatain's signet can unlock it."

The other replied, "But no one's found the signet, and Pym saw Pares and another soldier come this way before he and Lady Rejane disappeared. So—" the door swung open under his touch, as Ares had not locked it.

The two went in and made a hasty search by torchlight, then came out again carrying the (presumably) discarded chain mail, complete with sword. Away they went with it at a run. Once they were out of the garden, Ares raised up, scowling. He still needed the disguise of that mail. He certainly needed something to wear.

Aware that time was short, Ares ran in his dripping linen smock back into the cottage. One of the soldiers had left his torch in the sconce by the door. Glad for the light, at least, Ares grabbed a small blanket and loaded it with all the rest of the food on the table, including a bottle with a little bit of wine. While on his knees in front of the table, he glimpsed under the bed the belt, still holding the two sets of keys, that the sentries had missed seeing. He snatched that up to put it on.

Then, knotting the blanket with the foodstuffs, he looked around the cottage, hoping against hope to find something to wear. The mail shoes had been left behind, which he was glad to put on, but they did not constitute a convincing costume when worn with linen underwear. There was a chest by the far wall he had not noticed previously. The lock on it bore the same rosette as was on the door, so Ares used the signet on his hand to open it. Lifting the lid, he found a black robe and a hood.

Instantly, he recalled what Miers had said about Ulm's playing executioner. Grabbing up the robe along with the bundle of food, he paused by the door. With his wet footprints all over the floor, and the pilfered food table and chest, it would be obvious to the searchers who were to imminently arrive that their prey was nearby. But what if the sentry who left the torch had been careless with it? All Ares had to do was pull a lightweight hanging tapestry over the torch, as if it had been blown by the wind coming through the open door. This he did, and the tapestry caught fire promptly. Ares paused long enough to make sure that burning pieces fell on other furnishings in the room, so that by the time he had skulked to the brook, the cottage was burning robustly.

While he was crossing the footbridge, the bottle fell out of his loosely tied pack. Ares hastily retrieved it before it could roll off the bridge into the water—then realized that this was for his benefit: the little bit of wine would do him no good. Removing the cork, he drained the wine and filled the bottle from the brook. Corking it, he replaced it more securely in his blanket, along with the black robe. The whole he tied into a neat bundle, looking up at the sound of voices approaching.

So he slung the bundle over his shoulder and exited the garden by means of the back gate—that closest the cliffs. In front of him lay that short space of yard, then the narrow path that ran along the inside of the wall enclosing the fortress. Since the fortress was set so close to the cliffs, the moat formed a crescent moon, terminating at either side of the garden. No matter: he knew exactly what he was going to do from here. He peered around the corner of the garden wall to see numerous figures rushing toward the east garden gate.

Ares sighed a prayer of thanks for the intense darkness of the evening, which enabled him to climb up the rough stones of the encompassing wall unnoticed. Adjusting the pack for balance, he turned on the top of the wall to descend its cliff side, rendering himself just one shadow among many. He dropped tentatively to the two-foot ledge at the base of the wall, pausing to make sure of his balance before beginning a tentative descent down the cliff. Unfortunately, the armored shoes were poor for climbing a sheer rock face, so he was unable to find a foothold before the first wave of soldiers and servants carrying buckets arrived to fight the fire on the other side of the wall.

It was impossible, he realized, to climb far enough down these treacherous cliffs to avoid detection. Had he the proper equipment—ropes and shoes and daylight—it might have been done, but, Miers was right. Between the moat, which he dare not attempt in his weakened state, and the cliffs, there was no sneaking on or off this mountain.

Right now, all he could hope to do was hide. So, he knelt to withdraw the black robe from his bundle. Wrapping himself in it, he lay down snugly at the base of the stone wall. While the residents of the fortress endeavored to put out the fire on the other side of the garden wall, he went to sleep inches from the edge of the cliff.

He awoke when morning sunlight struck him full in the face. Wincing, he straightened from his contorted position against the rock wall, then fell back again as he almost lost his balance. Cautiously, he looked down over the cliff face, which he could now see in unnerving detail.

It was a vertical rock face with jagged cracks that ran up and down at irregular points. The slender, begrudging shelf on which he sat was the only horizontal footing that could be seen for several hundred feet in any direction. Ares felt a twinge of jealous admiration for the position of this fortress atop such a cliff—it was unassailable. Looking up from this vantage point on the edge, he could just see the top backside of the fortress, confirming that there was no exit down the cliffs. But the city clearly lay below, so there must be *some* route down. While he considered this, Ares breakfasted from his stolen store.

Thinking back to the night that the wardens brought him in, he vaguely remembered a side road that snaked away on the other side of the moat. That must be the road into town, as there was no crossing the moat but at the drawbridge (that he could see) and no route down this sheer cliff. The problem was, the only way to get to that road was over the drawbridge, which was exhaustively patrolled—especially now that Ulm was dead.

Now that Ulm was dead. . . . Ares looked down at the black robe that had helped hide him for the night. Ulm's death gave him a possible opening to make use of the fear associated with this robe. It was a huge risk, not at all certain to succeed, but the longer he stayed in the palace environs, the greater the likelihood he would be caught anyway—with never the opportunity to even find Henry.

Balancing on his narrow perch on the cliff, Ares tied the blanket with the remaining food around his waist, then drew the black robe down over it. Before putting on the hood, he crawled up to peer over the wall and make sure that no faces were turned toward this particular point on the cliffs at this particular time. Then he clambered up over the wall and dropped down to the path that ran between the wall and the garden. He pulled on the hood, adjusted his dislocated food pack, and began a stately walk down the path toward the front of the fortress.

# 13

Once Ares gained the path around the fortress, he took care to walk with a measured, heavy step. The keys on his belt were an unexpected boon here, as iron jangling against iron hinted at a hidden weapon (which he actually did not have). Also, the food-stuffed blanket added bulk under the robe, making him rather misshapen and all the more intimidating. The eyeholes in the hood were cut large enough for him to see adequately without exposing his scar. The only drawback was that the hood did restrict his peripheral vision and hearing, so he was tense listening for footfalls from behind or to the side.

The first Qarqarian he encountered was a servant exiting the garden with a wheelbarrow of burned debris. Seeing Ares, the poor man did a double take, then fell on his knees with a cry. Ares disdainfully passed him by on his stately march to the front gates.

He could hear a whispering crowd gather behind him, but he did not stop or turn around. Then appeared his first crucial test: a sentry came around the corner on an errand and jumped in surprise at the massive black figure rolling toward him. Ares fixed him with an iron gaze as the sentry stood rooted in the middle of the path. The manner in which Ares claimed the right of way could make or break his charade—stepping off the path was unacceptably weak, but too strong a show of force would elicit counterforce against him.

Coming upon the recruit, Ares paused to look down at him, obviously new and very young. He wore no mail, only the ornamental tabard of the palace guard. Frozen in terror, the sentry stared up at the cold, dark eyes under the hood. Then Ares reached out just far enough to knot his fist in the young man's tabard and lift him bodily with one hand only to drop him carelessly by the side of the path. Losing his footing in the landing, the sentry sat abruptly in the dirt, then scooted backwards crab-wise, all the while gaping at the black figure. With the obstruction removed, Ares continued up the path.

Having been alerted to the spectacle, other guards gathered on the path before him, but he did not alter his pace. The highest ranking among them, who looked to be wearing lieutenant's insignia, called, "Who are you seeking, Executioner?" Ares did not answer—but that question told him first, that the consentient opinion accepted him as genuine, and second, what to say when he must answer.

As he came upon the group, they parted to let him proceed unhindered. By the time he arrived at the front of the fortress, he had a large entourage following at a respectful distance. When he turned away from the fortress toward the manned drawbridge gates, he could hear expressions of relief rise from the crowd like a prayer.

Now for the big test: the drawbridge guards, of sterner stuff than the rest, watched impassively while he advanced. While not overtly threatening, they held their swords at the ready to indicate that he would not simply float by them over the drawbridge (which was lowered, as on any normal day). Scanning the bridge and surrounding wall, Ares counted twenty-two guards, all attending his approach. But the two who stood at the gateposts were obviously the senior guards, and the ones who must be persuaded to let him pass.

Ares drew up to within a few feet of them, stopping before they had to order him to. Moving his head in a pronounced manner, he looked first at one guard, then at the other. "What is your business, Executioner?" one demanded.

The fact that he used the dreaded title told Ares that his ploy had a good chance of success. In a hoarse, menacing whisper, neither Qarqarian nor Lystran, he replied, "I have been sent to avenge the blood of Surchatain Ulm. My path lies beyond."

The two guards glanced at each other, but there was no hesitation in their moving aside. The rest of the guards lowered their weapons in response, and Ares carried himself in a one-man procession across the drawbridge.

Almost immediately he was met with a quandary: the road beyond the drawbridge branched in opposite directions, and he did not know which branch led to the city below. If he hesitated, or took one fork and then doubled back, he would be exposed as an outsider. Sending up a prayer for divine guidance, he impulsively took the branch to the right, leading to an area of the fortress grounds that he had not yet seen. No one accosted him.

Progressing down this road at his usual unhurried pace, he was greatly heartened to see a merchant's cart coming up the road toward him, for it had to have come from the city. A further not-so-happy aspect of this encounter was that the cart took up most of the road, and Ares could hardly one-hand it off. As he was still within view of the fortress walls, he was still vulnerable to exposure as a fraud.

The merchant took care of the situation himself, however. Seeing the black figure bearing down on him, the man reined his carthorse off the road entirely, then threw himself from his seat and prostrated himself with his face in the dirt. Ares passed him without any acknowledgment whatsoever, for which the man breathed tremulous thanks. Little did he know that the man in black was also breathing thanks to the God of light, for this encounter told him how to find Henry.

As Ares continued down the road, he glimpsed a series of switchbacks leading down the mountain that he could not have seen from the cliff at the rear of the garden. Progressing, he discovered a gate and guardhouse at the head of the first switchback. But as these guards were focused on screening those who wished to gain entrance to the fortress rather than leave, the moment they saw him, they made haste to throw open the gate and stand aside. The terrain that he was passing through was admirably suited to the already impregnable defense of the fortress—it was barren but for scrub brush, grass, and the stumps of trees that had been felled. Therefore, anyone attempting to gain the fortress grounds by means other than the road had no cover to hide from the towers or guardhouses and nothing to scavenge for food or fuel.

By the time Ares had descended to the gate at the second switchback, the fortress at the mountain top was barely visible. But on the turn to the third switchback, he got his clearer view yet of the sheer cliffs to his right. The eagle pair that had made a nest in one narrow crevice looked to be the only creatures capable of mastering that formidable face. From this point, he also had an eagle's-eye view of the city. This proved so instructive that he stopped to study Hornbound's neat, square layout, particularly the road from the fortress leading into the city and the back road leading out along a portion of the outer wall. This was the wall that Miers had described as laying beyond (or rather below) the city of Hornbound. From what Miers had told him, Ares knew that this wall encompassed the whole mountaintop. So it also must be breached, eventually.

Past the third switchback, he was low enough on the mountain to come upon cultivated fields of quick-growing millet now being harvested. The field hands who saw him dropped their scythes in terror and hid among the stalks. Ares began to pass them in his usual ghostly manner, then reconsidered and detoured slightly to pick up a dropped scythe. The curved blade would be effective not only as a weapon, but as another visual clue to the nature of his mission.

Past the fourth checkpoint, the road straightened to the city. Beyond this, there were no further barriers to the streets, shops and homes of Hornbound. Here as well, Ares witnessed the generally terrified reaction to his appearance. As he passed into the heart of the city, he kept an eye out for an informant who best fit his criteria. He required someone of sufficient rank who was not too unnerved to answer a simple question.

Before long Ares spotted a likely candidate: a finely clothed noble was watching him in subdued alarm. When Ares turned toward him, he stiffened, but did not prostrate himself or run. Drawing within earshot, with his scythe held to his chest as an ornament, Ares hissed, "I seek the house of Lord Morand."

A look of relief, almost of eagerness, passed over the nobleman's face, and Ares perceived that he had asked directions from one of Morand's enemies. Composed, the man pointed to a side street. "Down that street past six houses—you'll come to the Crown Jewelers on the right. Lord Morand and his family live above the shop." As Ares turned away, he glimpsed the nobleman take something out of his shirt and kiss it in gratitude—obviously, a talisman of some sort. The nobleman suddenly called after him: "Remember me to my Lord Morand. I am Lord Heaviside, a loyal subject of my Lord Surchatain Ulm."

Issuing an animalistic growl in response, Ares went on his way, debating with himself whether the city knew of Ulm's death. The street cleared upon his approach; residents scattered like startled rats into the nearest holes. Shutters quietly closed over windows; doors were shut and bolted by unseen hands. Even before he got to the hanging wooden sign with the crown painted upon it, he saw the door beneath it slam shut.

Ares made a show of stopping before this door and turning toward it. With the blunt edge of the scythe, he delivered a rattling blow to the door. In a breathy croak, he uttered, "The household of Lord Morand is required. Show yourselves!" Then he stepped back to wait.

Moments later, the door creaked open and a richly dressed merchant appeared, white-faced and trembling. There also appeared, shooting out from between his legs, a short, stocky dog with a long snout and long ears pointing straight up. The small animal planted itself in front of his master and barked at Ares with all the ferocity twenty pounds could produce. Ares hissed at it, raising the scythe, but the householder quickly nudged it back inside with his foot. Turning, he said, "I am your humble servant Morand. Do with me as you will, but I beseech you to let my household be."

Ares craned his neck forward to suggest a ravenous predator. He croaked loudly, "Your household and all of your servants are required, Lord Morand."

"Yes, my Lord Executioner, but mercy, I beg you—I have been faithful to my Lord Surchatain Ulm—"

"Show your household!" Ares uttered, lifting his black-swathed arms.

Despair dripping from his every move, Morand backed up to reopen the door and wave shortly, gasping, "He requires everyone to appear."

One by one, the terrified family members emerged into the otherwise abandoned street. The dog attempted numerous dashes after them, but someone always shooed it back. There was Morand's wife, a proud, substantial woman who glared at Ares. Two sons, young men, emerged next, eyeing him with the fear of their father mixed with the prideful scorn of their mother. Following them, a beautiful young girl slipped out, her little hand seeking that of her older brother's. He gripped it, finding the strength from her pitiful grasp to mutely promise the Executioner that a hand stretched toward his sister must find its way over his own body.

After them the servants filed out one by one. They were less fearful but wary; being only servants, there was little likelihood that one of them had been accused of such an egregious crime as to be marked for public execution, but at the same time, if their master was executed, his household would likely be broken up, and what would become of them left open to question. Ares surveyed the steward, cook, and domestic servants as they lined up behind the family along the street.

The last one out was a thin, miserable adolescent boy dressed in soiled, too-small clothes. He slouched at the end of the row, looking indifferent in his misery to whatever loomed before him. At the sight of him, Ares' heart almost burst, and it was all he could do to stand still and not grab him up and shake him. For it was Henry.

When no one else emerged, Ares looked back to Lord Morand. "This is not all of your household," he hissed. The dog could be heard whining and scratching at the inside of the door.

"Yes, my Lord Executioner, I swear it is all of us. We stand at your mercy," Morand pleaded.

Ares turned his head as if dissatisfied, but condescended to say: "You have been accused of treachery by Lord Heaviside against my Lord Surchatain Ulm, who has been slain in his chambers."

Morand swayed on his feet and his wife gasped. As he was unable to utter a word, she exclaimed, "'Tis a lie! None has been truer to my Lord Surchatain Ulm than my husband. Ask the honored Counselor Viaud, and he will vouch for this house!"

Simply because Ares admired her courage, he nodded in her direction. "So he has said," he admitted in a gravelly, almost human voice (all this about Heaviside and Viaud being fiction, of course—to Ares' knowledge). The children glanced in wondering admiration at their mother, and some color began to return to Morand's face. "But because the accusation came from so high a personage, you are instructed to give up one of your household to me. Decide who that shall be," Ares instructed.

As Ares surmised would happen, Morand glanced immediately at the youngest, least valuable servant. "Take the boy, Henry," Morand urged in relief. A shade of regret passed over his wife's face, but neither she nor anyone else spoke up to save the boy's life.

Henry looked up vacantly. When Ares turned toward him and uttered, "Come," the boy's grey eyes watered slightly, but he shuffled forward until he stood in front of the terrible black figure. Not trusting himself to say anything yet, Ares laid a hand on Henry's shoulder and steered him on down the street toward the eastern edge of the city, bordered by wheat fields. As soon as they started off, Morand and his household surged back into his shop. Ares almost wished he could witness what would soon happen between him and Heaviside.

With his victim slogging before him, Ares headed out of the city on a straight path through continually emptying streets. Concentrating as he was on maintaining the charade until they reached cover, he was unaware of Henry's growing distress until they had left the city and crossed the foot path bordering the fields. Then, tears washing clean streaks down his grimy face, Henry looked up to plead, "Will it hurt? Will you do it quick so that it doesn't hurt?"

Ares glanced around, but the obstructive hood made it difficult for him to see if anyone was watching. Tossing the scythe down, he whispered, "Henry. Do not say anything; do not move. It's Ares." Henry froze in unbelieving hope, so Ares tugged on his hood just enough to expose a portion of his scar though an eyehole.

"Ares," Henry whimpered.

He tried to throw his arms around the bulky black Executioner, but Ares prevented him, whispering, "You are my prisoner until we can get to a hiding place, Henry. And we must move quickly before someone questions why we are not returning to the fortress. Now—"

He was interrupted by sudden ferocious barking. Wheeling, he and Henry saw the Morand family's stubborn brown dog challenging the awful Executioner over his property. "Puck! You followed me!" Henry exclaimed, dropping to his knees to gather up the muscled furball, who, mission accomplished, agreeably licked Henry's face and ears.

Breathing out in exasperation, Ares dropped beside them underneath a row of gently waving wheat. He pulled off the hood to look up and down the nearby path while Henry rubbed a spot on Puck's tummy that made his rear leg beat the air. "Henry, we need to get past the city wall. Do you know anything that would help us?" Ares said.

Henry screwed up his brow to think, still stunned by his deliverance. "Well, it is a little broken in places—I've heard talk that Ulm spends all he has on his army and his fortress so that he doesn't have enough to keep the wall in good repair—but you have to walk a long ways to find the spots. Ares . . . did you come here just to find me?"

"Yes," Ares said. "And Thom is bringing the army to get us both out. But we have to—" He broke off at the sound of someone coming up the footpath, so he and Henry, clutching Puck, scooted back to hide in the rows of wheat. Henry leaned over Puck to hold him absolutely still.

A field hand came into view, obviously neglecting his duties, for he looked as wary of getting caught as Ares and Henry were. They watched him pass in mild interest, then Ares nodded after him, whispering, "Follow. Quietly."

They emerged onto the road, crouching, and Henry bent to whisper, "Puck! Quiet." Eyes on Henry, the dog wagged his nub of a tail, then looked down the path at the wayward laborer. Ares shot a warning look to Henry before he turned to follow stealthily.

The three of them trailed the man to his destination: a large irrigation ditch filled with water and lined with stone. The ditch was equipped with an Archimedean screw that lifted water to a wooden trough running from ditch to fields. At this time of day, the area was deserted. So the fellow went digging among the rocks on the ditch's edge and removed a purloined flask. This he sampled with relish before stripping and easing himself into the water for a little midday relaxation.

Raising a cautionary hand to Henry, Ares crept forward to the place where the fellow had carelessly left his shirt, pants, and shoes. From behind the screw, Ares reached out to gather them in one hand, drawing them back along the ground toward him while his victim lounged in the pool, eyes closed. Then Ares and Henry retreated into the rows of wheat, accompanied soundlessly by Puck.

Ares had obvious plans for the clothes, but as the stalks shivered tellingly at any movement beneath them, he could not change right where he was. Cautiously standing to see over the growing wheat, he was then able to lead his companions toward the city wall. Fortuitously, he found one of those spots Henry had mentioned, where the mortar had loosened its hold on about two dozen stones that now lay in a heap at the base of the wall. While Henry and Puck stood watch, Ares rearranged the stones to provide temporary cover for the three of them.

Sitting behind their rocky shelter, Ares shucked off the armored shoes in relief—without hose, they were cutting into his feet. He likewise dispensed with the black robe and hood, revealing the bounty tied around his waist. He spread out the blanket, then he and Henry ate just enough to take the edge off their hunger, sharing bites with Puck. Ares scratched the dog's head between his ears in reluctant admiration as Puck chewed happily on a piece of cheese. "You're a feisty beast. No one else confronted the Executioner with as much pluck." Puck licked his hand in acknowledgment.

"Where did you get the Executioner's robe?" Henry asked.

"From the fortress," Ares answered. "Did Lord Morand know that Ulm is dead, Henry?"

The boy thought hard, picking crumbs off the blanket to eat—

something that Henry would never thought of doing eight weeks ago. "No, I don't think so. I never heard anyone say so. Oh . . . I feel like I'm coming out of a bad dream," he shuddered.

Ares lifted the bottle to let water trickle into his mouth, then handed it to Henry. First thing, Henry poured a little in his hand for Puck to lap. "Henry, we don't have water to waste," Ares reminded him.

"He's thirsty, Ares—he followed us a long way. Besides, Puck is really special," Henry protested.

Disinterested, Ares bundled up the rest of the food in the blanket, then glanced beyond their hiding place as he pulled off the soiled linen smock. He put on the stolen work clothes, eyeing Henry. "Why did you run away from Westford?"

Henry looked up quickly, then lowered his reddening face. "You were short with me at the dinner table. I just wanted to—get far enough away to make you worry a bit. But before I knew it, I was surrounded by these—creatures. They took my horse and put me in chains and marched me by foot miles and miles. . . ." His eyes started watering again.

"You told Morand your real name?" Ares said as a question. Trying on the shoes, he found them snug but adequate.

"I told everyone!" Henry exclaimed before remembering to keep his voice down. "I told them, 'I am Henry, Chatain of Lystra'—but no one believed me!"

"One did," Ares said, fingering Lazear's keys. "And that was enough."

He refastened the belt with both keyrings around his waist, then leaned back to look up at the wall, which was about ten feet high. The stones that had fallen off it at this point were not nearly enough to open up a breach—they were just a preliminary sign of disrepair. As far as Ares looked in either direction, he saw no opening, nor gate. "How did Morand bring you into the city?"

Henry squinted in thought. "It was late, and I was very tired, but . . . we passed by some kind of slave camp at the foot of the mountain. It was all very shabby, with rows of men in chains."

"The mines?" Ares asked.

"It must have been, though I saw nothing but long rows of shelters without walls, and great holes in the sides of the mountain with wooden beams in the mouths. There were torches and guards all around it. I heard Lord Morand tell someone that if ever Hornbound is attacked, the first thing the guards do is set fire to the wooden supports at the mouths of the mines, killing all slaves inside. He said it prevents them from joining the enemy and prevents the enemy from making use of the mines until Qarqar regains control of them."

"Isn't it costly to replace that many slaves?" Ares asked, brow raised.

"Yes, Lord Morand said, but they've only had to do it once. And it was less costly than losing Hornbound."

"What of the roads?" Ares asked.

"There is one road that cuts through the midst of this camp up the mountain, but we took another road that went around it up to the city gates, then to the fortress," Henry said.

"Once you were past the city gates on this road, did it lead through woods? And then end at the drawbridge over the moat around the fortress?" Ares asked.

"Yes," Henry nodded. He scratched Puck's ears as he talked, and the animal laid its long snout on his leg.

"This other road that cut through the camp. . . . Did it lead to the same gate in the city wall?" Ares asked.

"No," Henry frowned. "I couldn't see where it led—just somewhere up the mountain."

Ares thought about the left-hand fork of the road just past the drawbridge, and knew that it must be the termination of the road that ran through the midst of the mining camp. Qarqarian officials would want visiting dignitaries to just see the mining operations, not have to wade through them. Thus, two roads from the base of the mountain were necessary—and apparently, two gates.

Henry, meanwhile, was feeling the need to demonstrate Puck's abilities to his rescuer. "Look, Ares—I taught Puck some tricks. Watch." Laying a small rock in front of the dog, Henry commanded, "Hold, Puck." After a feint or two, Puck picked up the rock in his teeth. "Drop, Puck," Henry commanded. Puck dropped the rock.

"That's good, Henry, but—"

"No, wait! Watch. Hold, Puck," Henry instructed, tapping the rock. Puck picked it up again. "Take, Puck," Henry said, pointing to Ares. "Take to Ares. Ares!" Puck trotted over to Ares and dropped the rock in his lap. "See? I trained him myself."

Ares picked up the rock, tossing it lightly. "Henry . . . we have to get over the wall."

"All right," he answered tentatively.

Ares raised up enough from their hiding place to scan all around. "This looks like as good a time as any. Come—I will lift you up on my shoulders. Lay down flat on the wall and see what is on the other side."

"All right," he agreed.

After one more quick look around, Ares boosted him up to the top of the wall. As instructed, Henry went down on his belly, disappearing to Ares' view as he scooted over to the outside edge. Shortly, his head reappeared. "There's a drop of at least twenty feet on the other side. It looks hard and rocky."

"Is there a road or a path?" Ares asked.

"No, not that I can see."

"Can you see any place it looks safe to drop in either direction?"

Henry's head vanished again momentarily. When he came back, it was to say, "No."

"How wide is the wall, Henry?" Ares squinted up in the afternoon sunlight.

"About ten feet."

"All right. Come back down." Ares reached for him as Henry slid down feet first, then Ares lowered him to the ground. Weighing the black robe in his hand, Ares looked around. He wrapped the executioner's robe and hood around a rock, then stepped back and threw them over the wall.

With the bundle of food slung over his shoulder, Ares gestured to the foot path that ran along the perimeter of the fields about thirty feet inside the wall. As they gained the path, Puck happily trotted alongside. "We'll see if we can find a better place to go over the wall farther down. Will we raise suspicions walking this way?" Ares asked.

"No, not unless soldiers come along. They're suspicious of everybody. They question everybody," Henry said bitterly.

Ares glanced down at him. Where the collar of his shirt puckered out, Ares could see red welts covering his back. "It looks like you speak from experience," he said. At the light touch of his hand on the boy's back, Henry flinched. "Do you want to tell me what happened?"

"No," Henry said darkly.

Ares accepted that. But as he looked up, he spotted in the distance a long line of soldiers coming down the path toward them.

**a**res sucked in a sharp breath upon seeing the soldiers. There were at least fifty of them, and they were not restricting themselves to the footpath alone, but spreading out to search the fields as well. As far off as they were, the only reason Ares spotted them was because there were so many. But he and Henry had to move fast.

"All right, Henry—We go over the wall here, regardless what is on the other side," Ares said. Henry looked fearfully toward the oncoming troops. Thinking quickly, Ares stripped off his shirt to unbundle the food from the blanket and wrap in the shirt instead. "Take this. Up you go." Ares handed him the bundle of food with the water bottle before boosting him to the top of the wall. "Careful—the bottle is glass. Stay down. When I climb up, I'll lower you down the other side with the blanket."

"What about Puck?" Henry asked, peering down at him from the top of the wall.

Throwing the blanket over his shoulder, Ares looked back at the advancing soldiers. They would spot him at any moment. "We can't take him, Henry."

"We have to!" Henry cried, leaning over. "Ares, we have to take him!"

Ares dug his fingers into the mortar to begin scaling the wall.

"We can't," he grunted, inching his way up. "You can't hold on to him and the food and the blanket—"

"Yes, I can, Ares! I can! Ares, he's a slave, too!" Henry cried, tears pouring. Puck was standing on hind legs below Ares, scratching furiously at the wall as if trying to climb it after him.

Ares closed his ears against further pleas. But then a rock dislodged under his fingers, coming out of the wall. With this anchor suddenly gone, he fell, landing flat on his back, still gripping the rock. While he tried to regain his breath, Puck licked his face solicitously.

Gasping, Ares sat up, and Puck planted his stocky front legs on Ares' chest to regard him nose to nose. Muttering in exasperation under his breath, Ares stood and hoisted the dog. He held Puck against the wall over his head. "Can you reach him?"

"Yes!" Henry lay flat on the wall to reach down and grab Puck with both hands under his front legs, dragging him over the edge. As Ares repositioned the blanket and began to climb again, he glanced over his shoulder to see soldiers running toward them. They had been seen.

Ares scrabbled up the wall and flattened himself atop it, unraveling the blanket from around his neck and shoulder. "You take one end—"

"I'r rau iuh," Henry said. With the knotted shirt in his teeth and Puck under one arm, he wrapped the end of the blanket around his other fist and scooted off the wall. Ares lowered him bit by bit with the blanket until his feet touched the rocky ground. Without daring to see how close the soldiers were, Ares lowered himself over the wall to hang by his hands, then dropped the remaining few feet.

Collecting Henry and the blanket, with Puck alongside, Ares began descending the mountain slope directly away from the wall. It was not too steep, nor hard going, but there was precious little shelter from the sight of anyone on the wall—and why there hadn't been a guard patrolling atop it when they were forced to scale it, Ares couldn't imagine. They scooted down the mountainside, unleashing small rock slides as Ares led Henry in a jagged path, searching for the quickest route to safety.

Dropping past a ledge, Ares felt Henry follow him, but short

Puck gave a sharp bark, finding no way down. When Henry turned to grab him, Ares jerked them both down under the ledge. Since Puck had forced them to stop and look back, Ares spotted the soldier's helmet the moment it topped the wall.

The three of them lay panting under the ledge, then Ares peered ever so slightly over it. "Did they see us?" Henry gasped, clutching Puck.

"No," Ares said, almost in disbelief. "They're scanning from the wall now. We need to just sit here for a while." Breathing out, Henry pressed his face against the furry neck. Watching Puck lay contentedly in Henry's arms, Ares could have sworn the dog was grinning back at him.

Ares peered over the ledge periodically, watching the soldiers methodically move along the wall to survey the mountain below it. "Won't they just assume we're escaped servants? Not worth bothering about?" Ares asked.

Henry scowled. "Yes, they probably think that's what we are, and they will keep searching until they find us, to put us in the mines. They have so many slaves die in the mines that they're always looking for more."

"I suppose so," Ares muttered. "Especially if they have set fire to them recently. Or if they feed the ones who escape to the dogs."

Henry seemed to not hear him, as he was looking hard at the keyrings on Ares' belt, not for the first time. "Where did you get those?"

"One set is Lazear's, the trader who sold you to Lord Morand. The other I took from a warden," Ares said absently, watching over the ledge.

"Let me see them, Ares," Henry asked.

Reluctantly, Ares unbuckled the belt. "They are not toys, Henry."

Henry looked at him with a face grimy, gaunt, and years older than that of the boy who disappeared seven weeks ago. "After what I have been through, you think I am interested in *playing* with them?"

Ares took off the belt, handing it to him, and Henry intently studied both sets—three keys on one ring, four on the other. "I recognize this one. All the slavers carry one like it," he said.

Ares glanced down. "That is Lazear's keyring."

Henry observed, "But there is not one like it on the other keyring, the one you took from the warden. So it must be one that a warden would not use. And wardens don't handle chained slaves." Ares studied him now. "This one," Henry said, lifting a key on the warden's ring, "unlocks most rooms at the fortress, except for the Surchatain's rooms and the treasury. This," he said of the next key, "is a key to the dungeon. And this is a skeleton key that opens most doors in Hornbound."

Ares stared at him. "How do you know so much about the keys?"

"One of Lord Morand's duties was to be keeper of the keys for Counselor Viaud. Sometimes he left his keys with me, and I did play with them—although he made sure to tell me that if any were missing, he would cut me open to look for them," Henry said.

Ares glanced back at the wall, then turned to regard Henry again. "Since you are so well acquainted with the keys, you should carry them."

"Thank you, Ares," Henry said, passing the belt behind his back. It was far too large, so he doubled it around himself before buckling it. Then he remarked, "I also see that you are wearing the Surchatain's signet ring."

"Which I will continue to wear," Ares promised, shifting to look further along the wall.

"Ares—did you kill Ulm?"

"No," Ares replied. "He died by his own treachery. But I took the signet off his body."

Henry sank down, fingering the keys. "I am glad."

"All right—they've moved out of sight. We need to move, also," Ares said, standing. Puck hopped up, and Henry pulled himself to a stand.

For the rest of the day, they made their way down the sharp, rocky slope. The only vegetation was bramble or tufts of hardy grass sprouting from a crevice here or there. Ares doled out the water sparingly, so that Puck began to foam at the corners of his mouth. Although he made not a whimper, Henry picked him up to carry him.

By nightfall, they reached a small grove of larch that grew around a shallow pool. During spring thaws it was a small lake, but by this time of summer, two-thirds of it had evaporated away. Still, there was water to drink. While Ares and Henry knelt at the edge and cupped their hands to scoop up water, Puck had to lie flat on the edge, dangling his stubby front legs, to reach the water. Watching, Ares saw the rationale for the Creator's giving such a short dog such a long nose.

The small grove also offered suitable shelter to camp, as long as they did not have their hearts set on a fire. The three of them consumed the remainder of the food, which worried Ares somewhat. Stealing food increased their chances of getting caught, and it would be days—weeks, possibly—before Thom arrived.

After eating, Henry and Puck lay down together in between a pair of larches and went directly to sleep. Ares covered them with the blanket and covered that with loose soil, twigs and pine needles as camouflage. He redonned the work shirt, as the night was growing cool, then lay down near the boy and his dog. Ares glanced uneasily around the dark trees, then closed his eyes for weariness.

Hours later, in the dead of night, he was startled awake by Puck's sudden barking. "Hush! Quiet, Puck!" he hissed, but it was too late.

"There! In the trees!" someone shouted, and running footfalls drew near.

Ares rolled over to Henry to whisper, "Keep down, keep hidden—Thom will be here soon—" then he sprang up to run out in full view of the searchers and their torches.

"There he is!" one shouted. Having been seen, Ares took off as fast as he could over unknown terrain in darkness.

It did not take them long to catch him. He was able to run for only a few minutes before stumbling headlong into a depression that he had not seen. Sharp rocks cut into his hands, but he caught himself from landing on his face. Before he could get to his feet again, hands were grasping his arms and shoulders, yanking him up. He had just time to twist the signet with his thumb to the inside of his hand, hoping that the dirt would disguise the gold of the band.

But in closing the shackles over his wrists, the soldiers never bothered to inspect his hands. They probably would have searched him had it not been obvious that he carried nothing, wore nothing but the ragged shirt, pants, and shoes. The senior officer of the search party held up the torch to peer in Ares' bearded, scarred face. "So field work's too hard for you, eh?" he sneered. "We'll see if you prefer the mines."

The others laughed, and Ares wondered at their gaiety. But in marching him down a nearby road to the foot of the mountain, he gleaned from their discussion that miners were becoming so scarce, a generous bounty was offered for the procurement of healthy new ones, especially adult males.

After an hour's walk, they encountered another, larger road. Two hours' tramping down it brought them within view of the mining camp that Henry had described. Seeing it, Ares understood why they lost so many slaves. The only shelter provided them consisted of long rows of thatched roofs on posts, without even walls to keep out the rain, cold, or snow. The slaves were individually secured to one long chain running the length of each shelter. By means of these master chains, the slaves were handled in groups—taken down to the mines in the morning and returned to the shelters in the evening. They were not ever taken off the master chain unless they died. At this time of night, they were bedded down in dirty straw. Guards with torches were posted over them, about one per fifty slaves.

Ares was handed over to the mine master, who doled out the bounty silver to his captors. But before the newcomer was shackled to the master chain, there was a welcoming ritual in store for him. The mine master looked Ares up and down, feeling his shoulders and thumping his chest. "A good, strong one you be," he leered with black, broken teeth. "Strong ones are good for months of digging. But strong ones are troublesome, because they think they can escape. And you have got me up from my rest in the middle of the night to welcome you. So welcome you I shall, and wear you down a bit so that you're ready to work."

Walking away, he gestured to a subordinate, who in turn ordered that Ares' shirt be torn off him and his manacled hands hoisted on a bar over his head until his feet dangled off the ground.

Then they got out a whip, and set to work lashing his back until he had almost lost consciousness. After that initiation, he was taken to one of the shelters and hooked up to the master chain between two other slaves. He fell to the ground on his face and closed his eyes.

Earlier that evening in Westford, Renée, eyes red and swollen, sat listlessly at her vanity. She had spent the last several hours weeping as she had never wept before, until she was exhausted. Eleanor, her maid, had been dismissed from the room immediately after dinner, as the Chataine had far too much pride to cry in front of a servant. So now she was truly alone, and she felt it.

She rose from the chair to walk the denuded chambers. Oh, there was still furniture that some people would consider luxurious, but compared to what had been there before, it was nothing. A handful of dresses, a few pieces of jewelry, a few treasured knickknacks—these were all that occupied the roomy shelves and drawers of her great wardrobe, and the loss of the rest was as a condemnation of herself: she was no longer valued here.

Soon, she would be married off to whoever would take her, and sent away from Westford to live in parts unknown, among people who did not know her, accommodate her, or love her. The impending reality of what she had always dreaded, the realization of her worst fears was now staring back at her in the distorted reflection of the mirror (an inferior one offered by Giles in exchange for the fabulous gilded mirror that now resided in the treasury).

Renée then decided, in calmness of mind, that this would not be. She had one avenue yet to decide her own fate. Opening her wardrobe, she pressed a panel to reveal a secret drawer. In this drawer lay a gilded, bejeweled dirk, slender enough for a woman's hand to wield. Lifting the weapon, caressing it, Renée laid its sharp blade gently at the skin of her wrist.

Then she looked around in sudden regret—there were still beautiful things in this room, among them the magnificent rug at her feet. The idea of spoiling these treasures with bloodstains revolted her. So, concealing the dirk in the folds of her dress, she left her chambers and began to proceed downstairs. She passed servants who were as casual around her as if she were one of them and soldiers who did not stand at attention, as they did when Nicole passed. This was the final straw—that her inferiors knew of her debasement.

Renée paused to consider the irony of how Nicole, the peasant girl, usurped the position that Renée herself should have had. No matter, Renée sighed. What did anything matter anymore? Stopping at the foot of the great, curving staircase, she debated where to go. Eventually, she decided that bare ground absorbed blood with the least mess, as it had absorbed her father's, and probably her brother's. So she turned to walk the side corridor out of the palace to the path leading to the orchard. Perhaps, in taking this public route, she secretly hoped someone along the way cared enough to stop her and question her. But no one did.

The night was just cool enough to be pleasant, with the scent of newly set fruit carried on gentle breezes. The globed candles along the pathway gave a rather festive air to Renée's death march to the far end of the orchard near the pear trees. It made for such a poignant setting that she began to imagine herself attended by a host of unseen courtiers who wept silently as she passed. She was so caught up in the pathos of her imaginings that she failed to notice the very real guard who noticed her, then ran off to inform the Counselor of her whereabouts, as he had been instructed to do.

Renée stopped at the end of the path along smaller plantings, and looked back to confirm that no one else was in sight. Drawing a fortifying breath, she lifted the dagger to her slender throat. For some reason, she also looked up to the stars to breathe, "God, forgive me, but—You understand."

What happened next so confounded her senses that she was never quite sure that it really happened, but—a man in foreign soldier's attire appeared in front of her out of thin air as if bursting from a bubble. She gasped, badly startled—was this a ghost? But he proved himself flesh and blood, for after the first moment of being likewise confounded, he rushed upon her. Her instinct for survival reared up, and she slashed blindly at him with the dirk. She hit him somewhere, possibly on the hand, for he cried out in surprise, or pain, before coming at her with renewed force.

Screaming, Renée slashed again. The dirk went wide, cutting nothing but air. He grabbed her wrist with one hand and her throat with the other, bringing his face close to hers as he squeezed her wrist so that she was forced to drop the knife. Looking up at him with her disarming, limpid blue eyes, Renée thrust her knee into his groin with a force born of righteous fury at being handled against her will.

He doubled up in pain, and the air between them seemed to shudder. Suddenly he was gone again. Renée stared at the empty space that a living man had occupied a moment before, then she wheeled to begin running up the path toward the palace in delayed terror.

She ran smack into Carmine, who had been coming down the path toward her. Holding her arms, he stared at her white, chalkless face. "Chataine, what is it? Are you hurt?"

"Carmine! Oh! I'm losing my mind!" she exclaimed, bursting into tears.

His face changed slightly, and in her genuine distress, she did not realize that he thought she was bluffing. "Whatever has happened, dear Chataine?" he asked kindly.

"Oh, Carmine! A man just appeared—there—out of nowhere, and tried to take me! I fought him off, and—he disappeared again! What shall I do?" she cried.

Despite the fact that Carmine knew about the portal in a theoretical sense, he never for a moment imagined that it might somehow be connected with what she just now described. Rather, given her recent debasement, he was convinced that she had created this scenario in a desperate ploy for pity. So, in order to destroy whatever credibility she might still have in Westford, he played along: "Why, dear Chataine, I think you should report this at once."

"Who would believe me?" she cried.

"The Surchataine Nicole," he said with supernatural wisdom that even he did not know he possessed. "She is your friend, and will listen to you. But more than that, she is the highest authority available to us at this time." He knew that Renée's vanity required the most prestigious audience. And—he paid the Surchataine's guards well to tell him what was said in Nicole's chambers.

Dubious, but taking him at his word, Renée left him to hasten up the path.

Waving genially to her fleeing back, Carmine resumed walking down the cobbled path at a leisurely, contented pace. How fine a night it was! He lifted his nose to smell the scented air, and thought how pleasant it was to be avenged on the woman who had caused him so much grief and pain. For after tonight, she would be a laughingstock wherever she went.

Something on the ground caught his eye, and he bent to pick up the ornate, jeweled dirk. As he studied it, a shade of confusion, even alarm, passed over his face. For the dirk, obviously Renée's, bore traces of blood.

# 15

**N**icole had opened the door herself to Renée's frantic pounding, and now listened with grave face as the Chataine spilled out, "Oh, Nicole—you will never believe me, but the most distressing thing has happened. I was walking out in the orchard, and a man, some sort of soldier, appeared out of nowhere! He just—appeared out of thin air! I would have thought it was a ghost, but he grabbed me! I—I fought him off, and then—he disappeared again! Oh, dear Nicole, you must think—"

But Nicole had flung open the door to her receiving room and was demanding of the guard, "Who is the most senior officer that Thom left in charge?"

He stammered, "That would be—the Second Rhode, Surchataine. The Commander took the Second Oswald with him—"

"Send him up at once! Hurry!" she barked. Startled, the sentry took off at a run. Nicole turned back to Renée, who was dumbfounded but gratified, and said, "It was very wise and brave of you to come tell me this, Chataine. You may have saved us from invasion by Ulm."

"What?" Renée gasped. On impulse, she admitted, "Carmine told me to come tell you specifically."

"He knows about the portal," Nicole nodded.

"The . . . what?" Renée said weakly.

"It is too complicated to explain now. But Carmine knows, and sent you to me to save our lives," Nicole insisted. Renée's face grew thoughtful, even wondering.

The sentry announced the Second Rhode at the door. Nicole urged him inside. "Rhode, a strange soldier, probably a Qarqarian, came out of the portal into the orchard and attacked the Chataine. When she fought back, he retreated back into the portal."

She could almost see the hair on his neck rise. Turning to Renée, he said, "If you will, Chataine, please show me exactly where this took place." She nodded, assuming an air of importance. On their way out, Rhode instructed an aide to summon Captain Crager, sound a general alarm, and dispatch a unit from the Blue Regiment to the orchard at once. He only briefly saluted Nicole before disappearing down the corridor with Renée.

She led him, with Crager and the Blue unit, down the orchard path and pointed out the specific location of the appearance. Before they advanced farther, Rhode formed a human chain by having the men link hands, then he himself, on the end, stepped forward into the very spot that she indicated. Nothing happened. He walked all over the area, and still nothing happened.

By now Renée felt compelled to protest that she had not imagined it, but Rhode assured her, "I know of what you speak, Chataine. I myself have been in the portal." She shut her mouth in wonderment.

Although the portal appeared to be closed on this end at the time, Rhode posted a round-the-clock watch in the area. The men were to defend the palace with deadly force from any trespassers, but under no circumstances were they to enter the portal themselves. And they were to take care to stay clear of any disturbance in the air.

When all this was reported back to Nicole that night, she ratified Rhode's decision, and thanked him. Then she summoned the Counselor Carmine, who had to leave his bath and then dress to respond. When he appeared, bowing, she said, "Carmine, I cannot thank you enough for sending Renée to me with a firsthand report of the portal's opening in the orchard."

"The portal . . ." he said, his mouth hanging open.

"Yes," she said, pacing. "Your quick thinking has probably saved us from Ulm. Poor Renée was so shaken by what she saw, and so disbelieving, I fear that without your encouragement, she would have kept the matter to herself—until we were overrun and beyond help."

"The portal," he said, finally comprehending.

"Carmine, I am so grateful that you have forgiven Renée, or at least let the animosity between you bow to the greater imperative of saving Westford. And . . . I have been thinking. About Renée. I think I have been overly harsh with her, dear Carmine. I think we should restore her things. Giles really took too much away from her to begin with. Let us restore her chambers as they were. Tonight," she said decisively.

He began, "Certainly, Surchataine, our dear Chataine should be rewarded for her courage. But . . . you yourself know how very much she had, and—"

"Yes, yes, I know." She waved dismissively. "But Ares had decreed that she would be Chataine of Lystra for the rest of her life, and I have erred in taking that away from her." At the look of alarm that crossed his face, she hastened to add, "Your divorce stands. I will not force you to remarry her. But do restore her chambers. And when Ares returns, if he disagrees, he may reverse me. For Thom is bringing Ares home, Carmine. I just know it."

Ares lay on his face in foul-smelling straw, trying to breathe around the pain of his lacerated back. There was slight shuffling and moaning around him from the other slaves whose pains would not allow them any rest before they were herded back into the mines at sunrise. This meant, Ares knew, that he was facing his end. If Thom attacked during the day, when Ares was in the mines, then he would be one of hundreds of slaves suffocated to death. And the likelihood that Thom would attack during the day was, as close as Ares could calculate it, one hundred percent. Thom did not know about the Qarqarians' practice of burning the mine supports upon attack.

Closing his eyes, letting his scar rest on the prickly, rank straw, Ares whispered, "Lord God, see Henry home safely to Westford. Give Nicole wisdom to rule. Safeguard Bonnie and Sophie. . . ."

In his weariness, he slipped into something akin to sleep, but not quite.

Henry had lain very still, clutching Puck, when Ares had run out from the grove to be captured by the soldiers. But once they had taken him on the road, Henry had shuffled off his grave to follow. Although he lost sight of them ahead in the darkness, he knew that they were taking him to the mines. And Puck, sniffing the air, trotted confidently after their unseen quarry, pausing every now and then for Henry to catch up.

They walked for hours, Henry stumbling in exhaustion, until he simply dropped by the road in a stupor. Some time later, Puck woke him with a wet nose and a whimper, and Henry startled up. As nothing around them appeared amiss, Henry realized that the dog knew time was short. "Good boy! Good Puck. We have to find him before sunrise." Struggling to his feet, he whispered, "Find Ares, Puck." The dog trotted on down the road, and Henry staggered after him.

It was not too much longer that they came into view of the camp, with its long sideless shelters and torches burning low here and there. Henry ordered Puck to stop, and they lay in a depression in the ground to look around. In the dead hour before sunrise, the guards made their rounds sleepily; those slaves that suffered did so in silence, and those who were to die before morning passed quietly.

Eyes glazed, Henry looked over the lines of hundreds of sleeping slaves. Then he shifted to feel for the keyrings at his waist. In the blackness of late night, one by one, he fingered the keys, visualizing their shapes by the feel. Which one? Which one did he need here? Not the skeleton key—that went to doors. Not the dungeon key. This one—the one on the slave trader's keyring. The memory flashed through Henry's mind of the stinking, grinning demon holding the key up to Henry's face to taunt him: *"This one would set you free, boy."*

He unhooked that key from the keyring and put it under Puck's nose. "Puck, find Ares. Take to Ares. Quiet! Take to Ares, Puck."

The dog sniffed the key and picked it up gingerly in his teeth. Then he set off, padding softly across the ground toward the shelters. He stopped, looking back uncertainly to his young master, but Henry hissed, "Take to Ares, Puck!" So the dog trotted on toward the long rows of shelters with the key in his teeth. Coming to the first body lying prone under the first shelter, Puck sniffed his feet. Sniffing, he went down the long row of feet, one by one.

Ares opened his eyes at something wet in his ear. Barely raising his face from the hay, he smelled Puck's strong breath. Although he thought he was dreaming, he lifted up, and the shooting pains in his back assured him he was quite awake. "Puck! What . . . ?" Ares reached out to stroke his head. Without a sound, Puck nosed the hay beside Ares' face. Placing his hand on the spot, Ares felt the iron key where Puck had dropped it. Ares gripped it in one hand and squeezed Puck with the other. "Good Puck! Now go to Henry. Find Henry," he whispered. Puck trotted off into the night, nub wagging.

Ares bowed his head over the key, almost afraid to try it. If it did not work. . . . He breathed out a prayer, reconciling himself to whatever the outcome, and shifted to insert the key in the manacle on his left wrist. He attempted to turn the key first one way, then the other. When the cuff opened and fell away, he felt momentarily dizzy. He unlocked the other cuff, then began to think.

He could do little by himself. But if all the other slaves were unchained, they could easily overpower the guards by sheer numbers. To do so successfully, however, they must act in concert. Somehow, Ares must coordinate them without being detected. For him to move from person to person unlocking chains would certainly draw notice. But. . . .

Ares nudged the man on his left, but he would not waken, and Ares could not reach his wrists. So he quietly turned to the man on his right and shook his shoulder until he woke. Feeling for his wrist cuffs, Ares unlocked them, then handed him the key. As he did so, he instructed in a whisper: "You are to unlock the man next to you. Tell him to lie still until the guards come for us at sunrise, then we will attack as one. Tell him the Surchatain of Lystra commands this. He is to unlock his neighbor and repeat these words exactly. Do you understand?"

Feeling his unchained wrists, the man moaned, "Am I dreaming?"

Patiently, Ares repeated the words to him, adding, "We will not succeed unless everyone does this. Make sure your neighbor understands."

Shaking, the man took the key, which Ares was greatly reluctant to give up. That slave turned to the man on his other side, and Ares saw him unlocked. Beyond that man, however, Ares could see nothing else. So he lay back down to wait and pray that the slaves were aware enough to follow instructions. One break in the link, if it came early, would doom them all.

Waiting for sunrise, Ares slipped back into a daze. The raw wounds on his back burned with every movement. He knew he was not strong enough to take on all the guards here, or even half of them, should the other slaves fail to cooperate—if they ran rather than attacked, or if they refused to wait until the signal. . . . While his mind roamed restlessly over every contingency, Ares waited.

He was jolted awake by the sudden clanging of metal. When he raised up, early sunlight streamed in his face as a fat, surly guard ten feet away was taking up the master chain. "To the mines, lazy scum! Up, and let's see which of you dies today!" He yanked the chain to bring the slaves to their feet. Those to the left of Ares, who had not benefited from the key, struggled to a stand. But when the guard saw Ares unchained, he glowered as if someone had made a mistake. Reaching for the keyring at his side, he began, "Now what idiot—"

"Now!" Ares shouted. He lunged toward the guard, battering him with a shoulder to the stomach. While the guard lay rolling on the ground, Ares seized his short sword. Relieving him of further pain in this life, he then looked around to see how many slaves responded.

There was no telling, with the chaos all around him. The slaves that were free had scattered; those still chained were screaming to be free, and Ares could not determine at once how many there were of each. A trumpet alarm sounded, which was sure to draw soldiers from Hornbound, so he had to act fast. First, he threw the dead guard's keys to the closest slave who was still chained. Then he went guard hunting.

Assuming (correctly) that the slaves were unarmed, the guards were having little trouble hacking down those they caught. So at first Ares was virtually alone fighting them. Fortunately, they were relatively isolated, so he was able to come upon them unawares and kill them before they knew it. With each guard killed, Ares confiscated his weapon and tossed it toward the nearest able-bodied slave, shouting, "Fight! You have no chance unless you fight!"

Some got the message and took up weapons, scattering to attack anyone in view. Some who were too weak or scared to fight assisted in unlocking those who had not yet been freed. But a group of other slaves, armed, began gathering around Ares to support him.

This happened not a moment too soon, as the remainder of the guards collected, at least forty in all, to face down the uprising with long swords. They rushed upon Ares' band almost before they had a chance to come together, and a score of slaves were killed in the space of thirty seconds. Hampered in fighting with a short sword against the long swords, Ares grabbed up a dropped whip in his left hand. This he cracked in his opponent's face, or used it to whip the weapon out of his hand, until he could get close enough to reach his target with the short blade. And the first guard who died with a long sword in his hand lost it to Ares.

As the slaves were rallying behind Ares, fighting with what little strength or skill they possessed, a sudden deluge of rocks began pelting the guards. The slaves quickly backed away while the guards were beaten down by rocks being thrown at them from every direction. Ares looked behind him at a large semi-circle of slaves. They had set up a rather efficient line of conveying rocks hand-to-hand from a debris pile to the front row of strong throwers who delivered a relentless and effective barrage against the guards. In moments they were all down. A few minutes more, and they were entombed in a pile similar to the other rock piles scattered around the site.

With all immediate enemies subdued, the slaves looked around in a daze. This was the first opportunity Ares had to survey the mining camp as a whole. It was set up like a little village, virtually self-sufficient. The slave shelters had been built closest to the mouth of the mines. A nearby stream that issued from underneath the mountain powered the water wheel (and thereby the pumps). The refinery and smelter sat close by, accessible to the mining carts via wooden tracks. Behind the barracks, there was a large garden, as well as pig pens and chicken coops. While hungry slaves began gravitating toward the live meat, Ares looked toward the roads—there were two of them, as Henry had said. The one that ran through the midst of the camp was rough and narrow. A wide, paved road, farther off, ran around the perimeter of the camp. Both ascended the mountain in switchbacks toward the city above.

Pointing toward the nearest road, Ares whistled to get the slaves' attention and shouted, "We must block both roads! Bring carts and timber—anything you can find. This road and the main road to the city must be blocked before the army comes down from Hornbound!"

Understanding the fresh danger, the slaves began gathering materials to blockade both roads—until someone came out of the guards' barracks with a bundle clutched to his chest, and someone else cried, "Food! There is food in the barracks!" A mad dash ensued toward the barracks, and the blockade-building was abandoned.

Ares was one of the first to reach the barracks door. With the whip, he snapped the bundle out of the arms of the fleeing slave, who fell down. Then Ares turned in fury on the crowd of hungry slaves: "I will kill the next man who tries to eat while the roads remain open! To the roads! When the barricades are built, I will parcel out the food!"

"Who are you?" someone shouted.

"I am Ares, the Surchatain of Lystra!" Ares roared. "And I carry the signet of Qarqar, which I took off Ulm's dead body!" He raised his fist, adorned with the ring. "Now BUILD!"

They were convinced. To a man (of those who remained) they piled overturned mining carts, beams from the shelter, rocks and even the bodies of the guards across the roads, forming six-foot-high roadblocks that extended as much as twenty feet in either direction, until they met a natural obstruction in the terrain. The roadblock on the mining road was especially satisfactory, as they had placed it just past a curve in the road so that it was not apparent to someone descending until he was almost upon it. Also, there were boulders, crevices, and piles of waste timber that provided ample cover on each side.

When Ares was satisfied with the barricades, he gave permission for some of the older slaves to enter the barracks and get bread to parcel out to the slaves, a handful at a time. But while they were doing this, Ares looked up to see mounted troops, dressed in armor and red tabards, pouring down the mining road toward the camp like a river of fire.

# 16

**B**ecause Ares was staring intently at the mountain road, other slaves turned to look. And then even the hungriest among them forgot about food. "What shall we do, Surchatain?" muttered a young man at Ares' side. Early in the fighting, he had attached himself to Ares, and had not left his side since.

Ares turned to one of the designated food-bearers. "Are there any bows and quivers in the barracks?"

"A few, sir," the man replied, trembling.

"Bring them out," Ares instructed. "Get someone to help you bring them all to me. Make haste." As the man scurried away, Ares turned to shout, "Who can handle a bow? Come to me quickly if you can shoot!" A number volunteered.

When the weapons were brought out, Ares armed his volunteers and placed them, first, in the guard towers overlooking the camp, then in hiding alongside the road near the barricades. He ordered the rest of the slaves to gather all the rocks and weapons they could find and hide themselves along the road as well. To them all, he instructed that they hold their fire until the soldiers came upon the barricade. "Wait for my signal. Fire on my signal."

By the time Ares had everyone equipped and placed (counting them in the process), the soldiers had rounded the corner of the last switchback down the mountain. Armed with a bow and full quiver,

Ares stationed himself (with his young protégé) in the guard tower closest to the road. When he slung the quiver over his shoulder to climb the ladder up to the platform, searing pains reminded him of the lashes on his back. With that incentive, he gained the platform of the tower, nocked his bow and smiled grimly as the young man followed him step by step. "What is your name?"

"Timour, sir," he replied in slight awe.

"Timour, play the man today if you wish to see home. There are only a hundred and thirty-five of us poorly armed, poorly fed slaves to meet the army of Hornbound, however many thousands that may be," Ares warned him.

"My home is Hornbound," Timour replied to Ares' astonishment. "They took me out of my bed on a trumped-up charge to work the mines because I would not join the army. I do not think there are as many soldiers as you fear. They have lost many thousands fighting Lystra."

Ares studied him as he went on: "The mines do not yield the gold they used to, either, so they need more slaves to dig deeper and deeper, but the water has risen faster than we can pump it out. The mines are played out and the army is played out, so do not assume you cannot prevail with only a hundred thirty-five vengeful slaves."

"Well said," Ares admitted. Then he raised his bow and sighted down the arrow as the Qarqarians rounded the bend at a gallop. The barricade came as a full surprise, the front ranks crashing into it when the ranks behind were unable to stop in time.

Loosing the first arrow, Ares gave a shrill whistle, and a hundred other projectiles filled the air—arrows, knives, stones, mining tools—the soldiers who fell from their horses were trampled or crushed against the barricades; the more the horses panicked, the less their riders were able to find their way around the ends of the roadblock. Those few who did were dropped by an arrow, usually from Ares' bow. Thus, in the space of a half hour, all of the soldiers in that first wave fell dead or gravely wounded.

When the slaves comprehended their victory, they raised a hoarse cheer, clustering around Ares as he descended the guard tower. Indicative of how little Hornbound thought of the uprising, they had sent only a few hundred soldiers to deal with it. Knowing that a few from the rear guard had escaped back up the mountain—meaning that a second wave was imminent—Ares quieted the slaves. "All right," he said. "Those who volunteer for guard duty may eat first." So, very quickly, guards were set in place in the towers. Others were assigned to scavenge arms or rescue horses still milling behind the roadblock. A few others were given the task of parceling out the stored grain, beer, sausages and vegetables to the surviving slaves. But the bags of refined gold they found were brought to Ares.

These he set in the middle of the compound. "If no one touches it, I will divide it up among you after I have taken Hornbound. If it is pilfered, the thief dies, and none of you gets any of it." Thereafter, all of the slaves tiptoed around the bags in respect.

When, midafternoon, Ares finally sat to eat, he was joined by a stocky, bright-eyed visitor who bounded up to him with a happy bark. Ares put down his dinner to seize Puck, who squirmed in his arms. Then he looked over his shoulder as Henry approached. Sitting on the ground beside Ares, he sighed, "Do you have enough to share?"

Soon, Henry had a lap full of food and Puck had his very own sausage. "Where have you been?" Ares asked him. "You missed no little excitement."

"Hiding. And sleeping," Henry said faintly. "When Puck came back without the key, I had no way of knowing . . ." he trailed off, his eyes watering fiercely.

Ares gestured at the camp of former slaves, some eating or bathing. Many were finding clothes and arms for themselves off the bodies of the dead, but they took care to not appropriate anything resembling a Qarqarian uniform, which might prove inconvenient in another confrontation with the soldiers. "You freed all these, Henry," Ares told him. "You and Puck."

As Henry gazed over the camp, one of the slaves in a nearby watchtower called out. Ares ran over to scale the ladder and look up the mountain, using an eyeglass left by the previous guard. He saw the Qarqarian army coming down the main road from the city. Even at this distance, Ares could see that the horsemen were staying to the road, but foot soldiers were scaling down the mountain apart from the road, as he and Henry had done. This time, without question, there were thousands.

The only good sign he saw was that they appeared to be in no hurry. The main road, being a more circuitous route from the city to the camp, was miles longer than the camp road, and the army seemed to be approaching at a walk. Also, the men descending on foot would require the better part of a day from that point to reach the camp. So the slaves had time to prepare a defense . . . if Ares could plan one.

Leaning on the tower rail, Ares opened the west window of his mind for illumination. And what he saw was the morning sun pouring in through the window of the sun in the fortress at Hornbound, setting it aflame. That vision led him to remember how effective the trails of fire had been at Lord Welling's estate. Perhaps a variation on that strategy was in order. Nodding shortly to himself, he descended from the tower, gesturing the other guard-volunteer to follow him. On the ground, he whistled sharply to call all of the slaves to a tight circle around him.

Once they were gathered and attentive, he told them: "The standing army is coming down the main road now. Many are mounted, but many are descending on foot to bypass our barricade. So if you value your lives, do this quickly: tear down all the buildings and towers except for these two here—pile all the wood and straw you can find in a circle around the camp—I will mark out the circle. Is there wood in the smelter? Good—take it all—put everything that will burn on the wall, but do not set it on fire until I give the word. Some time soon, my army will be arriving from Westford. If we can hold off these soldiers until my Commander arrives, he will make short work of them. Now quickly—dismantle everything."

Armed with mining tools, the slaves scattered to comply, and Ares began drawing a line in the dirt around the two central guard towers where he wanted the wall of fire to be built. The long rows of slave shelters were the first to come down, the wooden posts laid out end to end to form the skeleton of the wall, with the straw atop it. The barracks flew apart like magic, and pallets, blankets, clothes, firewood and fagoting were added to the wall. (Ares found another shirt for himself, and entrusted a few emergency blankets to Henry's keeping. As for the remaining food, Ares left that to him to guard, as well.) Dead bodies, both of soldiers and slaves, were tossed upon the wall. Ares made them stop at this point and hammer vertical supports into the ground to hold the components together, building outward from the line in the dirt.

With raw enthusiasm, the slaves dismantled the smelter and refinery. Everything flammable went on the wall, while metal tools were placed in a separate pile as reserve weapons. The equipment in the mines—the wooden tracks, buckets, windlasses and pumps—were broken up and placed on the walls, which quickly grew to an impressive size. With the wealth of materials at hand, particularly the amount of wood in the smelter, Ares was able to make the walls much thicker than he originally planned—a good twelve feet thick. The camp area to be enclosed by this firewall was roughly two hundred feet in diameter.

In the midst of constructing the wall, Ares studied the stream that flowed out of the mountain, powering the water wheel. Though neither strong nor deep, it was definitely a liability in keeping their firewall going—all the Qarqarians had to do was douse an opening in the wall with water from this stream. While Ares was contemplating this problem, Timour had a suggestion: "If you like, sir, we can dam up the stream in the mountain. All we have to do is burn the shafts that extend from here [indicating a point on the mountain]—the earth will collapse on the stream bed within the mountain."

Ares looked at him. "Let us do that," he agreed. First, he had several large rain barrels moved to stand between the guard towers and filled with water from the stream. Then, while the firewall went up, the shafts were burned down. The stream slowed to a trickle before drying up completely. "This will also be our escape route," Ares said, indicating the dry stream bed, which was about five feet deep. "Lay these boards across, and cover them with earth—wet it down well, and stretch these iron tracks across, just so. Now continue the wall over it. If all goes well, we will have a tunnel under the wall to get out, should we need it."

The slaves worked with amazing energy and efficiency in tearing down every standing structure in the mining camp. The pens came down, but no one waited for the firewall to be lit to butcher and roast every last animal. In so doing, the slaves also found a large quantity of oil in the camp kitchen, which they brought out and poured over the wall. They cannibalized the mining road barricade, as it had already served its purpose, and added those materials to their firewall. In constructing it, they left an opening for bringing in food and supplies. This gap was to be closed last.

By the time they had made the wall as deep and wide as the materials allowed, the sun was setting. Ares climbed one guard tower to check the army's progress through the eyepiece, and discovered that, strange as it seemed, they appeared to be camping for the night halfway down the mountain. There was a ring of campfires, and not a single light descending the switchback. Ares lowered the eyepiece, brow wrinkling in thought. Because he had never fought slaves before, he had to do some mental stretching to understand the army's rationale.

After considerable thought on the matter, he realized that the army did not want to fight the slaves—they wanted to make them run. Having annihilated the first wave of soldiers, the slaves had the momentum of battle on their side. The army wanted to dispel that, to make them remember that they were just slaves facing a disciplined, armed force. If the soldiers could break the slaves' resolve to fight as a unit, they could pick them off individually, thus regaining control of the mines—and the gates of Hornbound—without further loss.

Ares hurried down from the tower to call the slaves together. He told them, "The battle is half won, for they loiter on the mountain, thinking to make us run. Unless they break camp to march on us at night—which I think unlikely—it will be morning before they come. And the longer they wait, the sooner they will meet up with my Commander and his army. All we need do is hold them beyond the firewall. . . ."

He trailed off, perceiving something amiss in the air. The wind kicked up; large drops of water came out of nowhere to randomly sprinkle the men. Looking up, he saw the clouds come together to blanket the night sky. From them issued an escalating number of drops that merged into a full summer shower. Dumbstruck, the slaves looked at each other, then at the firewall that they had spent the day constructing. At present, it was getting thoroughly soaked. What kind of protection would it be if they couldn't get it to burn?

As thunder rolled over the mountain, Ares saw the hope drain from their faces like the oil running down the wall. "This will not hamper us," he argued, looking from face to face. "Unless it rains all night, it will not prevent the wall burning. . . ."

The slaves began to slip away, looking for shelter. Henry and Puck were huddled together under one of the remaining towers, jealously guarding the blankets and food. Most important, Ares had left Henry in charge of the tinderbox, with which they would light the firewall.

After seeing that Henry was in control of his station, Ares climbed the tower to look up the mountain, but the low rain clouds obscured the army camp. While evening fell, Ares kept watch through the rain, and he and Timour took turns keeping watch through the night.

Early the following morning, Ares opened his eyes to see hazy light seeping through the cracks in the guard tower railing. He raised up from the rough-hewn planks of the platform, looking around for Timour, who was supposed to wake him for the fourth watch. The young man, having succumbed to exhaustion and the night, was slumped against the railing in a dead slumber. Mildly alarmed, Ares got to his feet to peer up the mountain. But as it was blanketed in morning mists, he saw nothing. Then he looked to the ground at the foot of the tower, and saw . . . nothing.

Stomach coiling, Ares climbed down from the tower, and Timour woke up. Hopping down from the ladder, Ares looked around at the deserted grounds. Puck, under the tower, raised up from beside Henry, who was still in possession of his modest store. Two other slaves were asleep near them. Ares darted over to the ladder of the other guard tower to climb it for a look—one slave was standing watch, and two were sleeping on the platform. Ares woke them, and called the three of them down. Then, with Timour behind him, he ducked out through the dry stream bed to look around.

The denuded camp was empty. The gold was gone, as was the rest of the food, blankets, clothing, tools—anything of value that had not been irretrievably built into the firewall. Ares hiked all around the camp to satisfy himself as to its complete barrenness before returning to the circle inside the firewall. Besides himself, Timour, Henry, and Puck, there remained exactly five slaves to fight the army of Qarqar. The good news was, it had stopped raining sometime during the night.

The small group silently looked to Ares. He stood before them and said, "We are all that remain. The others have evidently decided that they stand the best chance for survival to run and hide. I disagree—unless they have provisions to last them many days of traveling on foot, they will be easily overtaken on horseback, if not by the army, then by the slavers. And a slave carrying gold, without weapons or escort to defend it, is a sitting pigeon to the first man who finds him.

"I am certain that my Commander is coming soon. If he does not come in time to save us, however, I would still prefer to die fighting rather than running. Each of you now decide how you would rather die, for once the army moves, you have lost your luxury of choice," he finished.

After a brief silence, Timour pointed out, "If we were going to leave, Surchatain, we would have done so during the night."

Ares glanced away at the reminder of the obvious. "Ah, thank you, Timour," he said dryly. Sitting, and gesturing the others to sit, he said, "Henry, do you have enough breakfast to share?"

As it turned out, Henry had been just as busy as anyone yesterday, having gathered far more food than the small portion Ares had left with him. Henry opened his storehouse of bread, cheese, beer, and salted pork for the others. After a pause, Ares bowed his head to thank God for His mercies on this day, as on every other. Then they ate.

Ares sent a pair of guards up to each tower to report on the first movement of the army. While the morning sun rose warm in a cloudless sky, Ares gathered wood and kindling off the firewall to create a smaller, separate campfire, which required at least a half hour of patient striking with the flint in the tinderbox to light. When it came time to ignite the firewall, they must have a ready source.

Midmorning, Timour let out a yell: the army was on the move.

res scaled the tower ladder to look for himself. With the morning mists burned off, he could see that the army had progressed at least a mile from their camp of last night. Further, he could see that they had left most of their baggage behind in the camp, so as to move faster. Their Commander must have anticipated the fact that the majority of the slaves would flee, leaving the army with the easy task of gleaning stragglers here and there. "Well done, Timour," Ares said, patting his shoulder. "Keep watch. It will be several hours yet." Then he climbed down the ladder to draw Henry aside.

In a low voice, he told him, "Henry, I have been thinking. You and Puck have the best chance of escape, if you go—"

"And be caught by the slavers again?" Henry asked. "No, Ares. Never again. Never. Commander Thom will find my body next to yours, and know that I died fighting. Not as a slave."

Ares looked at him for a long time. "I have come to feel that . . . you really are my son. In spirit, you are my own."

"Is that why you came looking for me?" Henry asked.

"Yes, Henry. I came after my own," Ares said.

"Then you have found him, and I will not leave again."

For the next several hours, the small band kept watch on the army's progress. Evaluating their rate of travel, Ares calculated that the firewall should be lit when they passed the tree line about five miles from the barricade. He had little doubt at this point that it would burn nicely. He also kept a lookout for any foot soldiers who might appear off the main road, but he judged that, especially with last night's rain, they would probably not arrive before the main army. And any one or two who managed to breach the wall to see what was within would not survive to report their findings.

As the army neared the camp, evidently catching sight of the stripped grounds, the barricade, and the firewall, they picked up their pace. Ares leaned over the railing of the tower, watching as the horsemen of the vanguard reached the treeline. He ordered the other slaves down from the guard towers, so that they would not be an easy target for archers. The main body of the army reached the treeline, while the vanguard bore down on the barricade. Ares descended from the tower and nodded, "Now."

All the slaves, including Henry, took brands from the campfire and began applying them to the most flammable points along the firewall, beginning with the section that faced the main road. There was some sputtering and crackling, but the wood quickly ignited. As it turned out, the oil had not been washed away at all—merely dispersed more thoroughly throughout the wall, and left there when the water had evaporated away.

Shortly, the firewall was merrily crackling all the way around. Tongues of fire wrapped themselves around the fuel, growing larger and brighter. Ares watched the fire enclose a soldier's body until it became a human candle, and felt sudden pity for the wife or mother waiting at home.

While the army approached, Ares canvassed every section of the firewall, looking for holes, but there were none. It was rather disconcerting, being entirely surrounded by great, leaping flames that obscured the landscape round about. The last thing the slaves saw before the fire grew to obscure their view was the vanguard bearing down on them from around the ends of the barricade. Soon, even those glimpses were obscured by fire; the shouts, the trumpet calls, the tramping of the horses were all gradually drowned out by the increasing roar of the flames. Unnerved, Henry put his hands over his ears, being unprepared for how loud such a great bonfire was up close. Brave Puck whimpered and cowered at Henry's feet. Instinctively, the eight of them and Puck gathered under one tower in the center of the ring.

A shower of arrows came over the wall of fire, shot blindly by archers on the outside hoping to hit someone inside. The slaves lay flat on the ground and no one was hit. Soon, the archers hit upon the idea of sending flaming arrows into the guard towers, which were soon burning as fiercely as the wall. But they burned harmlessly to the ground—except that, in collapsing, they took out one water barrel. This turned out to be rather advantageous, in that the gush of water put out some of the flames when the charred platforms fell. The defenders tossed handfuls of dirt on them to snuff the rest. Rendered relatively flame-retardant by the water, the dirt, and the charred outer layer, the pieces were then pulled together as a shelter against further fire.

By this time, however, Puck was almost crazed with fear, wriggling and snapping to try to get out of Henry's arms and run—somewhere, anywhere, even into the fire. Ares dipped a blanket in another water barrel and tossed it over both boy and dog. Thereafter, they huddled quietly in the midst of the inferno.

The archers on the outside stopped shooting when they discovered that they were hitting their own comrades on the other side of the ring. By now the wall was fully engaged, and the heat and smoke were fierce. The flames shot upwards of thirty feet above the wall. Majestic columns of grey smoke rose, completely blocking out the sky. All of the slaves were panting and coughing, eyes pouring tears. There was only one other blanket. Ares wordlessly offered it to the others, but no one would accept it for himself when everyone else went unshielded. Timour, however, took the blanket and ripped it into pieces, which he dipped into the water and passed around for each man to wrap around his face. With this protection, they lay flat on the ground under charred pieces of wood . . . and waited. There was nothing else to do.

Except watch the escape tunnel in the dry stream bed. As Ares had predicted, a few soldiers found it and attempted to enter. It was almost unnecessary for Ares to guard it with his bow—the few men who tried to enter were on fire by the time they had passed the wall, so Ares' arrow (shot while he was flat on his stomach) merely hastened their end. It was rather sobering to realize that their theoretical escape route was, in fact, a death trap, but it hardly mattered now. The only escape for anyone within the ring would be to the waiting arms of whoever stood outside the wall when it finally burned down.

So the slaves lay waiting in composure, and some in prayer. One or two looked at the swords in their hands, contemplating their use, but Timour urged them to hold off on that last option till they knew there was no other escape. They knew that the soldiers beyond the firewall were not just waiting for the fire to burn down—the continuous, intense vibrations of the ground under them told him there was fierce activity going on all around them, and it seemed to go on for a long time. Ares lay still for so long, listening to the lulling vibrations, feeling himself grow woozy, that he almost drifted into blackness.

Something made him snap awake—whether it was the burning in his throat, or the realization that he must not succumb to sleep, he did not know—but all at once he was wide awake and looking around the smoky enclosure. He stumbled to the rain barrel to take a long drink and wet his face cloth, then looked over to see that Henry's blanket was ominously still. Finding a cuplike shard, he dipped it in the water and ran over to lift a corner of the blanket, now dry. "Henry. Henry!" The boy raised up groggily. "Here—drink. Give some to Puck. Stay awake—don't fall asleep."

When both were somewhat alert, Ares went around check-ing on the other slaves, urging them to drink. They came to slowly, and Ares poured the remainder of the water over them all.

By this time, some hours had passed—four? Five? Six?—since the lighting of the wall, and the flames were beginning to lose height and intensity, though smoke still obscured the sky. The group sat together watching the fire burn lower and lower, so that a horse was glimpsed there, a helmet here, a flash of shield beyond. Ares put his head to the ground again, and the vibrations he felt now were fewer, quieter. He sat up on his heels. There was a finality in the activity beyond the fire, but no absence of soldiers—any break in the firewall revealed another glimpse of spear or armor. They were gathering all around the enclosure. Then Ares spotted a standard, and his heart stood still.

Finally, great sections of the wall collapsed; the flames died down to heights of only four or five feet, and soldiers on the outside began shoveling dirt on the weakest sections. Henry sat staring, tears pouring down his blackened face. Puck, exhausted and overcome, lay in his lap panting. Timour gripped his bow with shaky hands, and Ares turned to smile at him. As Timour stared, confounded, at his self-satisfied expression, Ares nodded toward the encompassing army and asked, "What do you see, Timour?"

The young man blinked, and the other slaves looked around, struggling to see and understand. "They have changed colors," one blurted. That much was true: instead of red and gold tabards, they wore blue.

"They have changed standards," Timour said, squinting in disbelief. That also was true: instead of the sunface, the standards bore a lion and a cross.

"They have changed armies!" another slave exclaimed, as a pathway was opened up in the firewall for the Commander to step over the circle.

He approached Ares and saluted. "Greetings, Surchatain. I see that you have retrieved the Chatain Henry. Are you well?" Thom asked. He was so pleased to get to say all this that he delivered it in a perfectly flat voice, straight-faced.

"Never better, Commander," Ares sighed. "Come, let's see what you have done."

What Thom had done was arrive with his army right on time, as the Qarqarians had set themselves to relaxing until the firewall burned down. Having encountered several of the slaves who had run away last night, Thom knew exactly what was going on. The Qarqarian army, however, was completely surprised by the invaders who pinned them between the fire and the mountain. They were hewn down like summer hay.

While the remainder of the firewall burned itself out, Ares and his little band made a brief tour of the battleground with Thom, Oswald, Alphonso, and the other officers, including Ares' page Ben. Lystran soldiers were stripping the dead and piling bodies on one section of the firewall, now converted to a pyre. The mountain stream that the slaves had dammed burst up from the rocks on the other side of the camp, thus affording water to bathe and prepare the evening meal. Freed from the ring of fire, Puck revived, and soon found himself the hero of the camp, meeting friendly hands that petted him and fed him tidbits wherever he turned.

Bathed, with his wounds dressed, Ares sat with a dinner of beer, bread and quail, caught on the army's four-day march from Westford. He told a crowded ring of listeners about his activities since the portal delivered him and Nicole to Hornbound instead of Westford—of freeing the Lady Rejane and witnessing Ulm's death (showing them the signet he still wore) and of donning the executioner's robe to locate Henry at Lord Morand's house.

Then Henry related what he had done after Ares had been taken to the mines. But when he was asked what befell him after he had been captured by the slaver Lazear, he would not talk about it at all except to say, "I never thought I would ever see Westford again. Then Ares came as the Executioner, and I knew that I should go with him and not be afraid, even though I did not know it was him. I wasn't afraid of dying until we got farther and farther away from the Morands' house. They were actually kind to me, though I did not much appreciate it at the time. I could have been much worse off. Lord Morand saved my life by buying me."

"I'll remember that when we get into Hornbound," Ares said.

Oswald leaned forward to ask, "Who is in charge now that Ulm is dead?"

"I don't know," Ares said pensively, glancing at Henry as he devoured a bird. "What do you think, Henry? Who is likely to be in control now?"

"No one," Henry scoffed. "I would guess that Counselor Viaud, Steward Nairne, and Commander Nexo are battling among themselves—if the Commander did not die here."

Alphonso snorted, "The coward couldn't be bothered to quell a slave uprising. We checked the insignia of all the dead, and he's not among them." After a pause, he added, "You proved your mettle, Chatain. I think you will make a fine officer some day. What say you, Commander?"

Thom, who had urged placing a bounty on Henry's head, glanced up to admit, "He shows certain promise. Something else troubles me, however. If Commander Nexo is not here, then neither is the bulk of his army. We faced no more than fifteen hundred today. According to my informants, on any given day,

Qarqar's standing army numbers five times that."

Without pointing out Timour in particular, Ares observed, "Some of the slaves seemed to think that the army had suffered great losses fighting us."

"I certainly hope so," Thom grunted. "Even so, their own garrisoned troops should number many more. Either they are awaiting us behind the city walls of Hornbound, or . . . they are elsewhere." That is, they were somewhere that Thom's troops were not.

Ares considered this, then said, "We will find out tomorrow when we march on Hornbound." Then he gave Thom and Oswald a detailed description of the fortress, including the drawbridge, the moat, and the cliffs. They debated the best method of approach before unanimously agreeing on a full frontal assault.

Then they turned their attention to the best means of spanning the moat and getting the drawbridge down. After considerable discussion, they reluctantly agreed to shoot grappling hooks over the walls, allowing men to swing across the moat, scale the walls, and gain access to the drawbridge mechanism. Ares agreed to this maneuver only as a last resort because it wasted so many men, and the older he got, the more it hurt to lose men. With those essentials decided, they went to their bedrolls.

Before sunrise the next morning, the Lystrans were breaking camp in preparation of assaulting the fortress of Hornbound. The former slaves, especially Timour, were eager to participate, so all were dressed out in some form of armor. And since Henry wanted to go as well, he could hardly be left behind. But when he mounted up to join Thom and Ares at the front of the ranks, Puck dashed after his horse. This quickly became an unacceptable hazard, for if Puck didn't get himself trampled, he still darted among the horses' hooves, snapping at their fetlocks as if trying to herd them. So the dog was placed in a saddlebag behind Henry, and rode there happily, ears pricked and tongue lolling.

As the Lystran army had dismantled the barricade on the main road the previous day, they started up that road toward Hornbound. This broad, paved road snaked up the mountain in leisurely switchbacks adorned with statues and ornamental plantings along the way. Cut deep into the side of the mountain to maintain a level surface, it was clearly constructed to accommodate fine carriages. Finding the way easy and clear, Ares signaled his troops to a lope. He was most anxious to reach the city.

After only a few hours, they came to the gates of the city wall, which were closed. Ares had never seen these gates, as he, Henry and Puck had scooted over the city wall on the other side of the mountain. Scanning for archers along the wall, Ares shouted, "I am Ares, Surchatain of Lystra, and I demand that you open the gates to me!" There was no reply, nor could anyone be seen.

But like any well-trained army, the Lystrans had come prepared for the possibility of a cool reception. Ares gestured, and the troops parted to make way for the horsemen towing the battering ram. It was a simple device—a large straight tree, stripped of branches and fitted with an iron tip, mounted on wheels and powered by dozens of men. Numerous hands brought the ram within striking distance of the gates, and there was still no reply to Ares' challenge. The ram was brought crashing into the weakest point of the gates only twice before they splintered. Heavily armored Lystrans swarmed over the ram through the gates, where they met no resistance.

When the debris was cleared for horses, Ares rode through to see his men standing around with ready weapons and no one to strike. The city gates had been barred *from the inside* and left deserted. From this point on, Ares made sure that Henry was beside him, being the keeper of both information on Hornbound and the keys that would unlock most of the doors within.

The Lystrans proceeded at a gallop up the remaining length of switchback before the road straightened through the Surchatain's hunting woods. Passing through these woods where the portal had dumped him twice provoked indescribable feelings in Ares— exhilaration upon arriving at last with Thom and the army at his back, mixed with anxiety for Nicole and his daughters at home in Westford.

As they broke out of the woods to approach the drawbridge, Thom shouted, "Ho! A royal welcome."

Ares raised his hand for the company to stop. Silently, they eyed the unmanned watchtowers on the gateposts, the empty parapets, and the drawbridge standing open over the moat.

fter assessing the vacant greeting, Ares gestured forward, calling to his troops, "Arms at the ready!" The vanguard proceeded over the drawbridge with bows nocked and swords drawn.

They filed into the fortress courtyard, where still not a soul could be seen. Ares took in the empty dog pen, the barren grounds, the familiar southeastern tower. Then he studied the gilded, arched doors that stood ajar at the top of the steps. Growing agitated, he shouted, "I am Ares, Surchatain of Lystra! Show yourselves!"

At that point, a red-robed figure appeared in the great doorway, hands folded serenely in front. Henry immediately leaned over to tell Ares and Thom, "That is Counselor Viaud."

Ares dismounted and took the steps two at a time to reach him. Removing his helmet, Ares asked with a trace of sarcasm, "Do I stand before the new ruler and sole occupant of Hornbound, Counselor Viaud?" Thom also dismounted, drawing within hearing distance.

The Counselor inclined his head in a show of deference. "True, I am one of the remaining few, O mighty Ares. Slay me if you will, but before you do, you might wish to compel me to tell you where the army of Qarqar is at this time."

"Pray tell, good Counselor," Ares said.

"They are sacking Westford," Counselor Viaud replied.

"Impossible," Thom scoffed. "We would have spotted them anywhere within a hundred miles of Westford on the way here."

Viaud nodded sagely at Thom. "True, Commander, if the army had gone by the road which you came."

"There is no other by which an army can pass between here and Westford," Thom said stubbornly, though Ares discerned a jittery edge in his voice.

The Counselor replied, "No? Your Surchatain knows of what I speak, for he came here by means of it."

Ares went cold. "I would think you mean the portal, but you cannot. You cannot discern where it is in the forest, for it appears out of thin air."

"That is only a port, a by-way, and not the main gate. Shall I show you?" The Counselor extended his arm toward the interior of the palace.

Ares turned to give orders: Thom, Oswald, and Henry were to accompany him. Alphonso was to post guards throughout the first floor of the fortress and in the courtyard, and keep a chain of communication open between them and Ares' party. Then he turned to nod at the Counselor: "Proceed, if you please." Counselor Viaud led the four of them through the main floor of the fortress toward a large interior courtyard—something Ares had not seen before. He noted that most of the luxurious appointments had been stripped, and everyone else certainly had fled.

Exiting into the open air of the courtyard, they spotted a freestanding stone entryway that mirrored exactly the one carved on the hillside on the Road of Vanishing—only this one was complete. Also, this edifice defied normal laws of construction— shaped like a horseshoe, with the weight of the stone on top, it could not remain standing as it was . . . unless it was supported by unseen forces. "Here is the main mouth of the portal, by which all other openings are accessed. After you came by way of the portal to murder Surchatain Ulm, Commander Nexo took his troops by means of the portal to level your city," Viaud said pleasantly.

Ares studied the entryway silently, then looked at Oswald, who nodded, "It's thick with green, Surchatain. It looks to be open."

Viaud then suggested, "You may, of course, follow Nexo

through the portal with your own troops. Frankly, that is the only way I see of your getting back in time to find anything standing of Westford."

Ares looked at him. "Why would you aid me in defeating your own army?"

"My army?" Viaud raised his elegant eyebrows. "Pardon, Surchatain, no. Not mine. Commander Nexo is my sworn enemy. For him to return with Westford in hand will mean my death. I would certainly rather give Hornbound peaceably to you."

Ares evaluated him, then said, "Excuse me for a moment." Drawing the others out of Viaud's hearing, he said, "Well?"

Henry hissed, "Whatever he says, he's not telling you the whole truth. He's a snake, Ares. Don't listen to him."

Oswald said carefully, "I would rather not abide in the void again, 'twere it all the same to you, Surchatain."

Thom had a strange look on his face. "Surchatain, I. . . ." He faltered, and Ares studied him. "I ordered Counselor Vogelsong to study whatever was written about the portal and then go to the Road of Vanishing to see if he could close it. This one here . . . there's something not right about it. I would say that this structure is a newer copy of the carvings on the hillside—not the other way around. Ulm may have found an entrance here to exploit, but there is still much we do not know about it. I would advise against it, Surchatain."

Such caution coming from Thom in the face of a direct threat to Westford was extraordinary. So Ares asked, "What if Nexo has used it to reach Westford?"

"I believe I left the Second Rhode and Captain Crager with sufficient manpower to hold them off until we return," Thom said adamantly. "I agree with Henry: This is a trick."

Ares looked at the three of them, united in their opposition to using the portal, and returned to Viaud to say, "I have decided to avail myself of your kind offer of assistance. But I need a guide. So, if you will, good Counselor—show us the way." Ares extended his hand toward the entryway.

Viaud smiled, shaking his head. "You do not need me, Surchatain. Having traveled the portal yourself, you know that you need only speak your destination to get there."

"And what could be easier?" Ares murmured. "Step into the void, speak your wishes, and like magic—you are there! Without rain and sun and hardships of travel. Without miles of dust, choking thirst, blocked roads, muscles that seize up with weariness. Without the neverending effort of putting one foot in front of another hour after hour, eating stale bread and drinking dirty water, sleeping on rocks and shaking scorpions out of your blanket. Just speak your wishes and you are there!

"Only—it is a lie," Ares said. "Were such a shortcut possible, we would have an army unfit to fight once we got there. Ulm used the portal to transport his army to the very border of Lystra three years ago, and we crushed them like ripe grapes in the press. Why was that, good Counselor?"

"Ulm's deficiencies as a Commander have nothing to do with the portal, Surchatain Ares," Viaud said.

"If that is the case, then lead us," Ares repeated, gesturing to the entryway.

"Surchatain—!" Thom said in warning as the Counselor suddenly knocked Ares toward the portal. Normally, such a tap would not have budged him, but Viaud hit him between his breastplate fastenings directly on a lash wound, and Ares recoiled with the pain. He fell toward the portal, drawn by the tremendous suction of the opening. With a scream of rage, Henry pushed the Qarqarian. Both Viaud and Ares disappeared into the portal.

But Thom had grabbed Ares' arm while he was falling, and Oswald held onto Thom, whose arms looked to be cut off at the elbow where they crossed the threshold of the portal. Sinking to his knees, he grimaced with the effort of holding onto Ares with both hands. "It's closing!" Oswald grunted. "Pull, Commander! One—two—three—!" They hauled with a mighty effort, and even Henry held on to one of Oswald's trunklike legs to anchor him. Suddenly they were all rolling on the ground with Ares between them, gasping. There was that windless shudder, and the portal closed.

"That was a close one," Oswald muttered, sitting up. "I come to like this portal less and less—eh, Surchatain?" He looked down at Ares, who did not reply. "Surchatain, are you well? Ares? Can you hear me?"

The three of them leaned over Ares anxiously, as he did seem to be having difficulty coming back, so to speak—his face was blank and bloodless; even his scar was a dull brown rather than purple. Thom closed his eyes, breathing a prayer, and Ares blinked, groaned, and shook his head. "What was it, Ares? What did you see?" Henry whispered.

"It was . . ." Ares' words were thick and slurred. "There were hundreds—thousands—crowding into one another . . . thousands all crammed together. They nearly crushed me. . . ."

"Who, Surchatain? Who were they? Nexo's army?" Thom asked, leaning over him.

"I . . . I could not tell. There were too many of them," Ares groaned. He had to lie still for several minutes before he could even sit up. The others sat back in deep concentration, trying to understand.

"After blaming the portal for their defeat at the Battle of the Crossroads three years ago, I can hardly see them jumping into it again to attack Westford, regardless of what this Viaud says," Thom said flatly. "They fear it too much."

"Then where is their army, Commander?" Oswald asked.

Thom looked chagrined. "It would be possible . . . if they had advance warning that we were coming, it would be possible to bait us with a token army, then sneak by us in the night. Knowing the terrain, as we do not, they could have used a hidden road down the mountain and circumvented us to get to Wolfen Road, while we are parleying with their Counselor."

"Or they could be hiding in the city," Ares said slowly, "waiting for us to leave. The Counselor tells us they have taken the portal to Westford—the fortress is empty, so we chase off to Westford after them. Then they come out from the city cellars and retake Hornbound." Given this likely scenario, Thom gave orders, and riders set off down the road to the city to search every house, every inn, every barn that might harbor more than a handful of soldiers.

It took several hours longer for Ares to regain a little color and vitality. Finally standing, he said, "I do not understand why crossing the portal again should have weakened me so. Of course, it was crowded, and it would have been good of you to pull me out at once, instead of delaying." There was a mixture of bemusement, embarrassment, and chastisement in his voice.

Thom looked at him with a sickly expression that was so unlike his normally sedate face that Ares studied him. "How long did you think you were in there?" Thom asked.

"It felt like an hour or more," Ares shrugged.

"As I live, Surchatain, it was a matter of moments. Ten heartbeats," Thom asserted.

"Of course," Ares murmured. Then in a deliberate show of shaking it off, he said, "Let us go see what the scouts report from the city." And they went out to the front courtyard of the fortress.

As soon as they came down the steps, Puck bounded up to Henry. Holding him, he sat gazing at the gates so soberly that Ares asked, "Henry? Would you like to see the Morands again, to tell them goodbye?"

Henry blinked, looking up at him. "Yes, Ares." He got to his feet, hefting Puck. "Yes."

So Ares put him on his horse with Puck in the saddlebag and mounted a second horse beside him. They loped down the switchback to the city, seeing no guards in the towers nor merchants on the road. Upon entering Hornbound, they were met by Captain Yonge, who was coordinating the search. Saluting, he said, "Surchatain, we have almost finished canvassing the city, and have found nothing but a small contingent of city guards, as well as renegades and deserters, which I will bring to you. The citizens are quite fearful and cooperative."

"Very good," Ares said, though the sudden clenching of his fists indicated that it was not very good. If the Qarqarian army was not here, then they must be on their way to Westford—or already there—and Ares was wasting time.

As nothing more could be done until the search was completed, Ares and Henry rode down the side street toward the Morands' house. Having bathed and dressed in a regulation Lystran field uniform (only slightly baggy on him), Henry looked ready—no, eager—for this reunion.

The streets were as deserted as the first time Ares had come down this way, and he smiled grimly at the repetition of the scene. Drawing up to the Morands' door on his warhorse, with Henry similarly seated beside him, Ares called out, "Lord Morand! Ares, the Surchatain of Lystra, summons you and your household! Show yourselves!"

There was tumult within; Lord Morand, white and shaking all over, came out of the house and fell on his face in the filthy street. His wife and daughter followed him, curtsying deeply. The servants cringed behind them. And that was all. "Where are your sons?" Ares asked.

"Have mercy, Surchatain Ares," Morand moaned, lifting his face. "They were conscripted into the army against their will . . . to fight you."

Ares said sincerely, "I am sorry to hear that, because I cannot guarantee that their lives will be spared. But I have brought someone to say goodbye to you." And he nodded toward Henry.

For the first time, the Morands looked at the boy on the second horse. Morand's wife, Lady Della, gasped, "Henry?" and Lord Morand simply lowered his face back to the dirt.

Henry said, "I wanted to say goodbye because you were very kind to me. I told Ares that you saved my life by buying me." He looked at the Morands' daughter as he said this, who, in turn, was studying him in wonder.

Lady Della's eyes filled with tears. "You will forgive us for giving you up to the Executioner, Henry? However you escaped, I am glad you did."

"I was the Executioner," Ares said, smiling tightly. "I disguised myself to get Henry back."

"Why, my Lord Surchatain?" Lady Della breathed. Lord Morand sat up on his knees.

"Because he is my son," Ares said. Lord Morand toppled over again, having fainted.

"He told us," the girl murmured. "Mama, he told Stephan that he was Chatain of Lystra, but we didn't believe him." Lady Della stared at her daughter.

With a glance at Henry, Ares said, "It is rather fortunate for him that you didn't. But because you treated him kindly anyway, I give you your lives as a ransom. I will give instructions that none of your family be harmed during the occupation of your city. I am sorry that I cannot do the same for your sons."

There was a commotion up the street, and they turned to see a group of Lystran soldiers under Captain Yonge herding about a hundred Qarqarians toward Ares. Yonge barked at them to stop and drop to their knees, which they did. Then he rode over to salute Ares and say, "Surchatain, here are all that we found—"

"Stephan! That's Stephan and Sumner, Lord Morand's sons," Henry said, pointing.

Ares gestured, "Bring them to me."

The two young men were hustled to their feet and brought to stand before Ares on his horse. He leaned forward on the saddle. "Now why aren't you off fighting Lystra?" he asked dryly.

"Pardon, Surchatain," the oldest said, glancing between him and Henry. "We did not want to."

"Tell me what happened," Ares said.

Stephan replied, "Two days ago they came for us. They took us out of my father's workshop, and said that henceforth we would be soldiers. We were going to invade Lystra. They put us in uniforms and marched us up toward the fortress, where they began leaving by a secret route."

"Did you see this route? Do you know where it is?" Ares asked quickly.

"No, Surchatain. We were near the end of the ranks, and there was so much crowding and confusion that we were able to slip away into the millet fields. We have been hiding there ever since—until your men found us," Stephan said, red-faced.

"Can you estimate the number of soldiers that you saw?" Ares asked.

Stephan and Sumner studied each other, then Sumner said, "We were lined up five abreast along the road for at least a mile. Given barely two feet of space per soldier front and back, that would make for . . . thirteen thousand, two hundred."

Ares' breathing went shallow. "And that was two days ago?"

"Yes, Surchatain," Stephan replied.

Two days ago, Ares was watching what he believed to be the Qarqarian army coming down the main road toward the mining camp. But Thom estimated that he fought less than two thousand, which meant that over eleven thousand had bypassed the mining camp altogether to march on Westford.

Ares felt a nauseous admiration for Nexo's cunning—somehow, he had divined that it was a Lystran who had invaded the hunting woods. Possibly, he knew it to be Ares himself. Rather than expend the effort to capture him, Nexo allowed him to escape, then sat back waiting for the Lystran army to come rescue their Surchatain. When it arrived, Nexo abandoned Hornbound to go sack Westford. That done, he could come retake Hornbound—knowing secret exits and entrances that Ares did not.

He looked down as Sumner approached Henry's horse to pat Puck on his head. "So you really are the Chatain of Lystra," he murmured. Henry smiled benignly.

Ares turned to his Captain. "Yonge, these two young men are to be released to their mother," he said, nodding toward Lady Della. Bursting into tears, she opened her arms, and they rushed to her. Lord Morand picked himself up from the dirt. Ares continued, "Of the rest of these, whoever has a home may return to it, but you are to keep the guards under lock and key. Commander Thom will separate out those troops he wishes to remain here."

As Ares wheeled his horse around, Lady Della called, "Bless you, Surchatain Ares!"

He glanced back at her, and her daughter smiled, "Goodbye, Henry."

"Goodbye, Tesla," he murmured, abashed.

Ares was in such a rush to find Thom that he ran his horse back to the fortress, inadvertently leaving Henry to catch up. Henry did catch him, however, when Alphonso hailed him at the rear of the fortress compound near the garden entrance. "Surchatain, we found it!"

"What?" Ares demanded.

"The entrance to a secret tunnel on the backside of the mountain that's wide enough for three wagons across. The Commander just now sent a scout down it," Alphonso reported.

"Show me," Ares said tersely.

Ironically, or purposefully, the secret entrance stood directly across from the portal, appearing to mirror it. But while the portal was closed, Oswald took the opportunity to study this curious mirror image, and so observed unmistakable evidences of a real opening in the stone facade. When he began prying around it, he found that pressing the eye on the carved sun face that spanned the double doors unlatched them so that they could be pushed open. Beyond was the entrance to a genuine tunnel carved in the mountain, sloping downward at a steep—but not unmanageable—grade.

While Ares, Thom and Oswald stood at the tunnel mouth, the mounted scout that Thom had sent returned from its dark recesses, carrying a torch. "Surchatain," he saluted. "The tunnel leads down the back side of the mountain straight toward Wolfen Road. The exit does not lie within sight of the main road or the mining camp."

Ares' eyes glazed over. "Then Counselor Viaud told the truth, in a manner of speaking—the army did go through a portal. And if they left two days ago, as the Morand boys say, then they are bearing down on the gates of Westford now."

# 19

Leaving the Second Oswald and Lieutenant Alphonso with a force of a thousand to hold Hornbound, Ares, Thom, Buford, Henry (bearing Puck) and the remaining seven thousand Lystran soldiers set out that day for Westford. Timour, the former slave, requested and received permission to accompany them.

Early on the return trip, however, before even making camp that night, Ares made the decision to appoint himself leader of a scouting party that would ride in advance of the main army to Westford. An army of seven thousand could not hope to travel as fast as a small band, and Ares was anxious to reach Westford. (He did not stop to appreciate at the time what Thom had accomplished in bringing that army from Westford to Hornbound in a little over three days.) Fortunately, because of the terrain, a Qarqarian army of eleven thousand could not venture far off Wolfen Road and still reach Westford, so if Ares traveled fast enough, it was possible to catch them. (What the scouting party might do when they caught them was another question.) As Ares considered all this, a tiny temptation did rear its head to squeak out the suggestion that the circumstances were dire enough to throw caution to the wind and use the portal, but an instant remembrance of the strange conditions inside it crushed that thought once for all.

Therefore, appointing Captain Yonge in command of the army,

Ares selected Thom, Timour, Buford and Coyle the engineer to ride with him. Henry cried to go with them, but as he was not strong enough to keep up on horseback (especially with Puck) Ares convinced him to ride in a supply wagon on the return trip, thus conserving his strength in case he was needed to fight (so Ares told him). Henry was also somewhat consoled by the fact that Ben, who contrived to go everywhere with Ares, was also left behind.

Packing minimal supplies, the party of five appropriated the strongest horses and set out. Before leaving, Ares had reassured Captain Yonge that the party would backtrack immediately should they spot the Qarqarians. "Even I do not presume to think we five can take on eleven thousand," Ares said. But Timour was looking as if he had a mind to try.

It was the hardest two-and-a-half days of riding that Ares had experienced in a long time. They rode late into the night, ate without building a fire, slept for a few hours, then took to the road again before daylight. Ares felt the effects of his age as he ached in muscles that had never troubled him before. He found himself growing weary far too quickly. Upon every hour, he resorted to mentally measuring the distance they had come and what they had yet to cover.

The worst part, however, was restraining the persistent, unwanted imaginative speculations as to what was happening in Westford. He imagined Rhode's skeleton crew being overrun by the sheer numbers of Qarqarians, and the rampage that would follow. He sternly blocked out voiceless suggestions of what would be done with his beautiful Nicole and young daughters. His only means of defending them was to cover them with prayer continually, which gave him a measure of peace.

At the next rest stop, however, when he fell down from the saddle, he was disconcerted to find that he could not stop the trembling in his hands. Timour pretended not to notice. Thom was busy scanning the grounds; Buford passed around hard, crusty bread, and Coyle tied knots in a snapped leather rein with chapped fingers.

The party spoke little—riding full speed most of the day precluded it—but on the second day of travel, when they stopped at the Passage to water the horses, Thom said, "Surchatain, I don't understand this. This is the only road by which the Qarqarians could have come through the mountains, and with eleven thousand passing, we should have seen some signs of it—something. I've seen plenty of markings left by our army on the way to Hornbound, but as for any sign of their coming south . . . nothing! How could they pass and leave no marks?"

"I've no answers for you, Thom," Ares uttered. "I am having trouble thinking beyond this particular moment."

Looking over the rolling woodland that sloped gently toward the Sea, Coyle observed, "Wolfen Road is merely the easiest route from Hornbound to Westford—not necessarily the only one. They could have skirted along the southern edge of the Fastnesses and then followed the Passage south."

To a man, they all looked north toward the Fastnesses, then south toward Westford. "Surely that would add another day to their travel," Ares said tentatively.

"Likely so," Coyle allowed.

"But why would they do that?" Thom argued. "Why would they take a longer route in a surprise attack on Westford? Their imperative is haste."

"You're right, Thom," Ares sighed. "We must assume they are still before us. Come." He remounted with a groan, and the others followed.

Hours later, after miles of strenuous galloping in the midsummer sun, Thom shouted, "The towers of Westford!" and the horses pricked up their ears.

"Do you see smoke?" Ares called back, eyes watering. *Fatigue*, he told himself.

"No!" Thom said.

They rode on, tensely watching for signs of invasion. Because of vagaries in how the road was constructed in relation to the border of Lystra, they were technically in Scylla right now. But a marauding army from anywhere in the north would have passed this way, too. As the party pounded down the road through fields of green wheat, they scanned the countryside for evidence of plunder. But the young wheat waved placidly in the summer wind, and otherwise all was still.

They came upon the northern shore of Willowring Lake, and tears of exhaustion trickled down into Ares' scar. The ancient willows stretched their long, wrinkled arms over the shore as they always had, their slender, cast-off leaves dotting the water. The rush-like foliage of spent jonquils in their hollow waved and bowed merrily in the slight breeze, as they had for generations. There was nothing but tranquility here.

Then the party was crossing the ancient wooden bridge that Ares had rebuilt after Magnus' trebuchet had collapsed it—welcoming trumpets blared from the parapets of the palace, and all at once the five were riding through the great, iron-banded gates. Ares looked up in a stupor at the soldiers on the wall cheering his return, and Thom saluted back at them.

The party dismounted; Ares' knees buckled and he fell against his lathering horse. Beaming merchants and nobles rushed up to bow and grasp his hand; the more forward among them slapped him on his injured back. He vaguely felt the pain, but paid no attention to it. Rhode hastened into the courtyard, saluting smartly. Ares, observing the cleanness of his dress uniform, deduced that he had not been fighting an invading army.

Then Nicole, beautiful and healthy, appeared on the palace steps, her eyes wet and lips crimson. Ares must have disengaged from his horse and climbed the steps, though he did not remember doing so. The next thing he knew, he had her in his arms, pressing his bearded face into her soft, fragrant, abundant chestnut hair. He dimly heard her say to Thom, "I knew that you would bring him home to me. And what of Henry?"

"He is following with the army, Surchataine," Thom replied, tired but satisfied. She exhaled in gratitude, and word was passed along of the Surchatain's success.

There were squeals: "Papa! Papa!" Two little girls, identical but for their many differences, came rushing out the great doors to fling themselves upon him, chattering and blubbering. Bonnie was chattering while Sophie, to her chagrin, could only cry. Carmine, urbane and quite in control of his faculties, bowed in welcome. Then Ares blinked at Renée curtsying, "Welcome home, Surchatain."

That was the first time he had ever heard her refer to him by that title. She was dressed sedately (for her) with only minimal makeup on her face. In irritation, he replied, "What happened to 'Papa'?" Her great blue eyes widened in recognition of his enduring fondness for her. With ever so slight trembling, she approached as a member of the family to kiss his scarred cheek.

Thom, who had been talking to Rhode and Crager, turned to Ares. The Commander started to speak, then changed his mind: "Let us go inside to confer, Surchatain." Ares looked at him in irritation for the solicitous tone, then realized he was almost too tired to pick up his feet. Nicole took his arm to inconspicuously assist him up the steps.

The scouting party sat with those who welcomed them at a long table in the great hall, where wine, veal, crisp garden vegetables and hot, fresh bread were brought on golden dishes. Timour began to eat with the wonder of someone caught in a happy dream. Thom took a token sip of wine, but made sure Ares had begun to eat before he started to talk. Then he said, "Surchatain, Rhode says that the Qarqarian army has made no appearance, except for one."

"One appearance?" Ares asked in alarm, calculating where they might be now.

"One man," Thom corrected. "One man came through the portal and attacked the Chataine Renée in the orchard. She fought him off and reported the breach to the Surchataine, who posted a watch night and day. No one else appeared after that, either by portal or by road."

Ares absorbed that, then turned to Renée in mild wonder. "Well done, Chataine."

"It was nothing, Papa," she shrugged, tossing her blond ponytail in disdain, although word of her heroism in singlehandedly staving off an invasion had not ceased to be repeated and embellished throughout Westford, to her modest denials in public and her smug satisfaction in private.

Leaning on his elbows over his veal, Ares muttered, "They are not in Hornbound. They are not at Westford. They are not anywhere in between. Where are the eleven thousand Qarqarians?"

Rhode gestured to a soldier and Thom said, "There may be an answer forthcoming, Surchatain. As I told you, I charged

Counselor Vogelsong with studying all that was written about the portal and then seeing if he could close it. He just returned from the Road of Vanishing yesterday. I have sent for him to make his report to us."

Nicole whispered, "Eat, darling, while you wait for him." She tried not to let on how anxiously she was studying him.

In regard for her wishes, Ares lowered his head to eat. But when Vogelsong appeared, Ares laid the fork down again. "Sit, Counselor. What can you tell us about the portal, then?"

Taking a chair almost violently, Vogelsong seemed unable to contain his excitement or express coherently what he had learned: "Surchatain, it is most extraordinary. Once the Commander charged me with this serious responsibility, I ceased everything else to hunt for the most obscure writings about the Road of Evanescere—or Vanishing, as we call it. The portal itself is very ancient—no one knows who began carving the monument that marks it. But the manuscripts I located spoke of the portal as the entrance to a river of time—that, upon entering it, one enters into a stream of time that flows both forward and back."

"What?" Ares blinked.

Vogelsong gestured in his impatience. "In our earthly sphere, Surchatain, time flows only in one direction: from the past, through the present, to the future. But the portal is a door to another sphere in which time flows in many directions, like the branches of a great river."

"But . . . the time always seemed to be about the same when I got out as when I went in," Ares said slowly. "It was the place that changed."

"Exactly so, Surchatain," Vogelsong said eagerly. "How do we measure time, but by changing places? As the sun and moon travel in the sky, by these changes in position, do we mark the time that has passed. The realm of the portal dropped you in one current of time and released you at another—ergo, at a different place."

"So . . . a trip that would normally take three days took an instant instead," Thom said thoughtfully.

"Quite so, Commander," Vogelsong nodded.

"Who taught Ulm how to use the portal?" Thom demanded. "He's no scholar to have read all this."

Vogelsong admonished him, "One point at a time, if you please, Commander. And you forget that Ulm was Counselor to the Surchatain he murdered. He may well have been researching it for years."

"How was it that Oswald and I were the only ones who could see it?" Nicole asked.

Vogelsong turned respectfully to her. "I cannot say, Surchataine, except that some are gifted with spiritual sight to see that which others do not. Now, after learning all this, the question for me was: how do we close the portal? It is no more possible to affect the flow of time in that realm as this, but—how do we block entrance to that realm? It occurred to me, Surchatain, that we must block it by . . . blocking it," Vogelsong said.

"What?" Ares said tiredly.

"I took a team of masons out to the Road of Vanishing, and had constructed a stone wall blocking the hillside entrance to the portal," Vogelsong said simply. Thom and Ares stared at each other. "It appeared to work. When the portal opened, no one could get close enough to it to enter."

"Could you see the green light when it opened?" Ares asked.

"Yes, with the prism. Oh—I forgot to mention that the green light emanating from the portal distorts the light from a prism. That is how I could test the wall," Vogelsong said.

Thom leaned forward to lay his hand palm up and say, "I am keen to know what causes the portal to open and close."

Vogelsong's high brow wrinkled and he made sweeping gestures to illustrate: "Again, think of it as a broad, slow-moving river, Commander. There are swirls and eddies in that river that lap up on the riverbank, dislodging a stick or two, overflowing its banks in heavy rains. Boats or swimmers in the river create small disturbances that to a tadpole are tidal waves."

"What?" Ares repeated helplessly.

"I believe that the door opened and closed according to the eddies, caused in part by the number of people in the stream," Vogelsong explained.

"Counselor, is it possible that there are—ghosts? Human spirits caught in the stream, that require something solid to come out again?" Nicole asked timidly.

Vogelsong looked at her. "From what little I know of spirits, Surchataine, I would say that they surround us in every realm, and require what is solid to manifest their intentions. Thus we have hauntings."

"Then—" Ares was struggling with the Counselor's previous point—"the portal is not controlled by an evil presence? Nicole heard mocking laughter after we were dropped in Hornbound."

"Interesting observation, Surchatain. While my study shows clearly that the river of time is too strong a force to be manipulated even by mighty demons, it is still a favored pastime of earthbound sprites, or imps, to toy with mortals caught in its flow. I can well imagine that an imp would redirect you from your desired destination. I also imagine that their pranks made the portal highly unreliable for regular use, thus giving rise to the Qarqarians' fear of it. We fear what we cannot control," Vogelsong lectured.

While the others contemplated this, Vogelsong went on: "One thing puzzles me, however. After I had the wall built, I monitored the light with the prism. It grew brighter and brighter, as if the currants and eddies were growing in force and volume. But—"

"No one could come out," Ares said, suddenly pale. "Counselor, think hard—what day was it that you built the wall?"

"That would have been . . . four days ago. June eighteenth," Vogelsong said.

"That was the day the Qarqarians left Hornbound," Ares breathed. He then turned to Renée. "Chataine, what day was it that you were attacked?"

Renée looked startled, but Nicole answered, "That was the seventeenth of June."

Ares sat back limply. In a monotone, he said, "They sent a scout through the portal on the seventeenth to see if it would take him to Westford. It did, but the Chataine drove him back. He reported this, so the next day they departed for Westford *through the portal,* just as Viaud said. But that day, our Counselor built the wall over the primary portal on the Road of Vanishing. And somehow . . . that prevented anyone from exiting *anywhere.*"

Agape, Vogelsong nodded. "That is likely, for each outlet is inextricably bound up with the portal. In a way that we cannot understand, they are all one."

Face bloodless, Ares looked at Thom. "That is why it was so crowded in the portal at Hornbound. That is why Counselor Viaud tried to induce us to enter it. The army went in but could not come out again. They are still there—and so is he."

"Eleven thousand men," Thom whispered. "Counselor, if . . . if we take down the wall, will they be able to come out?"

Vogelsong looked stricken. "That is what I started to tell you—I monitored the light through the prism while it increased tenfold, then it reached some sort of threshold, and—vanished. It was as if the stream, being blocked at one point, diverted entirely to parts unknown. You asked me to close the portal, and I fear I have done so, for all time . . . at least in this realm."

Ares sank back, head reeling. "If Nexo had taken his army out of Hornbound through the secret tunnel in the mountain and marched down Wolfen Road to Westford, he would have succeeded. I would have arrived today to find my capital a burning heap. But that would have meant making that long march mile by mile, when he had proof that the portal would take them to my doorstep in an instant. He knew nothing of earthbound imps or eternal rivers—it was too tempting to take the shortcut. . . ." The others absorbed this silently, and he murmured, "I . . . think it is time for me to rest."

For the next fortnight, Ares lay recuperating in his chambers. Neither Carmine, nor Thom, nor Nicole ever spoke of the legend surrounding the fate of those who entered the portal, and Vogelsong apparently had not encountered it in his research. But they watched the Surchatain closely, and breathed a little easier when he began resuming his duties bit by bit.

Henry was received home with great celebration, especially after Ares had made known (and dictated for the history books) Henry and Puck's part in saving him. Chataine Melva was brought out of hiding back to Westford, and Ares laid careful plans for her assumption of the throne of Qarqar, with detailed agreements drawn up by Carmine that addressed the interests of both provinces.

But until such a time that Ares judged Melva ready to rule, he appointed a council of Qarqarian nobles, answerable to himself, that would serve as interim rulership. This council was headed by Lady Della. The mines were to be reopened, worked by paid laborers, and what army remained would diligently cooperate with Lystra and Scylla to suppress the slave trade that had thrived under Hornbound's previous patronage. Also, a wall was constructed around the portal at Hornbound, even though Vogelsong's prism showed no light emanating from it, either.

Klar, having received Ares' messengers with the purloined letter to Ulm, made anxious inquiries about his grandniece, the Lady Rejane. Ares explained to him the circumstances of her escape, but nothing further was known about her until months later, when she showed up at Weygand alone and bitterly disillusioned of love.

About that time, Ares offered Melva's hand to Henry in a future marriage, but after she threw a fit, insisting on choosing her own husband, Henry declined. And from then on, he began to pay special attention to Sophie. He took seriously and literally Ares' rationale for redeeming him, and threw himself into proving his worth as Ares' son. So he was out on the field with the army a great deal. Since he was gone so often to places Puck could not follow, the dog found a new companion in the Surchatain. Thereafter, Ares was never seen around the palace without stocky, nub-tailed Puck close at his heels.

Now that Carmine and Renée were divorced, they seemed to find each other suddenly irresistible. The palace gossips kept tabs on their secret encounters with great delight, and Ares would occasionally approach Nicole for an explanation as to this irrational behavior. She tried to explain it in terms of forbidden fruit, but when Ares pointed out that no one was prohibiting them from seeing each other, she gave up and ascribed it to Renée's game-playing, which he understood. But he made no further references to marrying her off to someone else.

As life settled into normalcy at Westford, reports from Hornbound dwindled. Lystran messengers were well-received, plied with alcohol, and sent off with variations of the same report. Carmine expressed his opinion that the citizen council was functioning a little too well, but Ares was so encumbered with governing Lystra that he subconsciously decided to overlook anything but overt aggression.

Nicole, meanwhile, found herself incapacitated by the residual fear from her voyages into the portal. The potential consequences of Ares' unwitting defiance of some unknown cosmic law taunted her relentlessly. The green light invaded her dreams, causing her to wake in a cold sweat; the memory of Carmine's warning weighed heavily on her heart, despite not being confirmed by anything Vogelsong had read. Every time she looked at Ares, or Rhode, or Oswald, she wondered how they would die. And as for herself—

It was almost too cruel for words that entering the portal in obedience to her husband, despite her strong reluctance, should result in the curse of her own death. Dread began to eat at her, sucking all joy and consolation from her life. Seeing that, Ares began to withdraw again, thinking that she feared another pregnancy.

Blindly searching for solace, Nicole wandered into his receiving room one day to pick up his little book again—the first one. Now that it was full, he was carrying around a second. So this one he left on the windowsill where he spent those early morning hours. Nicole read it through completely once again, and while it contained many beautiful and worthwhile thoughts, there was nothing that directly answered her fears. So she was left in darkness for a few weeks more.

But then the Eternal Maker of time and of life decided that she had wallowed enough in self-pity, and pointed her toward the light. Drawn again to Ares' receiving room when it happened to be unoccupied, she went over to the stand that held the old, fragile book of Scriptures and opened it. Her eye fell on this passage: "Christ hath redeemed us from the curse of the law, being made a curse for us; for it is written, 'Cursed is every one that hangeth on a tree.'"

Stunned, she stared at the passage as the darkness lifted. Then Ares entered with a map, preparatory to replacing it in its honeycombed slot. Upon seeing her, he paused in surprise. "Lady! What do you require?" he asked anxiously.

She turned slowly from the stand with the glimmers of a mischievous smile. "You have been lax in fulfilling your promise to me of late, my lord."

He looked dubiously hopeful, and said, "I have been very busy, Lady."

"Must I waylay you in a storeroom, with servants listening at the door?" she asked, coming up close to him.

"That will not be necessary, Lady," he said, kissing her hand tentatively. She withdrew her hand to turn to the bedchamber, glancing back at him over her shoulder. The map that he had carried in got dropped to the floor, where it rolled under the table, and there it sat for the next two hours.

(The story continues in *Dead Man's Token*.)

# GLOSSARY

**Alphonso** (al FONZ oh)—a lieutenant in the Lystran army

**Ares** (AIR eez)—Surchatain of Lystra, formerly Commander

**bailey**—the outside wall of a fortress, or the space enclosed by the wall

**Ben**—Ares' young page

**bistort**—a flowering plant that has many uses, both as food and medicine

**Bonnie**—daughter of Ares and Nicole, twin of Sophie

**Buford** (BYOU ford)—a lieutenant in the Lystran army

**Calle** (kail) **Valley**—province west of Lystra, famous for its vineyards and fairs, which Ares annexed after defeating its Surchatain in battle

**Candace**—Chataine Bonnie's maid

**Carmine** (CAR men)—Counselor at Westford, husband of Renée

**Chatain** (sha TAN)—son of the ruler of a province; the feminine is **Chataine** (sha TANE)

**Chiacos** (CHEE a cose)—a Polonti guide who served Ares briefly before disappearing

**Corona**—capital of Seleca

**Coyle** (coil)—an engineer of Westford

**Crager** (KRAY ger)—a Captain in the Lystran army

**Crescent Hollow**—capital of Calle Valley before that province was annexed to Lystra

**Deirdre** (DEE dra)—(1) wife of Roman the Great; (2) Commander Thom's wife

**Della, Lady**—Lord Morand's wife

**Eleanor**—Renée's maid

**Eugenia** (you JEN ee ah)—the province west of Lystra, ruled by Klar

**Eurus** (YUR is)—capital of Scylla

**Evanescere** (ee WAN es kery), **Road of**—Road of Vanishing; the northbound fork off the Pervalley Highway that runs through the corner of Eugenia toward Qarqar

**Faguy** (FAH gwee), **Lord**—a rich merchant of Calle Valley, loyal to Ares

**Fastnesses**—mountain range forming the partial border between Lystra/Qarqar and Scylla/Seleca

**garderobe** (GAR de robe)—a water closet, indoor commode

**Gathing**—a tailor of Westford

**Genevieve** (JEN e veeve)—Steward Giles' wife

**Georges** (JEOR jes)—dinner master at Westford

**Giles** (hard *g*, long *i*)—the Steward at the palace of Westford

**Green Lady**—the mountain range on the southern coast, which resembled a woman lying on her side

**Gretchen**—Ares' personal attendant and laundress

**Hauffe**—Carmine's personal attendant

**Heaviside, Lord**—a nobleman of Hornbound

**Henry**—former Chatain of Lystra, Renée's half-brother

**Herzl**—a warden of the Surchatain's woods at Hornbound

**Hornbound**—capital of Qarqar

**Huysum** (HI sum)—a Crescent Hollow servant

**Kara**—Chataine Sophie's maid

**Klar**—Surchatain of Eugenia

**Laymon**—a warden of the Surchatain's woods at Hornbound

**Lazear**—a slave trader

**Lystra** (LIS tra)—province once ruled by Roman the Great, now ruled by his descendant Ares

**Magnus** (MAG nus)—Surchatain of Scylla

**Melva**—Chataine of Qarqar, now under Ares' protection

**Merle** (murl)—head laundress at Westford

**Michaud** (MICK aud)—a Lystran soldier

**Miers**—a Lystran soldier, a former Qarqarian

**Morand, Lord**—a nobleman of Hornbound

**Nairne**—the Steward of Hornbound under Ulm

**Neruda**—a favorite horse of Ares', a black gelding

**Nexo**—Commander of the Qarqarian army

**Nicole** (ne COLE)—Ares' wife, Surchataine of Lystra

**Nicole's Harbor**—new port city on the coast of Lystra, so named by Ares

**Oswald**—Second in Command of the Lystran army under Commander Thom

**Paramore** (PAIR ah mor)—a lieutenant in the Lystran army

**parapet**—the top portion of the castle wall, behind which runs a walkway

**Pares** (PARE is)—Lady Rejane's lover, a Qarqarian soldier

**Passage**—the river marking the boundary between Lystra and Scylla

**persillade**—a soup made with parsley and potatoes

**Pervalley Highway**—the east-west road through Lystra, running south of the Poison Greens

**Poison Greens**—the notorious mountain range dividing Lystra and serving as a boundary between western Lystra and Qarqar

**Polontis** (po LAWN tis)—mountainous province far northeast of Lystra, home of the hardy, courageous, but unsophisticated **Polonti** (po LAWN tee)

**Preus** (proose), **Lord**—the premier dressmaker in Westford

**Puck**—the Morand family dog

**Purdy**—childhood friend of Nicole's, now overseer of livestock at Westford

**Qarqar** (KAR kar)—province to the northwest of Lystra

**Rejane** (re JANE), **Lady**—Ulm's mistress

**Renée** (ren AY)—wife of Carmine, half-sister of Henry

**Rhode** (road)—Second in Command of the Lystran army under Commander Thom

**Roerich** (ROE rick)—the administrator of Crescent Hollow

**Roman**—the first great Surchatain of Lystra; author of Roman's Law; great-great-grandfather of Ares

**Sacco**—a young Lystran soldier

**Savary** (SAV a rie)—the new physician at Westford

**Scylla** (SILL ah)—the province to the east of Lystra, ruled by Magnus

**Seleca** (SEL e kah)—once-great province to the northeast of Lystra, now impoverished and riddled with slave markets

**Shahn**—a Qarqarian guard

**Shryoc** (SHREYE ock)—Surchatain of Qarqar, Melva's father, murdered by Ulm

**Sophie**—daughter of Ares and Nicole, twin of Bonnie

**Soucie** (SOO see)—wife of the Second Rhode

**squab**—nestling pigeon

**Stephan**—son of Lord Morand of Hornbound

**Sumner**—another son of Lord Morand

**Surchatain** (SUR cha tan)—the ruler of a province; the feminine is **Surchataine** (SUR cha tane)

**Tesla**—daughter of Lord Morand

**Thom**—Commander of the army of Lystra

**Timour** (TIM or)—a Qarqarian slave

**Ulm**—Qarqarian usurper who had killed Melva's father and attacked Westford

**Ursula**—Nicole's maid

**Viaud** (VEE aud)—Counselor of Hornbound under Ulm

**Vivian, Lady**—Renée's mother

**Vogelsong** (VO gel song)—a new Counselor at Westford

**Welling, Lord**—a Callean nobleman whose estate was restored to him by Ares

**Westford**—capital of the province of Lystra

**Weygand** (WAY gand)—the capital of Eugenia

**Wigzell** (WIG zul)—formerly the palace physician at Westford

**Wirt**—a Lystran soldier

**Wolfen Road**— the road from Hornbound to Eurus

**Yonge** (yung)—a Captain of the Lystran army

# appendix

### Daryoles

This version of *daryoles* is a very basic and easy cheese tart with a slightly tangy flavor. You may find that omitting the bone marrow, or topping the pie with fruit jam, makes this dish more appealing.

In medieval times these pies were prepared in large wood-fired ovens. Rather than removing the pie crust from the oven to add the filling, the baker might pour the filling into the crust using a bowl attached to the end of a long-handled baker's peel. In this way many pies could be filled quickly, and the oven would not lose too much heat.

1  9-inch piecrust
2 pounds large curd cottage cheese
6 egg yolks
1 Tablespoon cooked bone marrow, chopped

Preheat the oven to 400 degrees F. Crisp the pie shell in the oven for 10 minutes.

Meanwhile, put the cottage cheese and egg yolks in a blender and blend to paste. Pour the mixture into a mixing bowl. Add the chopped bone marrow and stir to mix completely.

Remove the pie shell from the oven and fill it with the cheese mixture. Bake at 400 degrees F. for 10 minutes. Reduce heat to 325 degrees F. and bake 30 to 35 minutes more, or until a toothpick inserted in the center comes out clean. Remove the pie from the oven and let it stand 10 minutes before serving. Serve warm.

Makes 1 9-inch pie. 6 to 8 servings.

From Cindy Renfrow, *Take a Thousand Eggs or More: A Collection of 15th Century Recipes* 2nd edition, Vol. 1 (Unionville, NY: Royal Fireworks Press, 2003), p. 51.

See Cindy's website at http://www.thousandeggs.com

## Books by Robin Hardy

The Streiker Saga
*Streiker's Bride*
*Streiker: The Killdeer*
*Streiker's Morning Sun*

The Annals of Lystra
*Chataine's Guardian*
*Stone of Help*
*Liberation of Lystra*
(first published as *High Lord of Lystra*)

The Latter Annals of Lystra
*Nicole of Prie Mer*
*Ares of Westford*
*Prisoners of Hope*
*Road of Vanishing*
*Dead Man's Token* (coming October 2007)

The Sammy Series
*Sammy: Dallas Detective*
*Sammy: Women Troubles*
*Sammy: Working for a Living*
*Sammy: On Vacation*
*Sammy: Little Misunderstandings*
*Sammy: Ghosts* (coming July 2007)

*Padre* (a new edition and a sequel,
*His Strange Ways*, coming March 2007)

## Edited by Robin Hardy

*Sifted But Saved:*
*Classic Devotions by W.W. Melton*

Printed in the United States
59226LVS00001B/18